ROGUE'S ISLES

ROGUE'S ISLES

THOMAS GATELY BRIODY

ST. MARTIN'S PRESS
New York

Design by Sara Stemen

LIBRARY OF CONGRESS CATALOGING-IN-PUBLICATION DATA

Briody, Thomas Gately.
    Rogue's isles / Thomas Gately Briody.
        p.   cm.
    "A Thomas Dunne book."
    ISBN 0-312-13157-7
    I. Title.
PS3552.R4886R64   1995   95-1738
813'.54–dc20   CIP

First Edition: June 1995

10 9 8 7 6 5 4 3 2 1

To Karen, Tory, and Alex,
the joys of my life

ACKNOWLEDGMENTS

My sincere thanks to Tom Dunne and Neal Bascomb, and to Ed Novak, a truly great agent. Your guidance and encouragement has been invaluable.

Thanks also to Len O'Brien for steering me toward an old friend.

DISCLAIMER

The characters and plot in this book are pure fiction. Any similarity to real persons living or dead, elected, convicted, or merely toppled from power, is entirely coincidental.

Scenes depicting Virtual-Reality sex, while perhaps technically possible in this modern era, are essentially fantasy. The author has no knowledge of whether the equipment or machinery in fact exists, or where it might be obtained.

ROGUE'S ISLES

he last time anyone saw Frankie Falcone on Federal
Hill, he was ripping off a little old lady.

Her name was Anna Bianchini, but everyone on the hill
called her Little Anna. They would say, "Lil' Anna,
how you doin'?" or "Lil' Anna, whaddyouse want today?"
Or even, " 'D'jou hava good time, Lil' Anna? Thaa's nize."
Anna knew everybody and everybody knew Anna. She was
seventy-six, built like a football, five feet tall and half as wide.
She dressed in black head to foot, just the way she had since
her husband, Johnny, died of a heart attack nearly twenty
years earlier. She walked through the doors of Amerigo
Vespucci Loan and Investment Company and gave Frankie
just what he was looking for.

Anna came in twice a month, once to cash a government
check, then again to deposit the laborer's pension money
Johnny had earned. Nine in the morning on the first and the
fifteenth—like clockwork.

"Morning, Lil' Anna," sang Rosalie behind the teller's window, with the same cheery tone she used for all the regulars.
Frankie watched from just inside his office door.

"Mornin', Rosalie," Anna replied, her Rhode Island accent
making it sound more like *mo-ahninn*. Anna handed Rosalie
her deposit ticket, already filled out. The little widow always
took a handful of blanks with her when she left the bank,
then returned with one filled out for her next piece of business. Like they would make her rich. She must have had a
thousand blank tickets sitting in a drawer at home.

Rosalie stamped the check, scribbled on the pad she used

to keep track of transactions. Five hundred and eighty dollars and thirty-five cents.

"Little Anna!" Frankie said finally, coming out of his office.

"Eh, Frankie," she said. Her eyes lighted up at the sight of the handsome young banker. Frankie flashed his perfect white teeth. She was one of the old-time customers, since before he was born. Deep down, Frankie knew she didn't like him, that she'd helped make his life miserable when he was young. But Little Anna would now make him another fifty thousand dollars.

"How's the hand, Little Anna?"

She waved an arthritic set of fingers under his nose and rolled her eyes. "The pain nevah stops, y'know. I got a good docta, but he can only do so much. The curse of bein' old. But how's y'family? How's y'wife?"

"They're doin' real good," Frankie said. Anna knew it wasn't so. The Falcones had long since left the old neighborhood for a plush East Side condo and a house in Jamestown. But there were rumors on the Hill about Frankie and his wife: trouble in the home, trouble in the bed. It was fun to take Frankie and bust his balls, make him cover up.

"Bella, bella. Una bella famiglia." Then she spit out a cough. Frankie had to grab her arm to keep her standing straight.

"You all right, sweetheart?" She nodded, blinking startled tears away.

"Come on in my office. There's something I want to show you." His grip on her arm was strong.

"What's wrong?" She was frightened. The bank president inquired about her health; that was fine. But going in his office . . . Frankie closed the door.

"I just wanna do you a fay-va," he said, lapsing into the dialect of the Hill. He was sitting her down, gliding over to his plush leather seat behind the big cherry-wood desk. She stared at the pictures behind him on the wall: Frankie with politicians, Frankie with some businessmen, Frankie with his family, Frankie with big black kids who played ball for PC. He ain't one of us, she thought, but he's important, this banker is.

"Anna, how much interest you getting on your savings?"

"Seven and a half," she replied automatically. Anna watched the rate, because Johnny'd always said that's what you had to do. Watch the rate. A change of a tenth of a point can make you a few bucks. And a few bucks helps pay the bills.

"Anna, that's not enough. You could be doing better. We got a new account that pays eight point five. How much you have in your savings?" Frankie already knew. He'd checked her account that morning.

"Fifty towsend," she said. Frankie was already doing the math on a desktop calculator.

"Right, now you make tree towsend, seven hundred fifty," he said. "That's per yea-ah, simple interest." He pushed the calculator away and leaned back in his chair. "I can get you another five hundred a year, Lil' Anna. Bring it to four thou—four towsend, two fifty."

"What's the catch?" Johnny had always said you don't get nothin' for nothin' in this world. But then, another five hundred dollars would buy the grandkids a lot of presents.

"Anna, my Little Anna, have I ever steered you wrong? It's a special rate for long-term customers. How many years you been coming here now?"

"Since before you was born."

"That's right. Since before I was born," he said respectfully. Frankie smiled for a moment, then looked at her as if he was looking at someone dying, someone he pitied.

"It's okay, sweetheart. You don't have to change your account. I understand all the stress this is causing—"

The little widow's glare softened. She wished her own son had turned out so well, instead of going to work for the laborers' union. Just like his father, but without his father's drive. And another five hundred a year . . . I can get a new cable channel, she thought.

"Where do I sign?" she demanded.

"Anna, I don't want to push you into something you don't want."

"Gimme the paper."

"Maybe you should think about it."

"The paper, the paper," Anna said, insistent.

Frankie Falcone drew a paper from his desk, a form with lots of words. Anna didn't like to read. It made her eyes ache.

"Can you sign this, Anna?"

"I don't have my glasses."

"That's okay, dear. This just says you want to close out your old account and open a new one. I'll fill the paperwork out later."

Anna hesitated. Something wasn't right. But she needed to get to Alerio's before the midday crowd. And this banker was being so nice. Maybe she'd been wrong.

She reached out and took the pen. Her hand only shook a little when she signed.

"Oh, Anna. You're a sharp businesswoman. You know a deal when you see it," Frankie said with a laugh. "Now listen, dear, you're doing the right thing." He whisked the paper away and slid it into a drawer.

"Do I get a new passbook?"

"We'll send you it in the mail, but until then, your old one will do just fine."

Little Anna used her cane to get to her feet. She wobbled toward the bank entrance.

"Take care, Anna," Frankie called.

"Thanks. You come by and visit sometime."

"I'll bring you a muffin. You like muffins, Anna?" Rosalie, the teller, held the door as the elderly woman made her way back onto the street.

"Anything I can do, Mr. Falcone?" Rosalie asked.

"We were just having a little chat," Falcone said. "It's good for business."

He went back into his office and retrieved the paper from the drawer—three papers, actually, carbon-backed—a loan agreement saying that Anna Maria Bianchini had just borrowed money and agreed to put up her savings account as collateral. Frankie reached over and pulled the cover off an old Selectric typewriter, then slid the document down through the spool. Carefully, he aligned the numbers in the spaces provided and typed "50,000."

It wasn't the cleanest way of stealing money, but it was close. He had done it eight times in the last two weeks, a hundred times in the last year. He couldn't count how many times he'd tried it in the year before that. It was fast, it was simple, and it had always worked.

He knew someone was watching him. But others had watched before. When he was little, he saw his father supervise the workers counting money. Big bundles of tens, twenties, wrapped in bundles, stacked in rows, laid side to side and end to end. Crisp black-white-and-green paper in the big vault with AMERIGO VESPUCCI LOAN AND INVESTMENT painted in gold leaf on the front. Then they had watched from outside as men in slick suits and fedoras come in to the bank to do business. To little Frankie, they were just men his father knew. When he got older, he realized they were wise. They worked for a man named Patriarca, the man who ran a vending-machine company down the avenue. They were why the bank was watched.

Now others were watching—regulators, investigators, forensic accountants, prosecutors. Armed with books and calculators, wanting to see how Frankie did business. Raising their eyebrows about his loans and accounting methods. Trying to make him sweat.

But Frankie wasn't sweating much. He had planned well. The club had seen to that. A bad time was coming. But he would be taken care of. The club would see to that, too.

He slid a brown leather bag out from beneath his desk, his finger tracing the shoulder strap before he unzipped for one last check. Papers altogether, the numbers for the accounts together. A fresh new U.S. passport. He was almost ready.

Outside his office, he went to a cabinet and filed the loan forms. There was no need for approval; he was the president and could approve whatever he wanted. The tellers were still busy at two windows, and they paid no attention when the boss walked in to the tiny vault room. With two keys, he pulled open a heavy drawer loaded with one-hundred-dollar bills, neatly arranged in bundles of a hundred each. Frankie took five—Little Anna's loan. He stuffed them inside his suit jacket pockets, then took them back to his office.

Two minutes later, he came out.

"I'm gone for the day," he said.

"Bye, Mr. Falcone," the tellers chimed. "See you tomorrow."

"Yeah," Frankie said, "see you then."

He almost skipped through the parking lot, then climbed into a red Porsche 944. He barely glanced back at the bank his father had founded, had built into a neighborhood institution. A neighborhood where Frankie didn't belong, then or now.

He pulled onto Atwells, cutting off a delivery truck bound for the restaurants up the street. The driver made a fist and shouted something Frankie couldn't hear. His mind was on something else, someone else: Julia Roberts.

An old Roy Orbison tune rang through his mind as he imagined Julia strolling down Rodeo Drive in Beverly Hills. Pretty woman.

Frankie was in love.

He shifted into third, ran a light, drove through the arch with the huge pinecone that marked the entrance and exit to Federal Hill, and disappeared.

2

A vast there! I am the king of these waters and I require your gold and your women!"
The man was on the foredeck of a sailboat. He was yelling at a power yacht. He would have kept it up, but spray from a wave hit him full in the face.

"Aaagh." He spit dirty Narragansett Bay brine and cursed loud and long as he dangled from the standing rigging. The man was very drunk.

The power yacht roared past, cutting a massive wake and blasting Frank Sinatra so loudly it nearly drowned the noise of its engines. A swarthy helmsman wearing Vuarnets, no shirt, and a gut the size of Bermuda turned and saluted the sailboat with his finger.

"To the guns, lads. Let's give 'em a taste o' the grape. Come to think of it, give me a taste." The man on the sailboat's foredeck pulled at a bottle of white wine he held in his right hand. His left held on to the boat and he swung wildly with every passing wave, as if he would soon fall off and drown.

Michael Carolina almost hoped he would.

Ordinarily, Carolina didn't mind if day-charter guests went forward on *Maeve*. They were usually curious about how a traditional yacht looked, and wanted to touch the varnished wood and polished bronze and brass. *Maeve* was a tight, stiff, strong boat, a thirty-eight-foot double-ended cutter, built of red African mahogany, steamed and planked with bronze screws over white oak frames. Built to withstand the hazards of northern seas.

7

The cutter easily held ten passengers, but her deck was small enough that the passengers were never far from the captain. That was important on a day-charter vessel, where the passengers tended to know little about the dangers presented by wind and water. But today, the waves off Newport were three to five feet. The wind blew twenty knots. And the man on the foredeck was trouble. He had definitely had a few before coming aboard, and he had consumed more than half the wine bottle since leaving Bowen's Wharf. The voyage was less than an hour old.

"Sir, I think you've had enough," Carolina said, just loud enough to carry over the din of wind and waves.

"What's that?" The man cocked an ear, pretending he didn't understand. His friends, another middle-aged man with a paunch and two young blond women, laughed uproariously.

"Why don't you come on back to the cockpit and take a rest?" Carolina was used to obnoxious passengers. It was part of the charter business. But there were other guests that day, a father and two little girls and a dark-haired woman in her early forties. The father was preoccupied with his children. The woman watched Carolina with an expression that was both amused and sympathetic.

"You certainly have your hands full," she said. He grinned and shrugged, expertly balancing the ship's wheel, keeping one eye on passing yachts, the other on his wayward passenger.

"My mate is sick today," he said. "I've had his kind before."

"I doubt it," the woman said.

"Pardon me?"

"You don't know who that is?" The woman pointed at the man as he tilted the bottle toward his mouth and missed, splashing white wine all over his shirt.

"No," Carolina said. "Should I?"

"That," the lady said, "is Joey Giovannetti, the mayor of Providence."

"Oh," Carolina said, thinking, Oh shit.

"I believe the other man is his lawyer."

"Really."

"And I could be wrong," the dark-haired woman said, "but my guess is that those two women are working."

The two women were now squealing with delight as the man stumbled toward *Maeve*'s bowsprit. Obviously, they felt it was important to find the mayor's behavior amusing.

The wind was picking up, almost to twenty-five knots. *Maeve* had developed considerable heel.

"Do you sail?" Carolina asked the lady passenger.

"A bit. I can hold a course, if that's what you mean."

"That's what I meant," Carolina said, motioning for her to take the wheel. The woman slid behind the helm as he pointed to a buoy.

"Just hold her steady on that can off Beavertail."

"Good luck," the woman said as he climbed out of the cockpit.

He made his way forward on the boat's windward side. The mayor and his friends saw him coming. "Aargh! A mutineer," Giovannetti called, and climbed up on the bowsprit's end. The woman chuckled.

"I really don't think that's a good idea," Carolina said.

"What's that?" the mayor said, and took another swig of wine.

Carolina said nothing, but he took a step forward, until the two men were less than three feet apart.

"Listen, kid, you got a nice little ship he-ah," the mayor said. "Me and my friends, we just wanna have a little fun. They jus' wanna see what I look like as a figurehead."

The mayor's audience chuckled. "You're too much, Joey," one of the women said. Carolina smiled.

"I'm glad you want to have fun. That's why I'm in business," the charter captain replied. "But I also have a duty to make sure that you're safe, that the people back in that cockpit are safe. It won't do any of us much good if I have to go fish you out of the water. I'd like you to help me out."

"Yeah? Well, I'd like you," Giovannetti deadpanned, "to suck my dick."

The lawyer and two women found this to be the funniest thing they had heard all day. Carolina took another step forward, until he was just a foot away from the man. "Now, Mayor, what would your constituents say about that kind of language?"

The mayor's eyes widened. The women fell abruptly silent.

"You tr'eatenin' me?"

"No, sir. That's not a threat. Now, if I was to, say, tell you that I'm going to the papers and TV stations as soon as we get back to Newport and enlighten them about your boorish behavior, well, I guess *that* would be a threat."

Joey Giovannetti stared at the captain, as if trying to comprehend what had just been said. The mayor's cheeks were already red and raw with sun, wine, and salt water. Now they reddened further. Joey Giovannetti was being shown up.

He swung the bottle. Carolina ducked, heard the glass crash and shatter against a metal stanchion, felt shards fall against his back and splash down on to the deck. *Maeve*'s bow hit the bottom of a trough and began to swing up. Carolina reached up and grabbed Giovannetti, pulling him forward, using the motion to haul the man off the bowsprit. The politician sprawled.

"Hey, you can't do that," the lawyer called. He, too, was drunk, and he reached down to try to pull the captain away.

Michael Carolina turned and threw a short right hook, strong enough to stop the man, not enough to knock him down. The women retreated. The lawyer rubbed the side of his jaw where the punch had landed. Mayor Giovannetti spewed a string of obscenities.

10

"That's assault. I'm gonna sue," the lawyer said.

"I doubt it," Carolina replied. He kicked glass away from the mayor, just as Giovannetti kicked a leg out himself, nearly knocking Carolina over. Giovannetti rose and threw himself at the captain, this time swinging heavy, meaty fists. Carolina stepped aside. The mayor pitched forward, heading toward the boiling sea. The boat's lifelines caught him, and held, just a few feet from the water. Spray hit him again in the face.

Carolina reached for the collar of Giovannetti's polo shirt and hauled him back aboard.

"Do that again and I just might let you go."

From his back pocket, the young captain yanked out a piece of line a quarter of an inch thick. Within thirty seconds, he had neatly lashed the mayor's hands together. He let him lie on the foredeck.

"I tried to be polite," Carolina said, "You wouldn't let me. Now"—he looked at the fuming lawyer and the blondes—"the three of you will kindly go back to the cockpit and sit down until we get back to the pier. I believe the entertainment portion of our trip is over."

As the three of them moved back toward the stern, the mayor started to throw up. His vomit smelled strongly of alcohol. Carolina held Giovannetti's head but did not untie his hands.

When the mayor was down to dry heaves, Carolina leaned forward, close to his ear. "Your Honor, I think you have two choices. You can join your friends in the cockpit and be quiet and polite until we get back to Newport in about an hour. Or you can continue to be obnoxious and unpleasant, as you have been ever since we left the dock. If you take the second choice, I will leave you trussed up like a chicken here on the foredeck. It pitches and rolls more here, and you're bound to get sick again. But you'll survive. Personally, I'd opt for the cockpit. It's your call."

The mayor thought for only a moment. He was through being defiant.

"I'll do what you ask."

"That's great," Carolina said, and hoisted the man to his feet. "I think we'll all be much happier this way."

"Aren't you going to untie me?" Giovannetti asked as the captain led him back to the cockpit.

"Sorry," Carolina said, "I've seen too many politicians who go back on a promise."

Carolina released the mayor as soon as *Maeve* docked at Bowen's Wharf. Giovannetti didn't fight. As they climbed off the yacht, the lawyer turned to the charter captain.

"Make no mistake, we will sue."

"And I'll win," Carolina said. "I'm a licensed captain. We were at sea. I'm entitled to do whatever is necessary to protect the people on my ship. Check your treatise on admiralty law, counselor."

"I got witnesses," the mayor rasped, feeling safe now that he was back on solid ground. He gestured toward the two women, both checking their makeup a few feet away. "They'll say whatever I want. I'll have your balls for breakfast."

"I didn't know you had such peculiar dietary habits, Mayor," a female voice said.

Giovannetti turned to look at the dark-haired woman.

"Who are you?" the lawyer asked.

The woman ignored him and stared at the mayor, who was still wiping dried vomit from his chin. "Hi, Joey."

A look of recognition hit the mayor's face.

"You know, I really wish I'd brought a camera." The woman's eyes were merry. "I mean, a picture of you lying up on the foredeck like that. There are people in Providence who would kill for a photograph like that. What a shame," she said in mock sadness. "I guess they'll just have to take my word for it."

"I don't know who you are, madam, but this is none of your affair," the lawyer said, not knowing who she was but trying desperately to gain some control over the situation. The withering look she gave him told him he had failed.

"Oh, but indeed it is my affair, counselor. You and your group here just ruined a perfectly lovely afternoon sail. And even though this is my day off, I'm thinking there might be a story here—especially if you decide to file a complaint against this man." She nodded toward Carolina. "It really should be the other way around. Anyway, I'm sure we can find a way to do something with it."

Carolina listened and watched in amazement. The woman had reduced the mayor to a quivering mass of jelly.

"You wouldn't," Giovannetti said.

"In a heartbeat."

The two blondes were watching with annoyed looks. This mean old sailboat captain had spoiled their fun, and now this woman had captured the attention of their clients.

And Joey wasn't his usual sarcastic, confident self anymore. In fact, Joey was begging. "Come on, this is all off the record." The mayor attempted to laugh. It came out sounding like a dog being whipped.

"Mayor, you are who you are. How can your actions be off the record?" the woman said, suppressing a smile. "Of course, this is my day off. If you were just to go your way and allow Mr. Carolina to go his, I doubt anything will come of this."

It didn't take long for Joey Giovannetti to make up his mind.

"Come on, Sal, let's go get a drink," he said to the lawyer. They turned and started walking down the pier. The two women had to run to catch up.

"Nice seeing you, Joe," the woman called after him pleasantly.

Michael Carolina turned to the man with his two daughters. "I'd be happy to refund your money," he said. "I hope you'll come again. Problems like this one are really the exception." The man took the cash and led his children down the pier. "And the truth is, I ought to pay *you*," he said to the woman. "Thank you very much for getting me out of that."

"My pleasure," she said, "and I don't need a refund."

"I didn't get your name."

"Shirley. Shirley Templeton. Would you like a drink? I want to talk to you about a job."

They sat in the outdoor patio of the Black Pearl, drinking Sam Adams from the bottle. Shirley Templeton ordered a burger with chili and onions, no cheese. Hordes of late-summer and early-autumn tourists were still in Newport, milling about, watching the yachts and the yachties and the other tourists.

"Do you get teased much about your name?" Carolina asked.

"About as much as you do about yours," Shirley said. "What is it, Italian?"

Carolina nodded.

"That's good, good. Ethnic names are big here."

"Pardon me?"

"We have a lot of Italians in this state. They'll like your name." The woman reached into a giant purse and pulled out a bottle of vitamin C. She popped two and swilled them down with beer. The gulp was quite audible.

"Want one?"

"Uh, no thanks," Carolina said, mildly intrigued. "Why do I have this feeling I know what kind of job you have in mind?"

"I'm a news director," she said.

"I figured that when you mentioned to the mayor that there was a story."

"I work for Channel Three in Providence. Been there six months." She bit into the hamburger, chewed thoughtfully for a moment, then swallowed. "Nothing like a little scandal to liven things up," she said, "but then, everyone already knows how Joey drinks and whores. In Providence, nobody cares as long as he gets people jobs, picks the garbage up, and keeps the property taxes in line."

"Is that right."

"I'm looking for a reporter, an investigative reporter."

"You are."

"I want to hire you."

Carolina drank some beer himself. It tasted wonderfully cool and sharp going down. "Too bad," he said, "I was starting to like you."

"What do you mean?"

"If you want to hire me as a reporter, you know who I am. If you know who I am, you probably also know that I don't care for news directors, especially ones that want me to work for them."

Shirley took a huge bite of hamburger and dribbled only a small amount of chili. She picked up a paper napkin and delicately wiped her face.

"Maybe I can do something to change your mind," she said.

"I doubt it."

"Even so, I'd like to hire you."

"Why?"

"Lots of reasons."

"Such as?"

"Such as your Italian surname. Like I said, lots of Italians in Rhode Island."

"My mother was Irish."

"Even better. Lots of them, too."

"That's a wonderful journalistic reason."

"There are others," she said. "You look good, for one. Handsome. You make a nice appearance on-camera." She paused a moment to look at him again. His face was square, almost chiseled, and deeply tanned from months on the water. His black hair was thick and full, cut short so it would stay out of his face. He had long, thick lashes on the lids of deep brown eyes and a nose that fit the rest of his features. Not too big or too small. Just right.

"But those are just icing. You want to know the real reason."

"I'm dying to hear."

"Because you're the guy who nailed Larry Traynor," she said, her eyes boring into him. He didn't blink.

"I think every news director in the country has heard of you," she said.

"That"—he nodded—"is why I don't work in TV news anymore."

"I don't think so," Shirley said. "I think there are other reasons."

Michael Carolina concentrated on removing the label from his beer. The image of Sam Adams slowly peeled into his hand.

"You know, when I heard you were down here, I couldn't believe it. A network exec, a friend of mine, was here on vacation, saw you, and gave me a call. Is this what you've been doing since you quit?" She made a gesture over toward *Maeve.*

"Yup."

"How long in Newport?"

"Just this summer. Last summer, I did Nantucket. I guess I'll go back there next year. The network execs who vacation there don't know me."

"Where have you been in between?"

"The Caribbean—Saint Thomas, Saint Johns. The Leeward Islands, mostly. Wherever the customer wants to go."

"How long has it been now?"

"Two years."

"What's Traynor doing?"

"Life without parole," Carolina said. "It's not my favorite memory."

"Sorry."

They both were silent for a moment. Shirley finished her beer. She caught the waitress's eye, then shook her bottle. The waitress fetched another.

"So why did you do it?" Shirley said after another long pull at the bottle.

"Do what?"

"Don't be coy. You know."

Carolina watched a sailboat coming in and tying up, a long wooden schooner with roller-furled sails and a big dog standing near the bow.

"I guess I was naïve," he said. "I thought I'd be all right, as long as I stuck to the truth. He was molesting little kids. When I figured that out, I wanted to report it."

"And got fired for your trouble."

"That's right."

"Well, you still managed to get the story out. I've seen the tape of that newscast. Unbelievable."

"I'm sure Larry Traynor would agree with you."

"Would you do it again?"

"I'd like to think that I would," he said. "But I don't know."

"I could offer you this much," she said, handing him a slip of paper with a number on it. "No contract. You'd be scheduled to work Sunday through Thursday, but it's really a flexible shift. You come in when we need you."

"I made more in my last job."

"Providence is a smaller market. We're the number-three station, and New England is still in a recession. And," she said with a "tough shit" look, "you're in no position to bargain."

"The hell I'm not. I didn't come looking for work. You came looking for me."

Having made a statement she could not back up, Shirley was now smart enough to say nothing.

"Tell me what it's like to be a journalist here," Carolina said.

She brightened. "The best. You know, people have called this state a smudge beside the highway from New York to Cape Cod. But don't believe it. It's home to some of the most beautiful coastline in the Northeast, maybe the whole Eastern Seaboard."

"I haven't been past the Newport Bridge," Carolina said. "Charter guests always want to head toward Cuttyhunk or Block Island."

"Well, take a cruise up north, to Prudence Island or up Mount Hope Bay. Have you been to Providence?"

Carolina shook his head.

"Beautiful city. People talk about it like it's a mob capital. But there are wonderful restaurants, a full-time repertory theater, and some of the most magnificent Colonial homes in the United States."

"You sound like one of those people over at the Convention Bureau. What do you report? I mean, besides the mayor's philandering?"

"It's a reporter's heaven. This is more like a small feudal kingdom than it is a state. Everyone knows everyone, or knows someone who does. Everyone has a turf, and most everyone has a patron, or a lord to whom they owe allegiance. Favors get traded like baseball cards. People say Rhode Island is corrupt. And they're right. It is."

"Worse than Washington or Chicago?"

"Different. In most places, I think corruption is an acquired trait, something that you fall into or develop over time. Here, it almost seems hereditary. It's in the political DNA. Been this way for three hundred years. You know what the colonists used to call this place?"

"Refresh me."

"Rogue's Island."

"Charming."

"It is. Because even though there are thieves and scoundrels here, this is the most independent, most stimulating place I've ever been. I'm not saying this just because I want you to come work here. I really mean it."

He believed her. But Shirley wasn't finished.

"I know you're wondering, Why should I go to work for her? I'll tell you. Because you're flattered. Because you need the money—you're not getting rich running day charters in Newport. Because you're good. Because you like to write and break stories. And for all the shit that TV newspeople take from critics and the public, it's still the most exciting business in the world. And," she said, looking both grim and determined, "because you still have something to prove to all those people who remember you as some renegade reporter who gets people killed."

"Did you memorize all of that?" Carolina asked.

"Some," she said. "I figured you'd be wondering."

"You're right."

Carolina finished his beer. He looked at *Maeve*. She would need her bottom scraped and painted and her topsides varnished before long. A reporter's salary wasn't much, but it was more than he was making. And the work was steady.

"One condition," he said.

"What?" she asked, her eyes bright.

"When I get into a story, I don't quit. I don't back off. That's why you know about me. And if that's why you want to hire me, that's the deal we should make."

"I may regret this, but I agree."

"Okay," he said.

"Wonderful. I am absolutely delighted. Can you start tomorrow?"

"That soon?"

"We're shorthanded," she said. "And I know you can do the job."

Shirley paid the bill and walked back to the boat with him.

He noticed that she was pretty, with pale blue eyes. Unlike many women, she had been careful with her face, had kept it from being damaged by the sun.

And somehow, she seemed familiar.

"Have we met somewhere before?"

"No," she said, "but you might remember me."

His expression showed that he did not.

"I worked with Larry Traynor. Before you were hired." Now he did remember. He had seen her on archive tapes at his old station.

"The news director who fired you," she said matter-of-factly, "he fired me, too. Thought I was too old."

"Why did you get into management?"

"More control, I guess. We all have different ways of dealing with the pain this business can cause. You went off on that boat of yours. I became a news director."

In a strange way, Carolina thought, it made sense.

"It's a small business," Michael Carolina said.

"Ain't it?" she agreed, and popped another vitamin in her mouth. "See you tomorrow. Nine A.M. sharp."

He watched as she walked down the pier, and he thought that for a news director, she might be all right.

The man waited in the shadow of history.

It was a home built in 1805, a massive building of brick and stone and wood. No one had lived there for years—the place was too expensive to heat and maintain. At night, it sat empty and dark, a shield from the light of streetlamps, offering a place to hide and, tonight, to meet.

The waiting man heard the footsteps coming down the tiny alley. They were quick but uneven as the person approaching picked his way through broken cobblestones.

"Evening," the waiting man said, his voice just above a whisper, as the steps drew into conversation range.

"Y'have something?" the other man said in a voice that was deep and heavily accented.

"Civil as ever," the waiting man said, handing over a package. The man with the accent fumbled with the paper, then snapped a lighter. The flame briefly illuminated his face. It was round and ruddy. He had dark eyes and a mashed potato of a nose, one that had seen more than a few brawls. The waiting man knew his companion was supposed to be a terrorist. But he looked more like a common thug.

"It's all there," he said, gesturing at the bag, crammed full with twenty- and fifty-dollar bills.

"It better be. Is Falcone gone?"

"Yes, he's gone. This is the last of it. Your payment, I mean." The man snapped the lighter shut and darkness covered them both like a blanket.

"Anybody follow him?"

"No."

"Y'sure?"

"Yes."

"Yeh, I bet you are." The man with the accent coughed hard, thrust his hands in his pocket, fumbling for a cigarette.

"Don't smoke here. It's bad enough that you used the lighter."

"Fuck off." Accent's fingers found what they were looking for. He jammed the cigarette in the corner of his mouth and lit up. The butt's end glowed like a firefly.

"So," Accent said, his voice softening, "how's it feel to be a member of the club?"

"What would you know about it?" the waiting man said.

"Know enough," Accent said. "Know you're not a founding member."

"And you're not a member at all. Just an errand boy. Now, is there anything else?"

"Y'know, I hate your kind," Accent said, "you and your fancy clothes and airs. Talk like some fokkin' English barrister."

"My, that is dreadful. In the future, I will be careful not to offend your delicate sensibilities. Now, is there anything else?"

"There is, in fact," Accent said. "A little something from the other members."

"Well, what is it?"

Accent had his hands in the pockets of his brown leather jacket. He hunched slightly and looked down to the ground. "They want you to know . . ."

Accent swung his fist up and out. The blade entered the waiting man just above the navel, driving until it struck bone somewhere along the spine. Then Accent heaved. He lifted the man almost off the ground, until his heels left the sidewalk and only the toes of his shoes touched the ground. Accent watched as the man's mouth opened and he exhaled. He hung there, trying to cough, trying to speak, but making no sound.

The impaled man's head fell forward until his ear was inches from Accent's mouth. "They want you to know, sir, that the only members of this club are those who founded it."

Accent let the eight-inch steel blade slip, then watched as the waiting man folded gently onto the ground. He knew it would take a long time for him to die. It gave Accent a measure of comfort. He wiped the blade on the sleeve of the wounded man's tweed jacket before closing the knife and placing it back in his pocket. He removed the man's billfold. The police would believe it was a simple robbery, at least for the first few days.

He picked up the package. He had dropped it when he used the knife. At the same time, he realized the cigarette was still in his mouth, burned down almost to the filter. He had balanced it there all during the execution.

He moved off down the street and checked the front of his jacket to make sure the ash had not burned a hole. His steps were still quick. But this time, they were even.

t was the sounds he had missed the most. The whirling, high-pitched gibberish sound of tape on fast forward or rewind. The tapping on computer keyboards that had replaced the typewriters and wire-service machines of more ancient newsrooms. And phones ringing; people speaking urgently or patiently, reacting angrily or, on occasion, laughing. Michael Carolina remembered some advice an older reporter had given long ago. "Relax," he said, "it's only television."

The memory, and the sounds, were comforting. They did not exist on a boat, not on *Maeve*. For more than two years, he had managed to escape it all, only to find that on his first visit back to a newsroom he actually felt nostalgic.

"Morning!" Shirley Templeton sported a teal silk jumpsuit with gold buttons. The outfit was dazzling, until he took in the Reebok high-tops on her feet. Then she looked positively ludicrous. "Ready for your first day?" she asked, nearly bouncing as she headed toward her office. "We're just starting the morning meeting."

"How about some layups, first? Maybe a little one-on-one? You know, just to warm up."

"My, but you're clever. I'm glad I hired you. Maybe we can find a nice dry budget hearing to send you to."

Carolina recoiled in mock horror.

Shirley's office was polluted. A tobacco-smoke haze met him at waist level and extended above his head, like the smog line in some western city. He sat down and through the mist saw a pretty brunette rifling a copy of the *Providence*

Herald. Next to her was the source of the smog, a fat, balding man in his late thirties sucking on a Camel as if it was the straw coming out of a milk shake. Shirley reached for a pack of Merits.

"You didn't smoke yesterday," Carolina said.

"Yesterday, I was on your turf. Today, you're on mine," she replied, firing up.

A young woman blew into the room and almost tripped over Carolina's legs. She held a file crammed with press releases and newspaper clippings.

"I'd like everyone to meet our new reporter," Shirley said. "Michael Carolina, this is Tisha Billings." The brunette glanced up from her paper and offered a slash-mark smile.

"And Ron Davis." The fat man stuck a doughy fist out. "How ah ya."

"And this is Lilly Simmons, our assignment editor." The woman with the file was still fussing with her clippings, but she stopped and offered a smile. Her face had the look of near-total innocence. "Welcome to Channel Three," she said, brushing a strand of hair from her eyes.

"Mike's worked in Texas and the Midwest," Shirley said.

"What stations?" Tisha Billings asked, for the first time appearing interested in something besides the paper. Shirley interrupted before Carolina could answer.

"Why don't we get started? Lilly, what have we got?"

"Judge Monteiro gets sentenced at ten."

"That scumbag." Davis rolled his eyes.

"Monteiro was a superior-court judge," Templeton explained. "He took five-hundred dollar 'fees' for referring cases to lawyers—that is, until one of them got in tax trouble and agreed to wear a wire."

"Now Monteiro's got tax trouble, too," Davis said, "in addition to the state charges. I hear he could get five years. Probably have to serve them out of state. At least three guys doing life at the ACI want to nail his Portuguese ass."

"Ron, remember our little talk?"

"Sorry," Davis said, looking smug.

"Ron has not quite figured out that ethnic slurs are bad form around here," Shirley said to Carolina. "Someday, they might even be a firing offense." Davis's smug look evaporated.

"What's the ACI?" Carolina asked.

"Adult Correctional Institutions." Lilly said.

"My, you really are new here, aren't you?" Tisha said. Her voice was sweet. Too sweet.

"We've got the hooker scandal," Lilly said, fumbling with another file.

"Yeah!" Davis said.

"You are such a pig." Tisha Billings looked back at her paper.

"Channel Nine got an interview with one of the ladies last night," Lilly said. "I think they may have paid for it."

Shirley turned to Carolina once more. "Two weeks ago, the state police raided the house minority leader's office. Apparently, the reps were running a brothel right inside the State House. Six men arrested, three women."

"They were taking turns." Davis snickered.

"Two of the reps were Democrats," Lilly said. "It was bipartisan."

"And the hookers are on the payroll. They're apparently qualified for state pensions," Shirley added. "The Attorney General is suing to revoke."

"I hear that hooker on Channel Nine had a forty-five-inch bust," Davis said.

"Did I say he was a pig?" came Tisha's voice from behind the newspaper.

"What else?" Shirley wanted to finish the list. At the same moment, a beeper chirped. Lilly reached down and yanked the device off her belt, then read the digital printout.

"There's a body off Benefit Street. In an alley."

"Could be homeless," Tisha said.

"Let's find out," Shirley said. "Michael, you go to Benefit Street. It's a new story, so you may not need a lot of background."

"No problem," Carolina said.

"Ron, go to Monteiro." Davis unsuccessfully attempted to stifle a groan, obviously disappointed at losing the hooker story. "Tisha, see what you can dig up on the prostitutes. I want our own interview, if possible."

The meeting broke. Lilly scurried to find a photographer for Carolina. For a moment, Michael and Shirley were alone in her office.

"Is it always like this?" Carolina asked.

"Like what?"

"Corrupt judges. Prostitutes with pensions. And isn't Benefit Street the best—"

"The nicest street in the city? Yes."

"So you have a lot of homicides on the nicest street in the city?"

"No," Shirley said, laughing, "but we do today. We also have slow news days, like anywhere else. But like I said, you're going to like Rhode Island. It's fucking news heaven."

Benefit Street is one of the oldest in America, a long, mostly straight thoroughfare that runs north to south midway up a slope called College Hill. The road begins a few yards from the northernmost point of Narragansett Bay and stretches just over a mile.

Benefit Street is filled with the trappings of Colonial wealth, ancient homes made of brick and wood and mortar, stone and iron nails. The Rhode Island School of Design can be found there, along with the superior and supreme courts. Downhill lies the guts of Providence commerce: office buildings, banks, and city hall. Uphill stands the institution that gave College Hill its name. Upon its founding, the school was called Rhode Island College. Later, the name was changed to Brown University, after the slave-trading family that financed the school in an attempt to gain respectability.

Near the southern end of the street, a mass of police cruisers and an emergency vehicle clustered together like flies on a rotten piece of meat. And that is what the cops and EMTs were examining when Michael Carolina and a photographer pulled up.

"Nice." The photog wrinkled his nose as they approached the cluster of people standing at the edge of the alley. A whiff of bowel hit Carolina's nostrils, and he gagged.

The photographer's name was Bob. He hoisted the Sony Betacam to his shoulder. A cop who seemed to know him waved his hand.

"Don't botha," the officer said. "You won't put this on TV. It ain't family viewing."

Carolina peeked down the alley and knew the officer was right. Whoever it was had been gutted.

"Had to take two stray dogs off to be destroyed," the officer said. "They found him. Started to eat 'im."

The EMT crews were packing up to leave. Nothing could be done. A white van from the medical examiner's office was pulling up instead.

"Any idea who it is?" Carolina said to the cop.

"Who are you with?"

"Channel Three."

"I ain't supposed to say," the officer said. "And I don't know you."

Carolina looked at the men gathered behind the police line. A few detectives and an assistant medical examiner. Two deaners, men who move bodies and assist at autopsies, had emerged from the white van and were in the process of unloading a stretcher and a body bag. Carolina looked back at the uniformed officer standing next to him. The man's fingertips were yellowed. He saw the photographer, shooting the crowd and the police cars, waiting for the deaners to put a bag around the dead man so he could shoot that, too.

"Bobby."

"Yeah?" The photographer didn't look up; he was sizing up a shot.

"Got any cigarettes?"

A minute later, he went back to the officer, still standing next to the yellow police tape.

"Like a smoke?" He held out the pack. The officer thought for a minute, then pulled two from the carton, put one in his mouth, and stuck another behind his ear.

"Doin' me a fay-va, huh? No I s'pose you t'ink I gotta do one for you."

"I wouldn't mind."

The cop grunted and lit up.

"Find out who lives at Two sixty-four Williams Street."

Carolina scribbled the address down. "And don't forget who done you a fay-va," the cop said, sauntering away as he motioned the crowd to stand back.

The news car had a cellular phone. Lilly Simmons picked up on the first ring.

"Do you have a city directory?" Carolina asked.

"Sure."

"I think I have the victim's address."

"That was fast."

"Ready? Two sixty-four Williams Street."

There was a loud crack at the end of the line, like a phone dropping and hitting the floor. Carolina heard a jumble of voices at the other end, then what sounded like a shout.

"Hello, Lilly? Hello?"

"Michael?" Shirley Templeton was on the line.

"Yes. What happened?"

"Did you say Two sixty-four Williams Street?"

"Yeah, that's what I got from—that's the address I have. I think it belongs to the victim."

"That's the address of Frederick Simmons. He's the Rhode Island banking commissioner."

"No shit. Then this is a hell of a story."

"He's also Lilly's father."

Sergeant Donald Corvese knew blood. He had seen it in Olneyville as a beat cop, when drug dealers and clients disagreed over price. He had seen it in domestic disputes in South Providence and over in Fox Point and once at a fancy house on Blackstone Boulevard, where a wife grew tired of her physician husband's beatings and dispatched him with a pickax.

But Corvese had never seen anything like this. Not on Benefit Street. Not anywhere.

"Like Jack the fucking Ripper," Corvese muttered, stepping around the mess.

A police photographer, an officer assigned to the detective division, snapped pictures with a 35mm for evidence. He caught the face, eyes still wide open, the mouth shaped like an O, looking surprised at the people paying so much attention. The photographer coughed. "So this guy was a banker?"

"Bank *commissioner*. Don't you read the papers?"

"Sports section, that's it. I leave the rest of it at the office."

"If you read a little more, maybe you could solve a case on your own."

"Why would I want to do that? Then they wouldn't need you. So why was he in the papers?"

Corvese looked down and swore. There was blood all over his brand-new pair of brown wing tips. It would probably stain. "Some kinda shit about bank insurance. You know, how they got a big fund to back up deposits. Private fund. Buncha banks and credit unions contribute and pool the money in case one of 'em gets in trouble."

"Yeah?"

"Yeah. So this guy, he was some kinda white knight. Up

testifying about how dangerous private insurance is. Unhealthy for the economy, that kind of happy crap. 'Bout a year ago, he was in the papers every day for a month. Front page, business page. Above the fold."

"Above the fold? What's that?"

"Never mind. He got a lot of attention."

The photographer took some more pictures. They had swept the scene, talked to neighbors. But the alley was next to a closed-up house. No one had seen or heard a thing.

"Dead how long, you think?" the photographer asked.

"More than six. He's pretty stiff."

"Yeah, I'd say that's about right. Who saw him last?"

"His wife. He lives a couple blocks from here. She said he went for a walk last night, late. Eleven, eleven-thirty."

Corvese looked around, checked out the crowd gathered at the end of the alley. He used to hate the people. Parasites and carrion. But after years of seeing them at every crime scene, he'd grown accustomed to them.

"So what happened?" The photographer was putting his camera away.

"With what?"

"Sir Galahad here. Knight of the holy insurance premium."

"Oh that—yeah. I don't know. I think it just sort of died. Far as I know, we still got banks with private insurance in this state."

The deaners were standing by, looking at the two cops, awaiting their cue to move in and load up.

The photographer rewound the roll of film and popped it out of the camera. As he dropped the roll into a processing bag, he shook his head. "And you ask why I don't read the papers? It's too depressing. Nothing ever fucking changes, that's why."

Alerio's was a delicatessen and a pizza parlor. It was also a prime social center for those who lived on Federal Hill. The food was good and cheap. People were always stopping in to purchase fresh cavatelli and linguine or carbonara or pink sauce made fresh in the back. The prosciutto had just the right cure, the olives just the right tang. Best of all, it had not been discovered by the Yuppies from the East Side or the suburbs.

Still, Alerio's had history. A few years back, when men like Raymond L. S. Patriarca still controlled all the mob activities in New England, an incredibly stupid Irish gangster had violated the cardinal rule of turf. He attempted to move in on a local gambling operation being run from a tenement two doors down. Apparently unaware that the little betting parlor was in an Italian neighborhood and absolutely unaware that it was already under the protection of a patron, the man showed up one evening cracking knuckles, limbering his thick neck muscles, looking for a cut. Pay up or legs break and houses burn, the gangster warned.

A few days later, he disappeared. Just vanished. Where, no one knew. When the police finally noticed, they squeezed a few guys on the street, then a few more in jail. The cops even came around the neighborhood to ask questions. But no one knew a thing.

Two weeks after the Irish hood disappeared, his family got a package. It was wrapped in brown paper and left on the doorstep: a box of ashes.

That week, Alerio's began advertising a pesto pizza. The pie was called a "Shamrock Special." Made in the special "Shamrock Oven." The locals swore by it.

When anything happened on Federal Hill, the people at Alerio's were among the very first to know. So it only seemed right that they were the first to hear about the run at Amerigo Vespucci Loan and Investment.

Vinnie, behind the counter, got the call. His sister Rosalie worked in the bank and Vinnie kept all his money there.

"So you gonna take it out or what?" he said.

"I can't," his sister replied. "It's in your name."

"Well, do somethin'. You're my sista, fe'Chrissake!"

"I am doin' somethin', Vinnie. I'm callin' you, ain't I?"

Vinnie undid his apron and bolted out the door.

"Hey!" Senator Colantoni shouted after him. "Where you goin'? What about my lunch?" The phone rang again and Elisa, the waitress, picked up.

"Call for you, Senator."

Senator John Colantoni had represented the people of Federal Hill for two decades. Like all Rhode Island legislators, he earned just $300 a year from his work at the State House. But Colantoni had used his power and privilege in other ways. He had a cushy job with a city school department that paid a $50,000 annual salary for about ten hours' work each week. In his younger days the senator had been dismissed from the army as undesirable after six miserable weeks in basic training when he failed to master the art of close order drill. But his status as a "veteran" enabled him to apply for and receive a special state pension, authorized by secret legislative fiat. And while he maintained a legal residence near Atwells Avenue, Colantoni spent most of his idle hours in a palatial estate in West Cranston. The fact that the senator didn't really live on Federal Hill never seemed to bother his constituents, as long as he helped to maintain a number of no-show jobs for the right people, and as long as he remained accessible at places like Alerio's.

"Yeah?" he said, holding the phone in one hand and a bread stick in the other. In a moment, his face turned white. "How long's the line?" He paused. "Can y'get me a place in front?" He hung up.

Elisa was just setting a chicken cutlet with red sauce at his place. Colantoni ignored it as he ran to the door.

"Sorry, honey, legislative emergency."

Little Anna shuffled down Atwells Avenue. A man hurrying past nearly knocked her down.

"Hey!" she cried, and when she looked up, she realized it was Vinnie from Alerio's. Where was he going in such a hurry? She barely got herself straightened out when it happened again. Senator Colantoni.

"Sorry, Anna," he called as he rushed past.

"What's the rush?"

"Business, dear." He was almost running down the street.

Anna kept moving, thinking how maybe she should vote for someone else the next election. Men were so rude these days. She wondered whether it might be appropriate information for discussion on one of the radio talk shows she listened to in the morning and afternoon.

Then she saw the line.

It reached down the street like a serpent, growing every second or two as wives, workmen, and a few people in business suits jostled to take their places. They were pushing and shoving, mumbling and complaining—all waiting to get in to Amerigo Vespucci.

Anna had seen this once before. When she was sixteen, Papa had kept all his money in a bank. Then one day, the bank had closed. A few lucky people got the word about what was happening in time to get their money out. Papa wasn't one of them. The shame of having lost two thousand dollars stayed with him until the day he died.

But Amerigo Vespucci was insured, wasn't it? It said so on that seal at the door.

What if she was wrong?

The line was still growing, and so she took her place. She looked down the street and saw Vinnie poking his head out, trying to see if there was a way he could move up. She had been his customer for years, yet he had told her nothing.

A man tried to cut in front of Anna. She swung her cane, and connected. The wood made a popping sound as it landed on the back of his head.

"Bitch," he muttered, holding his head and slinking to the back of the line.

"Serves you right," Anna called after him.

The line moved forward, but slowly. And it was still growing. There were scuffles and more grumbling. It was one o'clock. Then one-thirty. Finally, Anna was getting close enough to see the door.

The yowl of an emergency vehicle rocked the crowd like a slap. A state police cruiser with two troopers inside. Then another. Then two state government cars pulled up outside the bank. Two men wearing gray suits and carrying black briefcases walked into the bank, trying to ignore the catcalls and oaths coming from those standing in line.

A few more minutes went by. The temperature dropped and suddenly it felt like rain. The line stopped moving.

An angry shout went up near the front.

Amerigo Vespucci Loan and Investment was closed.

One of the gray suits had locked the door. Two troopers were at his side. Safe inside the bank's tiny lobby, the man taped a sign to the door's glass window:

CLOSED PER ORDER OF
THE DEPARTMENT OF BUSINESS REGULATION.

"Where's Frank?" someone shouted. "Where's Frankie Falcone?" The man in the door shrugged and walked back into the bank.

The crowd did not disperse. It began to push at the door. It rocked back and forth. A glass bottle smashed and shattered against the bank's brick sides.

Little Anna did her best to fend people off with her cane. But it was dangerous on the street and no one paid her much attention. An elbow found its way to her head. Then she tripped, and was barely able to catch herself. There was a roar as more sirens came along, and Providence and state police spilled on the streets and alleys surrounding Amerigo Vespucci Loan and Investment. One of the officers saw Little Anna and helped move her across the street.

"Where's Frankie?" she asked him. "Where's my money?"

"Who can go cover a riot?" Shirley Templeton wanted to know. The silk jumpsuit was beginning to look a bit droopy since Shirley had taken over for Lilly in the morning.

Carolina was busy screening tape from the morning homicide. Lilly had actually agreed to do an interview about her father. Said how proud she was of him. How she could not understand why this would have happened. Detective Corvese eventually made a statement about the case. Carolina was still putting the piece together.

Shirley edged past his editing booth. Carolina knew that Davis was in the next one, bullshitting with a photographer. He had finished his story on Judge Monteiro, who had drawn four years after breaking into tears in open court. Now Shirley was telling him to head to Atwells Avenue.

"Pretty busy here on your first day," she said after Davis was gone.

"Certainly wasn't boring." He popped the tape out of the deck, preparing to go write a script. "I'm sorry about Lilly this morning."

"You couldn't have known. I'm sure she understands."

"She seems nice."

"She is. Smart, too. You must know what a tough job that is to fill."

It was. Assignment editors are the most overworked and underappreciated people in any television newsroom. Part journalist, part traffic cop, part negotiator. "Ever wonder what it's like?" an old one had once asked Carolina. "Go home tonight and get your clock radio and your stereo and put them together. Tune them all to different channels and turn them on. Get your telephone and call me. I'll give you a ring every ten to fifteen seconds. You might want to invite a couple of your neighbors over and have them stand over you and scream about what story they are covering, when are they leaving, whether there is a photographer available. That will almost give you an idea of what it's like."

"So what's happening? Where did Ron go?" Carolina asked.

"A bank just crashed. There was a run before it happened, I guess, and then a riot broke out when the state closed its doors. I hope Ron gets there in time for some decent interviews and video."

"What's the name of the bank?"

"Amerigo Vespucci Loan and Investment."

"Any idea what caused the crash?"

"Not yet."

Carolina looked at the videotape in the machine before him. It was year-old file video of Frederick Simmons testifying in front of a legislative committee on the issue of federal deposit insurance.

"Shirley, was Amerigo Vespucci federally insured?"

"No, it was private. That's why the state took it over."

Carolina went back to his desk. The drawers were empty. He had to grab a phone book from another reporter's cubicle. He called the Providence police and asked for the detective he'd met that morning.

"Corvese."

"Detective, Michael Carolina from Channel Three."

"Yeah?"

"We met this morning."

"Right. New kid on the block."

"That's the one."

"Doesn't smoke but gives 'em out."

"I do?"

"I wasn't born last month, kid. Watch out for cops like that, sometimes they get it wrong."

"I don't know what you mean."

"Yes you do. Anyway, if you play straight with me, I'll help you out. Deal?"

"Okay. Got a follow-up question."

"Go ahead."

"Are you looking for any connection between the death of Frederick Simmons and the collapse of Amerigo Vespucci Loan and Investment?"

"Vespucci is closed?"

"That's what we hear. I understand about a dozen of your units are up there trying to calm people down."

Corvese swore. "Would have been nice for them to tell us over in detectives."

"I take it, then, you haven't been looking."

"Not yet. We may now."

"I see."

"That was on background, by the way."

"All right."

"What made you think we would check into that?"

"Simmons's record last year on federal deposit insurance."

There was silence for moment. Then Corvese spoke. "Not bad, kid."

"Excuse me?"

"You're kinda like Yogi. Smarter than the average reporter."

Carolina laughed. "That's the first time I've been compared to a cartoon character." He heard the sound of a muffled voice on the other end of the line.

"Okay, Yogi. Wanna tip?"

"Sure."

"I have just been handed a fax from the state police. You know who Frankie Falcone is?"

"No. Should I?"

"He's the president of the now-closed Amerigo Vespucci Loan and Investment Company. He's wanted for questioning about the collapse of his bank. And no one has seen him for the last two days."

Carolina's piece that night was a knockout. It examined Simmons's death in the morning and the bank collapse in the afternoon. He worked in the historical material about Simmons and his public support of federal deposit insurance, how the effort might have prevented Vespucci's failure had it not died in committee. Then he connected the two problems with the information about the police looking for Falcone and trying to determine whether the collapse and the death were tied together.

The two competing stations treated the bank collapse and Simmons's death as totally separate stories.

"I hope Lilly watched," Shirley Templeton said. "You made her dad look like a hero."

"She may have had other things on her mind," Carolina said.

Tisha Billings tapped him on the shoulder.

"Haven't I read about you somewhere?"

"I don't know. Have you?" Carolina said.

"Didn't you work for a station where an anchor killed a lot of people?"

"Tisha," Shirley said, "I wanted to ask you something about your story. What happened to the interview with the prostitute? And didn't you see the memo about not reusing the file video of the reps zipping their flies as they were being arrested?"

"Let me explain," Billings said as Carolina slipped away.

The man with the accent worked for a partnership. In fact, it was more of a club, composed of three men who had known one another for years. One was Francis Xavier Falcone, banker turned fugitive. Another was a high-ranking member of the Rhode Island General Assembly. The third was standing in front of him in the living room of a magnificent home overlooking Narragansett Bay. The man swirled brandy in a snifter and looked out a picture window. He was angry. Simmons had been useful. His image as the enemy of private banking had been the perfect cover. But when Simmons had pushed for a piece of the club's action, his death had become a necessity. Too bad it had to coincide with the run at Vespucci.

The man sniffed the Courvoisier, then swirled the glass, staring as the brown liquid washed counterclockwise around the crystal base.

"I thought it would take longer than this."

"For what?" Accent asked.

"For the pieces to begin fitting together. For the cops and the fucking reporters to start figuring it out. If they ever figured it out at all."

Accent shrugged. "That's your business, not mine."

"You're wrong," the man in the window said. He turned back to Accent, standing impassively in his worn leather jacket. "You're going to make it your business."

Twilight was descending. It turned the bay into a slate of orange and pink. The man sniffed his brandy, checking its nose. It had been aged for years. Fine stuff.

"How did it go with Simmons?" the man said, sipping.

"The way I expected," Accent said. "I must say, he seemed a bit surprised when I stuck him."

The man made no sign that he had heard. He kept watching the water. The bay's colors were still changing, slowly turning to gray. Soon the gray would turn to black and he would go outside and listen instead of watching. But first he needed to give instructions.

"There's a new reporter at Channel Three. Has the last name of a state. He looks and sounds like a guinea to me. I want you to keep an eye on him."

"All right."

"If he shows more interest in Simmons or the bank, we might have a problem. And if that happens, it's your business. *Your business.* Do you understand?"

"Yes."

"You may have to divert his attention."

Accent grinned. "Of course."

"Permanently."

4

The phone lines burned at WAIL radio, where the Reverend Rasmus was holding court. The callers were all talking about Rasmus's favorite subject: the failure of government to protect the masses from their own stupidity.

Today the specific problem was a bank. Amerigo Vespucci L and I. Rasmus had never heard of it until seeing the headline of that morning's *Providence Herald*. But that didn't stop him from becoming an immediate expert.

"I had all my money there!" one caller whined.

"You have a right to get it all back," Rasmus answered as he sucked on a Coke.

"When?" the caller wanted to know.

"I hope it is soon, sir, soon. I will pray for your currency's swift return." When Rasmus spoke, his voice seemed like a blend between southern drawl and Brooklyn nasal—which made sense, since Rasmus really came from Brooklyn and his radio show evoked images of a fire-breathing Baptist minister.

"These heathen, sir, these heathen!" he shouted. "These heathen in the government of this sorry and afflicted state have a duty to you and to yours! An obligation to you and those like you! They must atone!" Actually, Rasmus hoped the bank stayed closed for months while the public screamed about thawing out frozen accounts. This financial crisis was good shit, he thought. People never got tired of talking about their money.

"Sarah from Warwick, are you ready to WAIL?" he said to the next caller.

"Isn't that insurance fund private?" Sarah asked.

"You tell me, Sarah." Rasmus slurped on the Coke again. He hadn't really bothered to read the whole *Herald* article.

"Well, that's what I understand. And if I'm a taxpayer, why should I have to pay for the failure of this privately insured institution? What'd it ever do for me?"

"What did it do for you?" Rasmus screamed. "That's precisely my point! Why should we pay for the greed of others? Who says it is up to us to pay for this mess?"

"Well . . . you just did—"

"Thank you, Sarah, and may God bless you. You're listening to the wailing of the people on WAIL, Talk Five seven oh. This is the most very Reverend Rasmus, and we'll be back after these messages from our God-fearing sponsors." Rasmus lit up a smoke as the station went into a break. The program director stuck his head inside the door of the foam-encrusted studio.

"Way to fire 'em up, Sol."

The talk host nodded and blew smoke rings. His real name was Sol Herskowitz. The only preaching he'd ever done was on this ten-thousand-watt AM channel, though he did hold a mail-order divinity degree from the Church of the Living Iguana in Death Valley, California. He'd applied after reading an ad in the back of *Rolling Stone,* and found the religious background useful when he looked for his first on-air job. Before the radio gig, Sol had sold cleaning products for Amway.

"Hey, what the fuck do we know about this banker, you know, Frankie Bird or whatever?"

"It's Falcone, Frankie *Falcone,* Sol. Whatever is in the paper is what we know." WAIL was a tight ship, management liked to say, which was much nicer than saying it was too cheap to hire reporters to staff a news department. So what was in the paper or appeared on TV provided the fodder for Sol's broadcast cannon. This troubled Sol to no end, because he knew that in order to succeed, he needed an edge on the region's other talk-show hosts. Fresh information. Something that would convince the audience that Rasmus was on the cutting edge of Rhode Island current events.

Sol tried to establish a relationship with some of the local media, tried to get reporters to clue him in on leaks and breaking stories. He'd promised beer and cigarettes, even a guest shot on his show. He couldn't understand why no one took him up on the offer.

"So you got no fucking clue as to who this Falcone character is?"

The PD shook his head and quietly closed the door.

"Stand by, Rev," a producer called.

The medieval groaning of a group of monks washed out of the speakers and signaled the masses that Rasmus, the Savonarola of Rhode Island, was back from commercials.

"My children"—Sol's lips brushed the foam-rubber microphone cover, almost caressing it, as if he was making love—"there has been a demon in our midst. A man who has used us and abused us for years and years. A man who has won our trust and our hearts and mostly"—his tone changed—"our MONEY." Rasmus paused for emphasis, and when he spoke again, it sounded as if his vocal cords had been strung across hot coals. "This man worked on Federal Hill, in the heart of our city, in the midst of our working classes, in the very bosom of the teeming masses. He said he was one of us, that he would help us save for the future, prepare for retirement. For the glory that awaits in the next life.

"And this man was Judas! He took our silver! Our thirty pieces! He took more than thirty pieces! He took it all!"

"You're mixing your religious metaphor, Rev," the producer called.

"I'm Jewish—New Testament ain't my bag," Sol responded, his hand pressing the mute button.

The Reverend Rasmus wiped away a fleck of spittle that

had formed at the right corner of his mouth. He took a breath and roared, "WHERE ARE YOU NOW, FRANK FALCONE, AND WHAT HAVE YOU DONE WITH OUR MONEY?"

Michael Carolina and every other reporter in Rhode Island were wondering the same thing. But not everyone could cover the story.

"I've been in town longer than he has," Tisha Billings complained to Shirley. "I have good sources with the cops." Tisha's one good source was a police sergeant who had tried to feel her up one night in a downtown bar. The good sergeant had indicated that plenty of other officers would also be willing to work as sources in exchange for certain favors. Tisha had blown him off, but with enough diplomacy to convince him he might have a chance someday.

"Tisha, you're a wonderful reporter," Shirley said, thinking that Tisha wouldn't be able to find her way out of a paper bag on this one. "But Mike got a good start on this yesterday. I have to give him a chance to see how far he can go. Want a vitamin?" She held out a huge jar of B tablets.

"I want that story," Tisha said, stomping out of the office. Carolina had to jump to get out of her way.

"What's with her?"

"Just some competitive spirit." Shirley shook her jar of B's. "Want one?"

"What the hell." Carolina popped a tablet in his mouth and swilled a little coffee from the mug he was carrying. "Why do you take so many of these?"

"I'm a lousy cook, love junk food, and work too much," she answered.

"That's sounds rehearsed."

"It is. Everybody asks me that."

"Don't they give you a lot of gas?"

"No one's complained."

Carolina couldn't think of any way to respond.

"So where can you go with this?"

"Oh, I've got a few ideas," he said, and sat (her.

Any investigative reporter who is worth a damn will admit that legwork is boring. Necessary, but boring.

It took Carolina three hours to get around town to the agencies he needed to check. At both the secretary of state's office and the Department of Business Regulation, he got a healthy dose of runaround.

"What do you want the records for?" a blue-haired clerk wanted to know.

"Do I need a reason?"

"You gotta fill out a sheet and say who you are and why you want 'em."

"Do you have a copy of the state's public records statute?"

"No."

"This is your lucky day. I do." Carolina withdrew the sheet from a folder and handed it to the woman. "If you can find the section where it says I have to tell you why I want the records, I'll be happy to comply."

The woman pushed the sheet away without looking at it. She didn't like being shown up.

"You gotta fill out the sheet or you don't get nothin'."

"Gee, I don't know if I can do that," Carolina said. "Maybe I can do something else. Maybe I can call my station and have them send a camera over. Then I can do a story about how civil servants are violating state law by refusing to allow a citizen to review a public document. You can be the star. Now, what's your name, so I can credit you on television?"

The clerk didn't give her name. She was already pulling the documents out of a file cabinet.

At the Department of Business Regulation, a clerk tried

another trick. "This is going to take some time. I'll need several hours, maybe even a day or two, to pull the reports you want and make sure it doesn't violate any state confidentiality laws." This clerk was a man in his forties. When he spoke, he rolled his eyes for no apparent reason.

"Here's a copy of the public records statute"—Carolina smiled back—"and the pertinent exemptions. That's funny, annual reports of state-chartered banks are not among them. I guess that solves the confidentiality problem. Oh yes, and here are the penalties for violating the provision. I believe there's a one-thousand-dollar fine against the organization and the individual state employee. Now, let's see, Mr. Moretti—am I pronouncing your name correctly?"

"Just a minute." The man was back in two minutes and dumped the reports on the counter.

Detective Corvese wasn't in when Carolina stopped at the police station. Then he went to the library and the Registry of Motor Vehicles.

But he couldn't find the connection. At noon, his beeper went off.

"What's up?" he asked when Shirley picked up the phone.

"Presser up at the statehouse at one o'clock. Governor has an announcement about Amerigo Vespucci. I'll send a shooter to meet you. Are you getting anywhere?"

"Not yet." He was leafing through the copies from the secretary of state's office and the annual reports from Vespucci. They listed just one president and CEO, Francis Xavier Falcone, and one director, who for all that Michael Carolina could see existed only on paper. One lousy director . . .

"I'll be damned," he said, nearly dropping the phone receiver. A woman with big hair and dragging a toddler flashed him a dirty look.

"What . . . what is it?"

"I don't want to get your hopes up," he said, "but if I'm

right, you're going to have a very unhappy employee. And another great story."

Governor Wilbur Dunleavy had made money in jewelry. Costume jewelry of the type sold in department stores across the country. In fact, Dunleavy did not really make the money himself. He had inherited it from a wealthy father and grandfather, who had both grown rich on the sweat of Irish, Italian, and Portuguese immigrants. The immigrants labored in the Dunleavy factories for just over minimum wage. From their labor, Dunleavy was able to live a privileged life. Family membership in the right clubs. Summers in Newport or on the islands. Good schools.

When young Wilbur was twelve, an unfortunate event occurred. He was guarding the goal in a lacrosse game and was struck in the groin by a shot launched with great speed from just outside the crease. The injury later proved traumatic to his psyche and his loins.

As he grew older and prepared to choose a career, Wilbur's father made it clear that he wanted his son to be more than just a jewelry executive.

"Look at the kids of that bootlegger up in Massachusetts," his father said. "Those Kennedys have the right idea. One's already in Congress, and his brothers are sure to follow. Bet one of them is going to be President someday. Irish Catholics. Goddamn. We can hold the world by the balls, if we don't let the dagos get in the way."

So Wilbur got into politics.

He spent the early part of his career learning the ropes, serving in the Rhode Island General Assembly. He developed an understanding of the status quo, the smoke-filled room, the parliamentary games and arm-twisting that are part and parcel of the legislative process. He took care of the people who had gotten him elected and would get him elected again. And whenever possible, he made sure that the state's business climate was conducive to the growth of the family business.

It was just the kind of experience needed to run the state of Rhode Island.

Not that candidate and then governor Dunleavy didn't talk a good game. The public loved to hear about reform and change, about cleaning up government and making sure that public officials towed the line. In debates, Dunleavy hammered the incumbent for political trade-offs and payoffs, for making back-room deals and telling front-room lies. When Dunleavy won, he threw all the previous administration's political appointees out and made a show of getting rid of a few of the more flagrant abusers in civil service: a transportation official who claimed a back disability but moonlighted as an insurance adjuster; a welfare department director who only came to work on payday. Dunleavy cleaned them out. He promised a new era for Rhode Island government.

Then he hired all his cronies. New era indeed.

While Dunleavy was more than a figurehead, true political insiders knew that he did not run the state. The job really belonged to his chief of staff, Johnny Rollins. Rollins was the ultimate political hack. He had started in college, doing everything from picking up handbills at the printers to sneaking around at night stealing the signs of candidates who had dared to challenge general assembly incumbents without party approval. Rollins slowly and carefully ascended the ranks, learning the ropes, developing a talent for figuring the angles on every issue, every dispute, every deal. He had a way of turning every matter to someone's advantage, usually his own.

And he did it all without ever actually holding elected office. That was what Rollins preferred: the power, not the limelight.

It was never really clear who had hitched his wagon to whom, Dunleavy to Rollins or vice versa. But somehow the tandem had worked. Worked fine. Until now.

Now a bank had failed, and the police were investigating the remarkable coincidence that the state banking commissioner had been gutted like a pig on the very same day. Somewhere far back in his mind, Wilbur Dunleavy saw visions of an attackman coming off a pick, taking a feed from a midfielder, winding up and cranking a shot at the goal.

"They're not gonna hit me," he said.

"What was that, sir?" Johnny Rollins said. Rollins always said "sir" when he felt the need to supplicate.

"Nothing. Is he checked out?"

"Yes, sir."

"And?"

"We've found nothing, sir. Nothing other than the ordinary relationship one would expect between a regulator and a banker."

"And what is that? In this state, 'ordinary relationship' could mean they're taking showers together, for Chrissake."

"As far as we can see, they're both dry, sir." The chief of staff chuckled.

"I'm not laughing, Rollins."

"No, sir. From what I can tell, their relationship was cordial. There is, uh, one small problem, sir."

"Beautiful. What is it?"

"Amerigo Vespucci hasn't had an audit for the past three years."

"Oh great. Just great. And I've been in office for what, two years and four months? That's just fucking fabulous, Rollins. How the hell do I deal with that?"

"Sir, I would suggest that you take a pro-active approach when you meet with the press."

"How am I supposed to be pro-active when we've got a bank shut down, its president missing, and my chief regulator dead? Tell me, Rollins, how do I pro-act?"

"Is that a word, sir?"

"Don't get smart with me."

"Sir, I suggest you announce a full investigation. Say as

much as you regret the tragic demise of Mr. Simmons, you are announcing a full-scale probe of his office and the way that it handled bank audits. You tell them that you are shocked to learn that no audits have been done on Vespucci for the past three years and that you intend to get to the bottom of the situation."

For the first time since his meeting with Rollins had begun, Wilbur Dunleavy seemed to relax.

"I like that. Full-scale investigation. Get to the bottom of it. Think that'll work?"

"May I suggest, sir, that you appoint me to head up the investigation?"

"Damned good idea. I like that, Johnny. We'll go out there and I'll fume and bang around, say I'm not going to stand for this sort of thing. Then I'll designate you to head up a commission. Press'll love this shit."

An aide knocked on the door of the office and slipped a note in John Rollins's hand. The chief of staff took his time unfolding it and gazing at its contents.

"What's that?" Dunleavy said.

Rollins coolly handed the paper to his boss. "The latest figure from the boys down at Vespucci. I took the liberty of asking them to report to me. I'm sorry, sir, but it looks like the news is not so good. About fourteen million is missing."

Dunleavy stared at a Buttersworth oil painting mounted above the office fireplace. Rollins watched his boss. He could never understand why, when faced with a tight spot, the governor always seemed to drop his hand to cover his balls.

5

The governor's ceremonial office is gilt-edged and covered with Persian carpet. It is filled with relics and souvenirs of Rhode Island history. A Gilbert Stuart portrait of George Washington, the one where the President has his mouth stuffed with cotton, hangs on one wall. Silver bowls and place settings from the battleship *Rhode Island* lie in a glass case at the center of the room. The outer doors open onto a balcony that offers a magnificent view of Providence's downtown.

Now the room was filled with television lights as crews from the three local TV stations and four stations from Boston prepared to tape the governor's press conference. In front of them, print and electronic journalists milled about, finding seats and quizzing one another on what they knew or what angle to pursue. For the locals, it was a matter of parry and thrust, trying to determine what the competition was doing while hiding one's own plans. There was a sense of paranoia, a neurosis that beset the reporters, each one fearing that someone else might just have an angle that others had failed to consider.

The out-of-towners didn't have as much at stake. It was a big story, sure, but they knew it would lead their newscasts only if there was nothing important in Boston. After all, this was only Rhode Island. The Boston reporters were quietly but markedly snide; they were slumming. Covering Providence was only a slight cut above working a story in Portland or Springfield.

Michael Carolina sat apart from them all. He was the new guy. There had been no time for introductions. And he worked for Channel 3, the station the other locals mocked, the doormat of the market.

"See that guy?" someone muttered. "That's the one who made the connection with Simmons."

"Yeah, I heard about that from my producer."

Carolina pretended not to hear.

The sound of still-camera motor drives roused him. Governor Wilbur Dunleavy had entered the room and moved gracefully behind the wooden podium with the state seal dressing the front. He shuffled a set of papers and tugged a pair of reading glasses from the breast pocket of his gray silk suit, giving the TV photographers time to roll some tape. Press aides squirreled about distributing releases.

"Ready?" Dunleavy said.

"Today I have ordered an immediate and full investigation of the Department of Business Regulation. I am shocked, *shocked*"—he gripped the podium sides—"to learn that for the last three years the department's banking division failed to conduct an audit of the financial condition of Amerigo Vespucci Loan and Investment Company. This situation is unusual, to say the least, and cannot be tolerated. In addition, it would appear that the condition of finances at Vespucci is far more severe than originally believed. State auditors have informed me that the amount of money that is missing is in excess of"—his voice dropped and the crowd of press leaned forward—". . . in excess of ten million dollars."

A print reporter let out a whistle. Camera strobes flashed. Dunleavy squared himself up and took a breath.

"Let me say at this point that I intend to get to the very bottom of this matter. I intend to find out what went wrong and why, and I assure the people of Rhode Island that this sort of situation will never happen again. To that end, I have asked Jack Rollins, my chief of staff, to take charge of the

DBR investigation. I am confident that Mr. Rollins will quickly and ably discover the roots of this problem. I will now accept your questions."

"How much more than ten million?" someone shouted.

"The precise figure is still changing."

"Over twelve million?" a TV reporter from Channel 9 asked.

"Possibly."

"Thirteen?"

"Don't know. We're working on it." The governor swallowed hard.

"Why aren't the state police getting involved?"

"They will if it's necessary."

"You don't think it's necessary now?"

"What about the FBI?" a radio reporter asked.

"One question at a time," Dunleavy asked. The assembled crowd reminded him of a pack of wild dogs. "I do not believe that this is a matter that comes within federal jurisdiction." I hope it doesn't, Dunleavy thought. Like all state executives, he had a healthy fear of agencies he could not control.

"Governor, does the name Simon Frederickson mean anything to you?"

Dunleavy turned to stare at the reporter seated in the front row. Michael Carolina smiled pleasantly.

"No," Dunleavy said.

"So no one by that name has ever worked in your administration?"

"Not to my knowledge." Dunleavy shot a look over to Rollins. Am I in trouble? the governor seemed to ask. Rollins gave an imperceptible shrug. The governor dropped his hand involuntarily, but caught himself before it reached his crotch.

"Any other questions?"

There were—about what the governor or other authorities knew about Frankie Falcone and what timetable had been set for returning depositors' funds. But there were no hard answers to give, and the reporters were still trying to understand how a multimillion dollar embezzlement had managed to escape the attention of state regulators. Carolina drew a finger across his throat, a signal to his photographer to stop rolling on the governor and instead shoot cutaways of the room. Carolina gathered his notes and the file he had started on the Amerigo Vespucci story.

"Got something?" a newspaper reporter asked, inquisitive but friendly.

"We'll see," Carolina said.

"Who's Simon Frederickson?" a reporter from Channel 9 asked him. She was less friendly.

Carolina shrugged. "Watch tonight. Maybe we'll both find out."

On his way out of the governor's office, Carolina felt a tap on his shoulder.

"I don't think we've met."

The reporter turned.

"I'm Jack Rollins, the governor's chief of staff."

"And new lead investigator," Carolina said, taking Rollins's extended hand. "Michael Carolina."

"What were you getting at back there? The Simon Frederickson question?"

"You're the man in charge of finding out what happened. Why don't you tell *me*?"

Rollins flushed slightly, then shook it off.

"I'm big enough to admit I don't know it all. I'm just getting started. Sounds like you may have something. But if you don't want to share . . ."

"Sorry," Carolina said, "I'm not used to answering questions, just asking them."

Rollins smiled. "You're pretty good at both, seems to me."

"Thank you." Carolina started to walk away, then stopped.

"I'd check Vespucci's incorporation papers," he said, "over at the secretary of state's."

"Why?" Rollins asked.

Carolina shook his head. "There's a limit to my generosity."

Rollins gave the reporter an appraising look, as if he was determining whether he should push a little bit further. Carolina noticed but said nothing. Finally, the chief of staff shrugged.

"Thanks," he said, "I owe you one."

Carolina smiled. "Not at all." He walked away.

Rollins called, "By the way, welcome to Rhode Island."

"Great to be here," Carolina said.

"This is incredible," Shirley Templeton said.

"I didn't notice it right away," Carolina said, running a hand through his hair. "But it's too much of a coincidence. Did you call her?"

"Of course. After we run it, everyone in town is going to be after them. She didn't know a thing."

"What about her mother?"

"Nothing. They have too many other problems to worry about."

"So we're going with this?"

"Hell yes. Here, have a vitamin."

At six, Channel 3's anchor introduced Carolina's story.

"The cases of a dead bank commissioner and a missing banker become more tangled tonight. Frederick Simmons was the respected chief regulator of Rhode Island's financial institutions. Then he was found murdered near Benefit Street yesterday. A few hours later, Amerigo Vespucci Loan and Investment Company closed after a run on deposits, and bank president Frankie Falcone is missing. Now, Channel Three has learned that Simmons and Falcone may have been business partners. Michael Carolina has the exclusive story on how death and disappearance have blended together."

" 'Death and disappearance,' I added that," Shirley said, smiling.

"Nice," Carolina said, trying not to wince.

The piece opened with the tape of Simmons body being loaded into the ME's van, then switched to some old file pictures of Frankie Falcone, looking every bit the banker in his Atwells Avenue office.

"Where'd you find that?" Carolina asked.

"We had an archive story about small banks from a few years back," Shirley answered.

The video of Falcone dissolved into the near-riot scene outside Vespucci the day before. Carolina noticed how several men ran past an elderly lady dressed in black. The woman had fallen down and was swinging at the men with her cane.

Then a graphic came on screen. It showed papers, the annual reports Carolina had obtained earlier in the day. Through the use of a television animation device called a DVE, one page seemed to slip out of the group. Then a name, Frank Falcone, lifted off the page and flew to the center of the screen. In another moment, another name flew front and center.

"Simon Frederickson is listed as the bank's sole director," Michael Carolina said, "but neither the telephone book, the Registry of Motor Vehicles, nor the state tax rolls show any listing of a Simon Frederickson in the state of Rhode Island." The tape cut to a shot of Wilbur Dunleavy, looking startled and bewildered, saying he knew no one named Simon Frederickson.

"The only clue," the track continued, "as to Frederickson's whereabouts or identity is on one Vespucci annual report that dates back three years. In it, Frederickson lists an address at Two sixty-four Williams Street in Providence."

The screen dissolved again, switching to a stand-up shot of Carolina on Williams Street. "That address belongs to Frederick Simmons. In that year, Simmons was named as Rhode Island's bank commissioner. We asked the Simmons family for comment on the similarity of the names, the address, and the possible connection between Frank Falcone and Frederick Simmons. Family members would only say that any such connection comes as a complete surprise."

"This is great!" Shirley was almost giggling. "No way it's a coincidence."

Tisha Billings stood at the office door, simmering.

"Who leaked that to you?"

Carolina smiled and said nothing.

"No one did. He dug it up," Templeton said.

Billings tossed her hair and stalked away.

"Call it a hunch, but I don't think she's all that thrilled that I work here," Carolina said.

"Don't worry about her. You have any plans for dinner?"

"No."

"Like red meat?"

"Excuse me?"

"Steak."

"Oh. On occasion."

"I know a place."

The Capital Grille looks like a turn-of-the-century New York steak house, which is precisely the look that the owner wanted. It is housed in an old railroad building just a quarter of a mile from the statehouse and thrives on a steady diet of lawmakers and lobbyists, deal makers and power brokers. Customers in turn thrive on a diet of aged beef, baseball-sized tomatoes, onions, and potatoes. If any of the patrons read reports about the health woes caused by rare steak and prime rib, they keep it to themselves. The Capital Grille is for those who love serious meat.

"You come here often?" Carolina said to Shirley.

"Maybe every few months," she replied. "Dinner is worth a day's pay, but the food is great and it's fun to watch who comes in."

It was the middle of the week, so the wait wasn't long. They were given a very visible spot in the feeding den, a table on the main floor. Behind them, an upper-level terrace afforded a view of those on the floor. In back, there were booths, for customers who preferred a more private place to devour their twenty-five-dollar steaks and creamed spinach.

"Who sits up there?" Carolina inclined his head.

"Those who want to see more than to be seen, I guess," Shirley said, "and those who are cutting deals."

"We don't look like we're cutting a deal?"

"No. We look like we're celebrating."

A waiter brought menus. "I've seen circus posters that were smaller," Carolina said, surveying the dozens of different cuts and selections. He lowered the menu in time to see a man pointing at him from a table near the restaurant's window. The man was sitting with two others. All three carried a look of importance. Carolina thought he heard one of them saying his name.

"I'm a little curious," Carolina said.

"About what?"

"About the three suits by the window."

Shirley turned her head, and the three men ducked quickly into conversation.

"State reps. One of them is the speaker of the house."

"Which one?"

"With his back to you. Dark hair. Name is Tommy Flannery."

As she spoke, the man turned and appeared to look across the room, as if he wanted to call a waiter. Carolina had the distinct feeling of being sized up.

"What's his reputation?"

"Better than some, worse than others. That general assembly is a sewer, so it's hard to differentiate. He doesn't care for the press. But as far as I know, he's clean. Wasn't involved in that whorehouse scandal."

Another waiter brought them water and asked if they wanted drinks.

"Chardonnay," Shirley Templeton said.

"Bourbon old-fashioned," Carolina said, "easy on the bitters."

They ordered when the drinks came. Carolina got buffalo steak with creamed spinach, a baked potato, and Caesar salad. Shirley ordered a Caesar, too, and prime rib with horseradish.

"You don't look like a beef eater," Carolina said as the waiter hurried away.

"What does a beef eater look like?" she asked, then leaned forward as if what she was about to say was confidential. "I'll take half of it home to the dog."

"Lucky dog."

They realized someone was standing over them.

"Talking about me again, Shirley?"

Tommy Flannery found his own joke to be very, very funny.

"How are you, Mr. Speaker?" Shirley said.

"Fine. How are things at the good ship *Lollipop*?"

"You know, Mr. Speaker, the first time I heard that joke, it was quite amusing. Now that I've heard it for twenty years, it's lost some of its punch. Have you met our new reporter?"

Carolina did not get up, but he shook firmly when Tom Flannery, speaker of the Rhode Island House of Representatives, offered a tanned hand.

"Saw your story tonight," Flannery said. "I've got a bill pending in the corporations committee that will make corporate officeholders' identities confidential except to shareholders and litigants."

"You believe the public shouldn't know when influential people have conflicts of interest?" Shirley Templeton asked.

"I believe corporate directors have a right to privacy," Flannery said. "I believe that good members of our business community are chilled from doing business in this state because news organizations smear them with sensational allegations and innuendo."

Flannery made the entire statement with no hint of embarrassment about his opinion.

"Where are you from, Mike?"

"Down south, Tom."

Flannery blinked but otherwise ignored the jab. "Where?"

"The Caribbean. I chartered a boat."

"A sea captain? Shirley, how appropriate."

"So how's the whorehouse scandal coming, Mr. Speaker? I know the investigation you ordered is going to be very thorough. Are you ready to talk about it yet, or are we still maintaining silence in order to protect the rights of the accused?"

Shirley's eye sparkled. Carolina could see how much she enjoyed giving it back to Flannery.

"It's all being handled by a committee, Shirl," Flannery said, keeping his cool. "You know I never get involved in such matters."

"Let us know when you're ready for an interview."

"Nice meeting you," Flannery said, nodding at Carolina.

"Oh, the same," Carolina replied.

The speaker left, shaking hands, chatting briefly with other diners as he made his way to the exit. The two minions he had not bothered to introduce trailed at a respectful distance.

"What an incredible asshole," Carolina said.

"I told you he doesn't like the press."

The Caesars arrived. Carolina took huge bites, stuffing bits of lettuce in his mouth, dabbing at a fleck of mustard and lemon juice on the edge of his lip. Shirley picked at the croutons.

"May I say something without being insulting?"

"You may, though I'm not sure that you will."

"It was a good piece tonight. You dug around and you found something. But you know—" She paused to crunch another crouton. "Doesn't it seem strange to you that Simmons was involved?"

"Of course. That's what makes it a good story."

"What I mean is, was he the only one? And how long was this thing being planned?"

"They're good questions," Carolina said. "I bet the police are wondering the same thing."

Shirley took a bite of salad and chewed thoughtfully. "The dates," she said.

"What dates?"

"How long has it been since Vespucci was audited?"

"Three years, according to the governor."

"But Dunleavy's only been in office for a little over two."

The steaks arrived. Shirley smeared horseradish across the prime rib. Carolina's buffalo cut had just a hint of pepper and garlic.

"So what you're suggesting is that things could have been happening at Vespucci before Dunleavy got elected," he said.

"Exactly."

They concentrated on their food. Shirley had made an interesting point.

"It seems to me," Carolina said after a moment, "that something this big couldn't be accomplished by just one government agency."

"What do you mean?"

"Well, Simmons obviously played a role. He was giving the appearance of being on top of the problem while he was really covering it up."

"That's what you reported." Shirley said.

"But what if the general assembly gave him what he said he wanted? What if they passed a law making federal deposit insurance mandatory?"

"That would have screwed up the plans to loot the bank."

"Exactly."

Shirley looked blank for a moment. "So what are you saying?"

Carolina ate more steak. "With all that public pressure from Simmons," he said, "I think someone had to make sure he'd fail."

"Someone else in government?" As soon as she said it, they both realized it wasn't a question.

They finished the meal and ordered coffee.

"So do you think the *Herald* will pick up on the story?"

"We fed it to Associated Press," Shirley said. "But the paper here is very funny. The editors watch all the newscasts, just to keep up on what's happening. But if a station breaks something first, the paper tries to ignore it for a while. They may wait a whole week and try to get some new detail, or sit on it for a couple of months and then run it like it's brand-new and they found out about it on their own."

"Sort of a pride thing?"

"There's a saying in these parts: If it isn't in the *Herald*, it isn't news. I'll tell you this. What the paper won't ever do—or hardly ever—is admit in print that someone else got the information first."

"Pretty arrogant."

"The *Herald* can afford to be. When it comes to print, the *Herald* is the ball game in Rhode Island. And you must admit, when we get beat by another station, we'll do anything to avoid admitting someone else got there first. The *Herald* just likes to think of itself as our direct competitor."

When they finished dinner, Shirley grabbed the check. "Station's treat," she said. "We never took you to dinner when you interviewed."

On the way out the door, she slipped an arm through his.

"Want to come over for a drink?"

"Why do I get the feeling that I'm dessert?"

"Mmmm. You could be," she said.

Her skin was warm. An image popped into Carolina's mind. Shirley Templeton having wild sex, then popping vitamins immediately after climax and asking, "Was it good for you?" Then there was another image: a smiling young woman on the deck of his boat, lying back, her face up in the sky, body drinking in the rays of the sun. Then another image, of the same young woman, screaming, trying to escape a madman with a knife . . . so long ago.

"So what do you think?" Shirley said.

"I'm sorry, what?"

"Want to come over?"

"I'm really tired, Shirl, and I've got to see to the boat. *Maeve*'s vents are open and the lines probably haven't been checked. . . ."

She put up a hand to stop him. "It's okay," she said.

"I'm sorry."

"Don't be."

They were standing next to her car, a red Toyota subcompact. It seemed too small for her, and when she climbed in, it looked as if she were folding herself into a suitcase.

"Tell me something," she said when she had started the engine. "Were you just thinking of someone else a moment ago?"

"No comment."

"I thought so," Shirley said.

"Do you want me to stay on this story?" Carolina asked.

"Are you kidding? You're the best new reporter to hit these parts in a long time. I hope you wring this one dry."

She slipped the clutch into first. "You know," she said, "I think a lot of people are wondering what you're going to find out next."

She drove away. Michael Carolina wondered, too.

6

Shirley was right.

The *Providence Herald* did not carry the story about Frankie Falcone's connection with the late Frederick Simmons/Simon Frederickson. The paper did, however, carry another story that Michael Carolina broke.

He saw it as he sat down at his desk. It was hard to miss, since it had been taped to the monitor screen on his computer. It was from the television section of the paper, with a big black headline that read like it came directly from the *National Enquirer*.

HE MELTED ANCHOR'S FACE
CHANNEL 3 HIRES NEW REPORTER
by Bill Guano

You may have seen a new face lately on Channel 3.

He's the kind of reporter who'll stop at nothing to get a story.

The kind of reporter who makes Geraldo Rivera look like Jimmy Olson.

His name is Michael Carolina. After the last stunt he pulled on TV, a lot of people thought he was off the air forever.

But Channel 3 news director Shirley Templeton says she hired Carolina to "give an added spark" to the last-place station in the Providence market.

Spark indeed. In his last job three years ago at a station in the Midwest, Carolina took over his station's signal and announced that the senior anchor was the prime suspect in a string of local murders.

When the anchor confronted him a few hours later, the intrepid Mr. Carolina maimed him with a pot of burning alcohol. Anchor flambé, if you will.

The anchor was eventually convicted and jailed. But Carolina's stunt burned his station so badly that he hasn't worked in the business since.

Until now.

Carolina could not be reached for comment. But a Channel 3 staffer who asked not to be identified called the hiring "a disgrace. They [management] have no ethics."

But then, ethics is not what local television news is about. It's about ratings. And money.

And right now, it looks like Channel 3's money is riding on a reporter with a burning talent. Or at least, a talent for burning.

"I tried to call you after I talked to him." Shirley was standing beside his desk.

"I don't have a phone yet. I need a cellular for the boat. 'Spark.' Nice choice of word."

Shirley gnawed on her lower lip. "Sorry. I guess it was just what he was looking for."

"I guess. What do you bet Ms. Billings is the unidentified source?"

"Could be. Tisha does not always work and play well with others. But there's no way to prove it, and it's a waste of time to try." She reached into the pocket of her dress for a jar of chewable C.

"Everyone who works on the air in this town gets nailed

by Guano. It's what he gets paid to do. This is his way of saying welcome to Rhode Island. He's an ass, but his paper loves him."

"I believe 'shithead' is the more appropriate translation." That made Shirley giggle as she popped the vitamin into her mouth.

"And I think *I* suffer because of my name," she said.

"You know, he's a lousy reporter. What he wrote is only half the story."

"You'll only encourage him if you call in a correction."

"Oh, I wouldn't do that."

"No? What would you do?"

Three hours later, William Guano was watching a soap opera at his desk at the *Herald*. A messenger dropped a package on his desk.

"What's this?"

"Do I look like a mind reader? Some guy left it."

Bill Guano had received raw hot dogs and fecal matter in the mail from sensitive TV news personnel who didn't care for the quality of his criticism. So he prepared himself before opening this new parcel, then removed its contents: a bottle of rubbing alcohol, a Bic lighter, and a note.

> Dear Billy,
> Here's to burning up the town.
>
> > Love,
> > Mike

In a law office on South Main Street, the Herald's TV column made Tommy Flannery laugh out loud. Everyone in the world had a skeleton in the closet, everyone. It was good to see one of those vultures get some of his own medicine.

The article also made Flannery think.

He had disliked Carolina from the moment they had met.

Smug. Disdainful. Like he was better than the speaker of the Rhode Island House. Fucking reporters got paid less than some his best hacks. But they worked harder, dug more, and didn't whine about their pensions or a job for a cousin who had just gotten out of the clink. Politics. It wasn't the hand-shakes or the long hours or the endless campaigning that made Flannery crazy. It was all the fucking *favors*. The favors always turned to skeletons that hung in his own closet.

But it was unusual to see a reporter with this kind of past. Most would push for a story but stop at the point where further reporting might hurt their careers.

Flannery hated journalists. But he admired testosterone. A TV reporter would need a lot of it to take down his own station's anchorman.

This guy had nerve. And smarts. Flannery had seen that from the way he connected up Simmons and Falcone inside of two days. Seen it in the way he held himself at the Grille, not flinching or turning away when he knew a bunch of law-makers were checking him out. A calm, wise, aggressive reporter.

Just what the Business Club did not need.

They had agreed that the elimination of Simmons would be necessary. The man had served a purpose, had helped to make things easier for the founding members. His death was useful, too. It made for an easy scapegoat. But Flannery and the other members had not expected anyone to unravel the connection between Simmons and the bank so quickly. Human error. An oversight.

"Where the hell is he?" he growled, forefinger punching the intercom to his secretary.

"Haven't seen him, sir," she replied.

He knew that she had no control over whether people arrived for their appointments on time. It didn't matter. She was paid to take abuse. The intercom chirped again.

"Sir, he just came in."

Flannery grunted acknowledgment. In a moment, his office door opened. The burly man with the accent stood before him, arms hanging, fingers half-curled: Igor with a leather jacket.

"Anyone see you arrive?"

"No one," Accent replied.

"Are you sure?"

"Yeh, I'm fokkin' sure."

"You may save the attitude for someone who doesn't pay your wages." Flannery didn't bother to watch the man's reaction. "Did you watch the news last night?"

"I read the paper this morning. 'Anchor flambé.' Clever." Accent admired innovative ways of inflicting pain.

"That's not what I'm talking about," Flannery said with exasperation. "I told you when the *Herald* gets whipped on a story, it often ignores other outlets. You have to watch what the bastard does."

"So what did he do?"

"Tied Simmons to Falcone."

Accent blinked. He had watched the news last night at the Rose Tattoo. The Tattoo employed a stripper named Sunburst, a nickname derived from the fiery color of her hair. She'd knelt between his legs as Carolina's piece was introduced. Accent had found it hard to concentrate on the television.

"How'd he do it?"

"A corporation filing–a public document. They were supposed to be cleaned up."

"Must have slipped through."

Accent was both embarrassed and aggravated. Tying up paperwork details was not his line of work. He vastly preferred the more physical aspects of his job.

"Where I come from, we don't mess with things like that."

"Well, this isn't where you come from. In this country, there are more subtle ways of controlling the people. And one of the ways is with information. People read the papers. Even more watch television. And they all talk to one another. And listen to one another. That's why someone like this guinea reporter Carolina can be dangerous. If we can't control the information he gets—and doesn't get—"

"Then we need to control him." Accent had heard the speech before. He knew the line by heart.

"Exactly." Flannery realized he was leaning across his desk, his knuckles turning white. He eased back and shuffled a few papers. "Fortunately, the connection won't do anyone much good. Falcone is gone. Simmons is dead."

Accent grunted agreement.

"But this reporter troubles me. He's a digger."

Accent nodded. "Your partner doesn't like him, either."

"Good. Then we agree. Do you know where to find him?" The speaker sounded nonchalant. It was a habit developed over the years in thousands of depositions and hundreds of trials and legislative hearings.

"Big boat down in Warwick," Accent said. "Keeps it in a marina."

"Really." So the reporter had not lied when he claimed to be a sea captain. "A charming way to live, I'm sure."

Accent said nothing. He had spent time aboard a freighter, running from his home. The better part of it had been spent in the bilge, sick as a dog. Why anyone would *volunteer* to live on a boat was beyond him.

"I would also imagine," the speaker went on, "that it could be quite hazardous. Boats sink. Lines can be cut. Engines explode. Fires occur. Almost anything could happen."

"Is this what the club wants?" Accent said.

"You've spoken to my partner. We would both be pleased."

"What about Falcone?"

"He's not here, is he? Besides, with a two-thirds vote, you have a clear majority."

"I'll see what I can do."

The leather-covered man turned to leave.

"Don't forget to watch the television," Flannery called. "We want no more mistakes."

Accent slipped out the door, pondering the best way to kill the reporter who lived on a boat.

The Reverend Rasmus had worked himself into a lather.

"Corruption! Corruption is the evil that grips this state. It is a grip like a vice, squeezing us like teenage boys squeezing pimples before the prom!"

Sol's producer rolled her eyes. The analogy was just plain gross.

"Corruption is worse than any serpent's poison, more powerful than the plagues of Egypt! It has locked us in its death embrace, hugged us, and crushed us. My brothers and sisters, we are being *screwed* by the corruption of our businessmen and our elected officials!"

Sol looked up from the studio board, to see the general manager standing at the window. The man looked like he could use a quart of Maalox. Sol realized he had just pole-vaulted over the line of acceptable on-air diatribe.

"Please forgive my poor choice of word," he whispered to the mike. "My fervor, my desire to root out this evil got the better of me. But my friends, we must remember that this higher power has not abandoned us. We suffer the pain of this terrible crisis at Amerigo Vespucci. We are locked out of our accounts and our safe-deposit boxes. Our passbooks and statements have turned to trash, meaningless slips of paper that remind us of our humiliation.

"But brothers and sisters, we must also acknowledge the gift we have been given. The sign sent by the Almighty that in the midst of this darkness and pain, we have not been forgotten. I am speaking of the death of that unholy and vile bank commissioner, Frederick Simmons! The man who made a deal with the devil's surrogate, the slimy, sleazy, and sniveling Frankie Falcone!"

Sol hit the mute button and swilled some Coke.

"And now God has sent us a disciple," he began again, "a prophet, a man who has shown us where the evil lurks. A man who knows which stone must next be uncovered so that we may trample and stomp and grind up the vermin that crawls beneath. Not some policeman or accountant or government official. No! Just"—he paused—"just a simple journalist. A reporter. I speak of a new reporter at Channel Three. I speak of Michael Carolina!"

"Jesus, what a suck-up job," the GM murmured to the producer.

"I know," she said, shaking her head. "He's hoping to get Carolina on the show. Maybe share some information."

"Fat chance."

Still, the GM had to admit, this quasireligious radio was working miracles for WAIL's numbers. Arbitron overnights showed a two-point jump since the bank collapse. Even the eighteen to thirty-fours were up for Rasmus, though the GM couldn't believe that the younger crowd actually took the show seriously. Maybe it was the sheer nonsense of it all.

It was almost noon, and Rasmus finished his shift. His producer went off, mumbling about how it was time to get a real job.

"Not bad, eh, babe?" Sol Herskowitz said as he breezed out the studio door. "For a Jewish guy from Brooklyn, I mean."

"Don't call me babe," the GM said.

"I thought that's how radio people talked"—Sol pouted—"you know, showbiz."

"Maybe in New York and L.A. Not in Providence. That reminds me. Maybe Imus and that creep Howard Stern can say 'screwed' on the air. Next time you do it, you'll be playing classic rock in Presque Isle, Maine. Am I clear?"

The Reverend Rasmus nodded meekly. He had not yet seen his show's ratings. The GM was in no hurry to tell him.

"So, what do you think of my appeal to that new reporter?" Sol asked, trying to change the subject.

"I think you're wasting your time. Reporters don't share sources and information with radio talk-show hosts. Especially radically religious radio talk-show hosts."

"But I can get him more attention! I'll let him on the show! More people listen to him, more people will watch him."

The GM walked away. It was amazing that this idiot could be so good with a mike and so ignorant at the same time.

"Just watch the language—babe," he called over his shoulder.

But Sol wasn't listening. He was thinking of how he could finagle a meeting with the new reporter at Channel 3.

7

eople get into the TV news business for two reasons. The right one is to tell stories that enrich and inform viewers' lives. The wrong one is to be seen, to be famous, to make money.

Usually those who work in television news will admit privately to choosing the profession for a combination of the right and wrong reasons. It is all a matter of balance.

Tisha Billings had no balance. Privately, she would admit that she didn't give a shit about journalism. She got into TV because she wanted to be a star.

She had grown up in Greenwich, Connecticut, and decided to be an anchorwoman after reading about Jane Pauley in a copy of *Glamour*. It had been a bad week. She had lost the lead in a high school musical to a younger, more talented student. She'd been kicked off the cheerleading squad for smoking pot during halftime of a football game. And Daddy, in his first real attempt at disciplining his daughter in seventeen years, had informed Tisha that the combination of poor grades, laziness, and the fact that he had just shelled out two grand to send her out of state for an abortion meant that she would not be getting a BMW for her eighteenth birthday. She would have to settle for a Ford Escort instead.

Daddy just didn't understand, she thought.

Tisha went on to an undistinguished career at a private college and majored in electronic communications. She took the minimum required courses in English (two) and political science, economics, and history (none). When Tisha graduated with a C+ average, she did not know Beirut from Baton Rouge or a state court from city hall.

She did, however, know what a camera was, as well as an anchor desk. She had beautiful thick brown hair and model's smile, clear skin, and deep blue eyes. A news director in Portland, Maine, took one look at her résumé tape and hired her over the phone.

Still, looks only went so far. The TV news business was competitive. And unlike many other young, beautiful women who managed to rise quickly in television, Tisha was sorely lacking in positive attitude. She complained about covering outdoor stories in cold weather. She sometimes liked to call in sick. And instead of trying to kiss up to the boss, she often whined about not getting the chance to anchor. In short, Tisha had everything news directors wanted to see on-screen and everything news directors despised when the cameras were turned off. "She's the kind of woman," one male news executive once said, "who you'd kill to sleep with and then you'd just kill."

As a result, in her three years in the business, Tisha had gone only from Portland to Providence. She had not received the anticipated offer from NBC or CBS, or even a station in New York or Boston. Tisha decided she needed help. Someone to make the connection at West Fifty-seventh or 30 Rock. She found an agent and paid him 10 percent of her salary. In exchange, he offered a piece of advice: Get a big story to put on your reel.

So far, the biggest story she'd done was the statehouse hooker scandal. Her success had been dubious. The elected reps wouldn't talk. The cops wouldn't talk. And the working girls wouldn't talk. The prostitutes were all poorer, less attractive, and less educated than the young reporter. But the women sensed that more than anyone else, Tisha was using them. One by one, they turned her down flat.

"This girl is trash," one said to another as Tisha stalked

away after yet another rejection. "I know," the other replied. "I'd do an interview with the right reporter. But with her, it just seems so . . . tawdry."

Tisha needed another story.

And this new reporter Carolina had spoiled her chance. Despite her ignorance about the affairs of government and her appalling lack of formal journalistic training, Tisha Billings had confidence. She was sure that she could break any story that came along. It was all a matter of being in the right place at the best possible moment. Wasn't that what happened with that man Woodward she once heard about in History of Reporting 101? He was just in the right spot when those burglars were arraigned. The same was true of many others, and if this creep Carolina would get out of the way, it would be true for her.

She had taken a step in the right direction, she thought, by leaking to that slug of a television critic. Billy Guano was hot for her, had been since he got a good close look down her dress at a media Christmas party at the governor's house. Guano was lazy, too. Didn't even know there was a new reporter at Channel 3 until she called and told him. But Billy loved gossip and had a good memory about scandals at TV stations. And Carolina's name was hard to forget.

"I can't believe he's working in Providence," the TV critic exclaimed.

"Neither can I," Tisha said, pretending to be more horrified than aggravated.

"Did you ever see the tape of what he did? When he named the anchor as a murder suspect?"

"No. How was it?"

"Wild. Unbelievable. I've got a copy. You're welcome to come over and see it," he said, then added, "strictly for professional reasons."

"Oh, you're sweet," she lied, thinking, He probably just wants another look at my tits. "But I've got early-morning cut-ins this week, and if I don't get nine hours sleep, I'll look like hell."

"Oh. Okay. Then how about a background quote about the new guy?"

Gossip always made her feel better. Vicious professional gossip was the best. So she'd pretended to be scandalized by Carolina's presence in the newsroom.

"You know," Guano said, "you're so much better than that station. I know you're going places. One day, you're just going to take off."

If she had been sitting with him at that moment, Tisha would have let the little weasel cop a feel.

Unfortunately, the news management at Channel 3 did not agree with the TV critic's assessment. And on the day Guano's column ran, Tisha was not assigned to dig and cover breaking events on the Vespucci story. She was, however, given a sidebar: to interview victims of the bank collapse. Shirley had tracked down a widow who lived on Federal Hill.

"Her life savings were in Vespucci," she said.

"Who gives a shit?" Tisha muttered.

"What did you say?"

"I said, 'What a pity.' "

"I thought that's what you said."

Tisha was assigned a photographer named Earl. Earl was sixty years old and had worked at Channel 3 almost since the day the station went on the air. In his younger days, Earl had been a dependable, albeit unremarkable, photojournalist. His biggest claim to fame had been staking out the Hyannis compound in 1963, waiting to see if a young President would be buried on the family estate. But at the last minute, the plans had changed and the President was laid to rest in Arlington. Life was like that, Earl reasoned. Missed appointments, missed opportunities. If it didn't happen here, it would happen somewhere else. After John Kennedy died,

Earl decided to take it easy, perhaps correctly assuming that in the long run, no single story was really that important.

It was not a philosophy that blended well with Tisha Billings's drive to replace Joan Lunden or Katie Couric.

"Let's go. We're late," she snapped as Earl loaded camera gear into a news car.

"We are not. I checked," Earl said, stowing a tripod at his usual leisurely pace.

"I'll drive," she said, snatching the keys from his safari jacket pocket.

Despite having lived and worked in Providence for over a year, Tisha still managed to get lost trying to find Federal Hill. And she ran two lights.

"You know, if you're media, the cops'll let you park anywhere in town," Earl said, "but if you kill someone running a light, they're likely to write you a ticket."

"Shut up."

Tisha had trouble parallel parking in front of the tenement where the woman lived. She left the vehicle with the nose sticking halfway into the street.

"Can you help with the gear?" Earl asked as he unloaded.

"No." She left him struggling and climbed the stairs to the second floor. There was no doorbell. She banged three times on the screen, waited, and banged again.

"Take it easy on that door!" an elderly female voice said from inside.

"I'm looking for Mrs. Bun-jeen-ee," Tisha said, trying to read the name she'd scribbled in her notebook.

"Who?"

"Mrs. Anna Bun-jeen-eye."

"Who are you?"

"I'm from Channel Three."

"An' I'm real impressed. Now, who are you?" Tisha saw an elderly woman carrying a cane and a look of suspicion emerge from the darkened apartment.

"I'm Tisha Billings. I believe someone from my station called?"

The door opened slowly.

"You gonna help me get my money?" the old lady said, her tone and expression now transformed to a healthy blend of hope and greed.

"May we come in?"

"Break out some ID." The lady sounded like she'd watched too many reality-based police shows. Tisha fumbled for a press card.

"There you go, Mrs. Bun-jeen-eye."

"Bianchini!" the old woman said. She examined the police photo on the ID. "Not a very good picture."

Tisha flinched.

Earl had reached the second floor and began dropping his gear to get out his own identification.

"Don't botha," Anna said, looking at the camera. She stepped away from the door. Tisha moved inside, somehow failing to notice when the screen door hit Earl squarely in the face.

The apartment was dark, the furniture worn. There were pictures on a bookshelf—a wedding photograph, another of an old man in a T-shirt. A crucifix hung over the door to the kitchen.

"You gonna pay me for this?" Anna said as Earl set up.

"How long have you lived here?" Tisha replied.

"I should get money for my stor-vee."

"Do you have any children?"

"You ain't answerin' my question, girlie."

"We don't work that way," Earl muttered.

"Who asked you?" Anna rasped. "You're gettin' paid to work that fancy camera."

"What he meant was that maybe we can help you get your money back," Tisha said, knowing that if the old lady didn't talk, they'd only have to go find someone else who would.

"I'm ready," Earl said.

"Let's make it fast," Anna said, relenting. "I got Channel Nine coming in half an hour."

The camera lights came on and Anna cranked the faucets. The tears fell like rain as she told how her life's savings were tied up in Amerigo Vespucci Loan and Investment.

"How much?" Tisha asked.

Anna wailed.

"More than a hundred thousand?"

Anna moaned, then gagged.

"How long did you know Frankie Falcone?"

"Since he was a *bambino*." She sobbed, every bit the old Italian grandmother. Then she stopped and dead-eyed the camera. "I always knew he was no good, *un stronzo, un porco dio*." The accent grew more and more pronounced with each new syllable. *"Un figlio di putta."*

Earl smirked. Tisha had no idea what Anna was saying.

"If you knew he was no good, why did you keep your money in his bank?"

Anna was silent, but only for a moment. Then she began wailing all over again. Every time Tisha asked another question, the wailing became louder. Anna Bianchini was clearly long on sob and short on fact. After ten minutes of tape, Tisha gave up. The tears stopped as soon as the camera lights were off.

"Am I good or what?" Anna said.

"Oh yes, just fine," Billings said as she checked her own makeup for a cutaway.

"You wanna shoot setup? Me sewing? Cooking? More crying?"

"We're okay, thanks," Tisha said.

"How 'bout me prayin', looking at the cross, heah?"

"No, we're fine."

"I got a nephew works in cable," the widow said.

"How nice for you," Tisha said.

"When's it gonna be on?"

"Maybe six."

"I wanna tape."

"Buy a VCR." The interview over, Tisha no longer saw any need for courtesy.

"They should have sent that new guy, Carolina. The one they mentioned on the radio. I got somethin' to tell him."

Tisha was suddenly pleasant again.

"Tell me. I'll pass it along."

Anna cackled in derision.

"Girlie, I been scammed for every cent I had. By the best. An' I know one thing. You ain't in that class."

Earl whistled as he left the apartment. He didn't even mind lugging all the gear on his own. Thank the Lord, he thought, for little bits of justice.

"Why should I tell you anything?"

The man was in his thirties but looked ten years older. His hair was unkempt, his collar loose, his tie askew. He looked like he had not slept for days, and Michael Carolina could tell he was seriously pissed at a reporter's intrusion.

"I mean, what are you gonna do? Help me get these people their money back? You can't. An' you're just lookin' for a story, anyway. Probably about how screwed up the regulators are. How we let an embezzler get away."

"All I'm trying to find out is how Amerigo Vespucci worked. And about Frankie."

The man leaned back in his chair, resigned to the fact that for the moment his work was interrupted. "How the hell did you get in here?"

The two men were inside Frankie Falcone's private office at Vespucci.

"Just walked in."

There were regulators all over the closed bank, and two state troopers at the door. Carolina found his way in when a state car pulled up and a woman got out. She opened the trunk and began to remove boxes. There were nearly a dozen, all empty, probably for the removal of records and any other documents the bank might have. The woman picked up an armload, piled so high, she could not see in front of herself.

"Need some help?" Carolina had said.

"Thanks," the woman said, not even looking at him. The reporter piled boxes in front of his own face and carried them through the door. The troopers and other workers barely gave him a second glance.

Frankie Falcone's office had paper stacked on his desk and his bookshelves, on the chairs and the floor. The man with the unkempt hair was seated behind the desk. He dug under the papers and pulled out an ashtray, then started to pat his jacket.

"They'll kill you," Carolina said as the man lit up.

"Not if these records do it first. What's your name?"

"Carolina. Michael Carolina."

"Jimmy DeVaro," the man said. "I'm an assistant examiner with DBR. You Italian?"

"Half."

"Name like that, you'd have to be. Look, I gotta tell ya, I admire your nerve. But I also gotta tell ya, I don't like the press. Always lookin' to nail someone. Always lookin' to expose somethin' and be a hero. Maybe next time, you're gonna nail me. Whether there's anything there or not."

"I'm not here to nail anyone."

"An' there's another thing. I don't like the way you people whine about deadlines. Always whinin' that you need somethin' now, like the sun rises and sets on you. I got plenty of problems of my own."

"I'm sure you do."

"I don't need to hear about yours."

"No you don't."

"Glad to see you understand."

"So tell me about your problems."

The man took a long, deep drag. "You're pretty good, you know? Just sittin' there lettin' me vent."

Carolina smiled, as if to say, You got me. Jimmy DeVaro chuckled. Then he shrugged, as if what were happening no longer mattered. When he spoke again, Carolina could feel the stress wash over him.

"What kind of problems . . . paper problems, money problems. I got a dead boss, and his secret partner is a fugitive. The governor's office calls about six times a day, wanting to know when we're gonna have a final number, how much is missing, what records are left, what records are missing. 'What can we tell the press?' they ask. 'We need something to tell the press. We need something to tell the depositors.' I got state senators and political contributors walking in on me, asking' for special favors. And in the middle of this, I'm supposed to figure out what the hell happened." DeVaro took another drag. "And in the middle of that, I got you."

"So what's taking so long?" Carolina asked.

DeVaro burst out laughing. Carolina joined him.

When they finished laughing, DeVaro leaned back in his chair. "You really want to know what's going on? What happened?"

"It beats covering a fire."

DeVaro shook his finger like a teacher scolding a child.

"Oh boy, you don't know. This is one hell of a fire. A big, bad paper fire."

"Tell me how he got the money."

"Lot of different ways. We're still figurin' 'em out."

"What do you know so far?"

DeVaro flicked ash on the floor. "I think I got a handle on one of the slickest. You know how interest rates are set?"

"Off the prime."

"That's right. The Federal Reserve sets the prime rate for

lending and borrowing money. Commercial banks adjust their rates in accord with the Fed. You wanna borrow money, it's at a rate that's higher than the prime. You wanna save money, like in a money market or with a CD, it's at a rate lower than prime."

"That's how banks make money. What does that have to do with Frankie?"

"I'm getting to that. One of the things you used to notice about Amerigo Vespucci, this pissy little Federal Hill bank, was its savings interest rates. They were always high."

"How high?"

"Way high. Sometimes higher than prime. And in the last six months, always higher than prime. Sometimes by more than a point."

"Must have attracted a lot of customers."

"It did. Tons of them. And tons of cash. This bank, it does most of its business right here on Federal Hill. Real family institution. Founded by Frankie's father. You got hundreds of people, families, businesspeople, retirees, and all of them looking for the best rate of return they can get. Especially the retirees, 'cause many of them live off the interest.

"So Frankie, he's talking to these people, pulling 'em in, tellin' 'em what great yields they're gonna get by going with his bank and his higher interest rates. 'You're getting ten percent? Come see me; I'll get you ten point five. Prime's at eight? For you, I got a special deal. Nine.' "

"And what happens?"

"This." DeVaro shoved a mass of papers toward Carolina. The reporter looked them over. "But these aren't account applications. They look like they're for loans."

"Very good. You picked that up very quickly. Now you wanna know a fascinating coincidence?"

"What?"

"The loan papers just happen to have been signed on the same day as the new savings accounts and CDs were supposed to be opened. We know that because we've called some of the customers whose names are on those loan papers. Not a single one knows anything about a loan, only about new accounts with higher interest rates."

"So what happened to the money?"

"The borrowers with their names on the paper never got it."

"And Frankie did."

DeVaro half-grinned and touched his forefinger to his nose.

"Now. Do you wanna see the beauty of it?"

"What do you mean?"

"The beauty of this—in casual terms—is how clean it looks to a casual observer."

"How?"

"When you take money out of a bank, you have to put something on a balance sheet to show why. Usually it's one of three things . . . some cash, or a check, or a loan. *Something* goes on that balance sheet to account for whatever's going out. So when you first look at this, it appears as though Vespucci has its house in order. The settlement sheets all reflect that there is money in the bank that covers the cash being loaned out. Only the customers"—he paused for a last drag on his cigarette—"don't get the cash."

"Frankie does," Carolina said.

"That's right."

"How did you catch on?"

"Hasn't been easy. First, Vespucci is part of a privately insured group in the state. Their board got a law passed a few years back that lets them do their own examinations. But this year, even that group got overwhelmed, and they asked for some help. As if we have lots of staff. Budget cuts wiped out half my department over the last three years."

"Really?"

"You didn't know that? Well, then, I did something useful

today. We been waiting for one of you reporters to do a story about how our department wasn't doing its job."

"Who was responsible for that?"

"General assembly, near as I can tell. Come July each year, we'd always find out things were a little tighter. And—we were always told the private insurance fund could do its own reviews."

"The fund your office is supposed to regulate?"

"Yeah. Fox watchin' the henhouse, so to speak."

Carolina scribbled notes.

"Tell me how Simmons influenced things."

Jimmy DeVaro snorted. "What a piece of work that guy was. He testifies in public that all the banks should go to federal insurance. But when we want to do exams, he holds us back."

"I thought you said the privately insured group inspected all the private banks."

"They do. But we had some oversight control. There were provisions in the law to let us come in if we weren't satisfied with the private group's reports."

"And were you satisfied?"

"I wasn't. The reports were always incomplete. There were a couple of times in the last two years when I wanted to get in here and take a look around."

"Here at Vespucci?"

DeVaro nodded.

"Did you?"

"Once."

"What did you find?"

"I spent a week. Every night when I came back, Simmons called me in. Wanted a full report. And Frankie, he wasn't exactly giving us his full cooperation. So I tell Simmons. Tell him when papers are missing, or if the numbers don't seem to quite add up. Tell him that Frankie is stalling, saying his accountant is working on the papers, that we'll get them.

Simmons was a pretty good actor, you know? He acted plenty frustrated, and I believed him. But he also said we needed to be patient. Looking back now, it all seems to make sense."

"What?"

"Every morning of that week, when we went back in there, it seemed like Frankie knew exactly what we were going to do next. It never made sense to me. Now it does."

"So you never knew they were partners?"

"Nobody knew. Not until it was on the news."

"So how did you figure out that this was a gimmick?" the reporter said, touching the phony loan papers.

"Don't you think this is one hell of a coincidence, all these loans bein' taken out on the same day these people supposedly openin' new accounts? You got a better theory, I'd like to hear it."

Carolina scribbled more notes. "Let me see if I have this right. You're saying that Frankie Falcone embezzled up to fifteen million dollars by duping people into opening or transferring into new savings accounts."

"Yeah, and then—"

"And then unwittingly signing loan papers that correspond to those accounts?"

"That's it." DeVaro nodded.

"And then, instead of giving the customers the money, he kept it for himself."

"Right."

"Because the customers didn't know they had loans in the first place."

"Now don't get me wrong. I don't know if this is the only way he did it. But it's one of them."

Carolina checked his notes for a minute. They were solid. He felt as though he understood how part of the embezzlement had worked.

"Tell me who you blame for all this," he said.

DeVaro thought for a moment. "Falcone for one. Simmons, too, I guess. But you know, I think about my old civics lessons, about how government works. The legislature is supposed to hold the purse strings, right? And the executive branch is supposed to make sure the right people are in place for the right jobs." DeVaro sat back and looked at Carolina expectantly.

"So you say the whole government failed?" Carolina prodded.

"I didn't say that. You did," DeVaro replied.

Carolina smiled.

"What's going to happen to those customers now?"

"To be honest, I don't know. I just get paid to find out what happened. But I can tell you that this bank doesn't even come close to having enough assets to cover everyone."

Carolina said nothing. In the silence, the two men thought about all the people cheated out of their savings.

"Funny thing, though," DeVaro said.

"What?"

"This is one of the ultimate con games."

"How do you mean?"

"You ever hear that saying, If it's too good to be true, it probably is? That's what you got right here. Bunch of people who figure they've found an easy way to make a little more on a buck than the next guy. And nearly all of them think that they're pals with the banker and that's why they're gettin' a deal.

"If you use common sense, you know that banks can't offer that kind of rate for very long and stay afloat. Anybody that thinks straight wouldn't put their money in. But I guess greed gets in the way of straight thinking."

"I don't suppose you'd let me put some of this on tape?"

"Not a chance," DeVaro said. "You can quote me, though—on background."

Carolina stepped back for a moment, looking around the office. There were still pictures on the wall, plaques and commendations. A bookshelf behind DeVaro was filled with knickknacks and souvenirs—a box of candies, a small Italian flag, a cream-colored ceramic bottle.

"How much do you know about Frankie Falcone?"

"You mean personally?"

Carolina nodded.

"He was a big spender, that's for sure. Hot cars, fancy dinners, that kind of thing. Lots of business ventures."

"Did he drink?"

"I suppose. Why?"

"May I see that bottle behind you?"

DeVaro turned around, saw what Carolina had noticed, and handed him the bottle. The reporter yanked off the cork and sniffed. The fumes were overwhelming.

"What is it?" DeVaro asked.

"Poitin," Carolina said. "Irish moonshine. Potato whiskey. Tastes like turpentine and about three times as strong. It's made in Ireland, but it's illegal there. They sell it to tourists to take home."

"Never heard of it."

"No reason you should have, a nice Italian boy like yourself."

"So what's a Federal Hill banker doing with a bottle of this stuff?" DeVaro said as he took the bottle and sniffed. As he did, a small white card fluttered to the floor. It had been stuck underneath the bottle. Carolina bent and picked it up.

"To Frankie," it said, "with thanks from the Business Club."

Carolina's piece that night laid out the loan/savings–account scam that Frank Falcone had allegedly used to make millions. The report contained half a dozen graphics and pieces of animation to make the piece understandable. Carolina also managed to find a few depositors who admitted that they had signed papers, thinking they were opening new accounts with Vespucci.

Tisha Billings's piece was a lackluster effort that consisted primarily of Anna Bianchini imitating a waterfall. But tears were tears, and in television news, broadcasting sadness was almost as good as broadcasting anger. Shirley proclaimed that she was happy with both stories.

"I don't see what the big deal is about *your* story," Billings said as Carolina picked up his jacket and prepared to leave. "You were just in the right place at the right time."

"Thanks, Tisha. I really liked your piece too."

"You've got a lot of nerve waltzing in here and trying to steal the biggest news in town."

"I'm sorry. I'll try not to do a good job anymore so that you'll feel more comfortable."

"You're sleeping with her, aren't you?" Tisha said, inclining her head toward Shirley's office. Carolina stopped and looked at her.

"Tisha, do you know what the prime rate is?"

"The what?"

"I thought so," he said, and walked out the door.

8

H e's doing it again!"

Accent stood, impassive, beefy hands stuck in his leather jacket pockets, eyes fixed on the ceiling. He had begun to understand the rhythm of his work. Each time that reporter Carolina did a story, he was summoned—first by this man, then Flannery. Now back to this man again. Accent felt like a Ping-Pong ball.

"These things do take a bit of time," he said. He knew why the man was angry. Sunburst had an early show, and Accent had watched the Channel 3 news at six.

"We don't *have* time. Every day he's finding something else. Now he knows how Falcone was working inside the bank." I'll have to do something about that, the man said to himself. That assistant examiner should have kept his mouth shut.

Accent spoke again. "I told you I'd take care of it. It's a matter of knowing where he is and what he's going to do. Habits. Things you can predict. Then you know where to set the trap."

"So what's taking so long?"

"He's new to the area. Still figurin' the ins and outs, gettin' a good look at the turf."

"Too good a look. I want him stopped. We need to send a message to all those other media shits that this is one to stay away from."

"Aye."

The man was late. He needed to attend to the affairs of government.

"When can I expect you to complete this task?"

"As soon as it's reasonable for me to do it."

"Do you have any idea of how?"

"I do."

"And?"

"That's for me to know, not you. It's not you that's stickin' your neck out."

"Just get it done."

Accent was not trying to delay. He had good intentions, at least, good intentions for a terrorist. He wanted to do the job right, and on the first try.

He remembered his last try. Working in the old country, attempting to lay down a prosecutor who was too successful for his own good. The man had convicted several of Accent's colleagues and was making real headway against what the prime minister called "an organized criminal element."

Accent had used a crude combination of gasoline and nails and fertilizer, and an even cruder detonation device that would trigger the explosive the first time it was jostled or shoved. He'd fixed it to the underside of the prosecutor's car, the theory being that the man would open the door, climb in, shut the door, and visit the clouds.

He had parked just a block down the street to witness the event. The man's car was parked just outside his home. As soon as it happened, Accent planned to drive out of town, to an isolated pay telephone, and advise the media of who had just detonated the bomb and why.

He never counted on the three boys kicking the soccer ball down the street. Never expected them to take their game right past the car's door. Accent watched as the kids angled for position by the car, then saw one of them trip and fall.

The street had been white with light, then black and red with smoke and flame.

The boy who fell was lucky, killed instantly by a spray of nails. The second lost his legs; the third, an arm and half his face. Both survivors were burned over 80 percent of their bodies. Accent read in the papers how one of them had begged to die.

He never made the call claiming responsibility, but everyone knew. The prosecutor who cheated death swore he would bring the bomber to justice.

The hazards of war, Accent had said. His colleagues agreed. Regardless, the bomber had now become a liability to the cause. He had acted alone, but if caught, he would be a symbol for everyone involved in the movement. The leader of the cell in which Accent worked thought it best for the terrorist to get as far away as possible.

He had left the same night on a freighter, hidden deep in a compartment of the ship's hold. "Stay away for a couple years," the cell leader said, "till the heat's turned down a bit."

It hadn't been hard to hook up in America. There were plenty of countrymen who had come before him who understood what he did, who were sympathetic to the cause. A fraction even had use for Accent's line of work. They were willing to overlook the accidental deaths or maimings that were an occasional hazard of the job.

Deep down, Accent told himself, he was still loyal to the cause. But he also knew how much he enjoyed the work of a professional thug—the intimidation, the beatings, the knife and gun work, and the occasional murder or bombing. Accent took a great deal of professional pride in his ability and reputation. And in this thumbprint of a state, a state smaller than his own country, a few select men made good use of him.

There was one substantial difference in the work he did in America, he thought to himself as he drove down I-95 from Providence to Warwick, then turned off toward the roads that would lead to the marinas. Here, he had better equipment. Sophisticated timing devices and wiring material. And C-4, the Play-Doh–like substance that easily molded into a variety of shapes and sizes, that would blow open a safe, or take the roof off a church and reduce the foundation to rubble. Or throw a car from one lane of traffic into another.

Or blow a sailboat out of the water.

He turned into the gravel lot of a marina on the north end of Greenwich Bay, the smaller indentation inside Narragansett Bay where hundreds of Rhode Islanders kept powerboats and sailboats for weekend daytrips. The place wasn't busy midweek, and certainly not at this time of year. Many of the yachts were already being hauled for the winter season.

Accent had scouted the marina once, even bought himself a nylon jacket and deck shoes to avoid looking out of place. He lifted a canvas bag from the seat next to him and headed down the pier. A long, tall, varnished mast poked out of the water ahead of him.

There were big powerboats tied up along the pier, but no people in sight. Accent looked straight ahead, using only peripheral vision to see if he was being watched. As he neared the end of the pier, he slowed down and then stopped, as if he was looking for something. Then he jumped, as if slightly startled. From a distance, he knew it would look like he had found the yacht he was seeking, perhaps dropping by to visit a friend.

He sprang onto the deck and noticed that the hatch was closed only by a screen to keep insects out. A tiny lock appeared above it, holding the top of the hatch in place over the slides that formed the boat's door. Accent fished a tiny metal device from his pocket. It took all of thirty seconds to pop the lock. He dropped down into the cabin and set to work.

Tisha Billings looked up *prime rate* in the dictionary. It didn't make her feel better.

Michael Carolina had spoiled her chance to make a big score on the Vespucci story. Tisha wanted to get even. She spent the night pondering how to do it. But after a full evening of brooding and sulking, the best thought she could come up with was to break some new angle. But what angle?

Despite her newfound knowledge about prime rates, Tisha understood next to nothing about banks and the ways they worked. She understood that banks were places to get money from, places where Daddy would deposit checks and where she could cash her own checks. She also knew that banks sent out overdraft notices and threatening letters when she maxed out her credit card at Jordan Marsh. But Tisha had no idea how banks loaned money or made a profit. The thought of spending any time learning how the process worked was more than she could bear.

Indeed, when confronted by the prospect of doing any kind of serious work, Tisha's resolve quickly weakened. She had no appetite for digging, for making calls or looking at documents. She wanted a big story. But she didn't know where to start.

Then Tisha had an idea.

It was not a brilliant idea. For Tisha and for many others who worked in television, original thought was a rare commodity. But this idea, if successful, would permit her to short-cut the legwork that was generally necessary to produce a groundbreaking story.

The fact that the idea called for the commission of a felony didn't bother her in the least.

It depended on whether Michael Carolina left his notes at home.

She had seen him carrying reporter's notebooks. He seemed to fill them at a rapid pace. And he wasn't leaving them at the office, perhaps out of fear that someone like Tisha would want to have a look at them. So she decided that he must be keeping them someplace else.

Which brought her to the marina in Warwick.

While Tisha knew little about finance, she did know something about boats. If she had learned anything during her years growing up in Greenwich and visiting local yacht clubs, it was that wooden boats are a pain in the ass. She knew they required endless hours of labor sanding, varnishing, painting, and polishing. Her own father owned a fiberglass powerboat, but she remembered other yacht types screaming and yelling at boatyard workers to hurry up, to do a better job, to get that brightwork done because they wanted to go sailing that weekend.

She also remembered that wooden boats generally had ports and hatches open, to let air flow and prevent mold or mildew. She had heard Shirley talking about Carolina's run-in with the mayor, about the boat and all the varnished wood and polished brass. She was sure she'd have no trouble getting inside it and having a look around.

Tisha parked at the end of the marina lot, strolled down the piers, looking around, only slightly self-conscious. A man working on a powerboat engine gave her the once-over. She ignored him. A guard in the shack asked her if she wanted some help.

"Fuck off," she said.

The guard went back to reading a paperback.

After walking down three piers, she saw a wooden yacht that looked about the right size. She moved toward it, re-membering how Shirley had said that Carolina's boat had a name that began with M. *Maeve.*

For all of her knowledge, Tisha hated boats. She'd spent too much time throwing up on Long Island Sound as a child. But this trip had a purpose. Kind of like a shopping expedition, she thought. And this boat wasn't going anywhere. She saw the open hatch, looked around, then climbed aboard and slid down into the cabin.

It was a tidy-looking place. The galley was clean, the table in the saloon shiny and bare. She looked around for any ob-vious signs of where someone might keep notes. Didn't these big yachts have some kind of table where the owner kept charts and a radio? She turned to her right.

"Oh," she said, startled.

"Hullo," Accent said.

Tisha Billings had finally found a big story. The only trouble would be figuring out a way to live long enough to tell it.

The Reverend Rasmus just had to meet this guy Carolina.

Sol Herskowitz had enjoyed great success as an Amway salesman. Persistence and a positive attitude—Sol had both in spades. He enjoyed the challenge of taking a reluctant stranger and bringing him around to another point of view, even if the only purpose was to close on a few cases of soap. But now there was more on the line. Sol was convinced that his future as the evangelical savior of Rhode Island (and his shot at boosting WAIL to number one in the Arbitron drive time) was by making contact with someone who could get him the news before the public read it in the paper or saw it on TV. Someone reliable, not one of those quacks who called in, like Freddie from Central Falls or Edna in Pawtucket or Anna from Federal Hill. He needed juice, serious juice, to make his show work.

Finding out where Carolina lived had not been easy. The guy didn't have a house. Didn't even have a telephone. But the receptionist at Channel 3 suffered from the long-standing belief that she was underpaid. A twenty-dollar bill bought Sol an address list for everyone in the newsroom.

The Reverend Rasmus just knew he was going to like this guy. Knew the guy was going to like him. It was all just a matter of the two of them getting together and having a little chat.

He parked his car in the marina lot and headed toward the piers. He'd worn his best jacket and tie, combed his hair, and shined his shoes. Salesmen, he knew very well, had to make a good impression.

The powerboats were impressive. Sol liked the big sport-fishermen, with the tuna towers and double steering, one in the cabin and one up topside so you could catch some sun. He liked to imagine himself off the coast of Florida with a couple of hot blondes, trolling for black marlin and drinking Heinies in green bottles. If only he could make this radio gig pay off. Maybe he could get a shot at a station in New York or Miami. The guard in the shack ignored him. Just another loser dreaming about owning a boat.

Finally, Sol saw the North Sea cutter, tied up between two big power yachts. Nice-looking boat, he thought. Too bad I don't know how to sail.

She had been tasty, Accent decided. A bit unpleasant, but personality didn't really interest him. He had plunged right in and had his fill, then left her quivering in the saloon. Too bad she wasn't a redhead, he thought. I might've taken her with me.

The terrorist told himself he had learned his lesson from the unpleasant bombing experience in the old country. Don't take any chances. Here in America, they had the finer things in life, like a remote-control detonation device. Accent had returned to his car, a nondescript white Chevrolet Lumina, not too new, not too beat-up. He pulled out of the lot, drove out of the marina, and turned left. A quarter mile down the road, he saw the house with a FOR SALE sign in front. A check with the Realtor had determined that the house was empty, the owner moved to another city. It was lovely, the Realtor said, with a beautiful view of Greenwich Bay and a nearby marina and lots of privacy. Everything that Accent needed.

He pulled into the driveway and followed it to the end, by the side of the house. Then he got out and walked around to the back. There was no one in sight.

From a wooden deck off the back of the house, he had an unobstructed view of the marina and *Maeve,* three hundred yards away. Accent pulled a pair of binoculars from under his seat and trained them on the yacht, just in time to see a man in a jacket and tie descending the companionway.

"Hello? I mean, ahoy? Anybody here?"

Sol Herskowitz had not become the leading soap salesman in New Jersey by being shy. Besides, it was possible that Carolina had not heard him. He stepped on to the boat's deck and then into the cockpit. He peeked into the cabin; it looked dark and empty.

"Hello?"

Nothing.

"What the fuck," Sol muttered, and climbed down the hatch.

The weather report had called for mostly sunny skies, with the possibility of showers late in the afternoon. As the day progressed, the forecasters revised and suggested the rain might arrive early, with the chance of a downpour.

Michael Carolina had left his portlights open and the forward hatch ajar. The last thing he wanted was to come home that evening to a flooded cabin. He pulled into the marina just in time to see a man climbing down the hatch of *Maeve*.

Carolina got out of his car and moved toward the guard shack at a trot.

"Did you see that guy?"

"Who?" the guard asked, looking up from his book.

"The one who just climbed down the hatch of my boat."

The guard put his book down. "Sorry. I guess . . ."

"Yeah, I know. You weren't paying attention. You got a stick or something?"

The kid handed him a flashlight that must have weighed at least three pounds. It was long and slender and heavy enough to do damage.

"Want me to come with you?" the kid asked.

Carolina shook his head. "It's probably just someone who likes boats."

Then he remembered he had locked the hatch door.

"Listen," he said, "I'm going to take a walk down there. If I wave this thing, you call the cops. All right?"

The kid nodded.

It took a moment for Sol's eyes to adjust to the lack of light. But the cabin looked nice, lots of wood and varnish.

"Anybody home?"

He thought he heard a groan from the saloon.

"Am I interrupting something?" Sol called. No response.

After a few more seconds, he heard another sound. Definitely a groan. And not, as he had thought a moment before, from someone having sex. He took a step. There. By the table, lying on the settee. A very beautiful, very nude young woman. Tied to the mast.

Sol did a double take. So this reporter's a little kinky. He's still got good taste.

Was it Carolina?

Accent couldn't believe his bad luck. He had not counted on the reporter coming home this early. Doesn't he work during the day?

Or was it someone else? If that was so, then all his work would be for nothing. That was the problem with this business. Something always screwed things up, usually when you least expected it.

Ten seconds passed. Whoever it was, Accent knew, he was sure to discover the other uninvited guest aboard the yacht. If anyone found her now, it would ruin everything. That woman had seen his face, and other parts. His hand moved over the radio transmitter on the seat beside him.

Carolina had dealt with intruders on *Maeve* before. For some reason, people who would never dream of setting foot inside someone's home when no one answered the door found it perfectly acceptable to walk aboard a stranger's boat unannounced and uninvited. Once confronted, such intruders usually left very quickly, but the experience was never pleasant. Carolina hefted the flashlight in his hands, hoping he would not have to use it. Why are people so fascinated with other people's boats? he asked himself. I really ought to get an apart—

The force of the blast knocked him off his feet. He could feel himself in the air for just a moment, then heard a crashing sound as water exploded past his ears. It took a moment before he realized he was underwater. He exhaled and rose to the surface, too shocked to wipe the hair from his eyes.

He felt something hard behind him and reached back to grab it. The wooden edge of a finger pier. He took his free hand and pushed the hair and slimy marina water away from his face.

Just in time to see his beloved sailboat burning to the waterline.

9

She was so hot, with the wind from the vent blowing under her dress.

Her face was ecstatic, lips red, mouth open, eyes shut. Just the hint of a giggle caught in her throat. Platinum blond and tight, smooth white skin.

Frankie Falcone had logged on. Now he was about to get off on Marilyn Monroe.

She was walking toward him. Away from the vent, the dress collapsed like a parachute on the ground. The dress slipped off her shoulders, down, easing past the hips, till it fell gently to the pavement.

She wore nothing underneath, and she was pouting now, calling his name, hand sliding up his shoulder, fingers lightly touching his chin, cupping, then lightly moving around to caress the back of his neck.

"I've been waiting for you," she whispered. "Where have you been?"

Frankie Falcone seized her tiny waist and lifted her in the air. She was light as a feather. In fact, she weighed nothing at all. When she settled upon him, he could feel her legs wrapping around and her arms on his shoulders. There was no strain. No pull from gravity. He backed her up against a wall. Then banged away.

It was the second time that day, the third time that week. He'd done Marilyn before Bo Derek. But after Sharon Stone.

Instead of making love to a woman, Frankie Falcone was making love to a machine. The woman he held was light because she did not exist. At least, not in the flesh. Instead she was created inside the helmet Frankie wore, her image made real by way of computer chip.

While the woman weighed nothing, the helmet weighed a ton. It made intercourse difficult unless you were standing up. The combination of electronic gear and computer chips and protective plastic was heavy and awkward on his head. He looked like a giant praying mantis. If he wasn't careful, he'd get neck strain again. That was the toughest thing about coming. The first time, he'd needed traction and physical therapy for three full days.

"How did it happen?" the doctor had asked in heavily accented English.

"High-impact aerobics," Frankie replied.

It wasn't all that far from the truth. He wore nothing above the waist save the helmet. His legs and feet were bare. But around his hips, he wore a Gore-Tex–like thong, plugged into the computer disc drive in the same way as a color monitor or a keyboard. In front of the thong, a cylindrical container about the size of a banana was attached by glue and solder. The computer could send ten thousand electronic impulses per second into his groin. The cylinder was washable and had a zippered opening to catch any of the expected secretions. A chip-driven diaper-vibrator–it gave a whole new meaning to the word *joystick*.

"Oooh, baby, Daddy is so good to me."

Frankie had programmed the dialogue himself.

He was thrusting, heaving, giving it his all as she cooed and sighed at just the right moments. A thousand-dollar call girl could not have done better. He pressed on, his face and eyes intent on the image of Marilyn, her eyelids fluttering as she dragged a moist tongue across her rich red lips. He cried out, convulsed, fought to hold his head up against the weight of the headgear.

Frankie's bout with the seven-year itch was over in less than five minutes.

She was still there, sighing and grinning, telling him he was the best, begging him not to leave, to make it once more.

"Not now, baby. Maybe later today."

She was still pouting as he flipped the computer off. Marilyn disappeared with barely a blip.

"God, I love that program," he murmured to himself.

It took a moment to undo the chin strap and step out of the diaper. He unhooked it from the telephone cord, then strutted to the kitchen and tossed it in the sink. Someday, he thought as he ran hot water, with cellular, I won't need the phone cord at all.

When the diaper was soaking, Frankie walked out of the villa and into an open-air shower. Despite its primitive looks, the water pressure was excellent; he let the cool jets massage his back and abdomen, then washed all over. He realized that he ached from all the sex. Too much of a good thing, he thought to himself as he toweled off and reached for a white terry-cloth robe.

Frankie had never been good with women. Beneath his fairly good looks lay enough insecurity to fill a dump truck. He still remembered with a great deal of pain his misery in high school, his shyness when it came to asking girls for dates.

Once, he wanted to take pretty young woman from the Hill to a prom. She was a year younger, with long, curly hair and deep brown eyes that always seemed to be hiding a secret. He had watched her walking to school, laughing and gossiping with her friends. Once, outside a shop on Atwells, he had bumped into her by accident. She giggled when he said, "Excuse me," then made her way across the busy street toward her mother's house. The eyes still held the secret.

He spent days thinking about what he would say. He practiced in front of a mirror. He desperately wanted it all to be perfect.

He asked her on a Friday afternoon a month before the prom. She was walking home from the bus stop and he had to wait until her friends had turned off to go home. But one girl stayed with her. She noticed he was following, and she turned, stared, almost smirking.

"What, Frankie?" she asked, and he blurted out his question. She smiled, looked down, laughed. It wasn't kind.

"My mother'd kill me if I went out with a half-breed."

It was then that he realized what the secret was. In her eyes, he could see the cruelty, the disdain, of the entire neighborhood.

He had gotten over that, he told himself.

An older black man appeared on the patio.

"Will you be wanting lunch today?"

"By the pool, Orland."

The servant nodded and disappeared into the villa. Whatever thoughts he had of his boss's bizarre sexual habits were kept to himself.

Frankie Falcone sat on a carved wood chair as the servant laid a table with fruit and bread, then beef and cheese. It was simple food, but filling, and he gazed at the water. It was one of the best parts of staying near Galway—the water that could look smooth as glass one day, then boil like a pot the next. He glanced back at the villa behind him. Its white-plastered walls and tiled roof were the envy of the locals, who were used to more common-looking dwellings. But this rich American wasn't afraid to live well.

Frankie had everything he needed here—shelter, servants, a fine view. And companionship anytime he wanted, all at the touch of a button.

The virtual-reality equipment had not come cheap. Nearly a million alone, plus fifty thousand for the right electrical hookups to make it work in this ancient land. But it offered all the comforts he needed and none of the hazards. He had sex with whomever he wished. There was no need for candlelit dinners, movie or theater tickets. No social requirement that he drive someone home and behave like a gentleman.

No mandate that he wear a condom or wait for a partner to install birth control or check into someone's medical history for signs of disease. No fear that a high-priced prostitute might blackmail him or attempt to rip him off. And he didn't have to ask for a date.

The machine asked for none of that. Just a little electricity and a good imagination. For Frankie's dollar, microchip sex had the real thing beat.

He took a piece of cheese, hard cheddar, and as he ate, he thought about all that it had taken to get him to this point in his life. All those years growing up on the Hill, learning the family business from his father and the men he worked with. When he was old enough, his father passed the business on. But Frankie controlled the money on the Hill. Helped decide who got a loan and who didn't. Took in the pay and the Social Security and even the welfare checks. Smiled at the men and the women, pinched the cheeks of their children. Deep down, he felt nothing for them except scorn.

Orland brought dessert, some kind of creamy pudding. Vanilla flavor, he thought, as he sucked on the spoon. Idly, he looked out at the water again and thought about the club— the Business Club, founded years ago by three men looking for an angle, for a way to get ahead. Each had found his own way, but all had stayed in touch with the other members, the relationship cemented not so much on friendship as on greed. Now they had all been paid. Now he was free.

His thoughts drifted to Sharon Stone. The way that she took a white scarf and tied Michael Douglas to the bed in that movie. Bouncing up and down, back and forth. Hot thighs and calves flexing. Orange light. Music pounding all around them. Sound track.

Yeah.

Marilyn will have to wait, he thought, as he went into the villa in search of a scarf.

It would take two days to positively identify Tisha Billings's remains.

A yachtsman found an eye and two teeth inside his Zodiac. A quahogger, a clam digger, retrieved two legs, amputated just above the knee, in the forward section of his power skiff.

Still, police had a good idea of who they were trying to piece together before they confirmed the ID. Tisha's car was in the parking lot and the marina attendant clearly recalled an ill-tempered woman matching her description walking on the docks within an hour of the explosion. After viewing a Channel Three publicity photo of the reporter, the attendant said he was sure.

Ordinarily, Tisha Billings would have been considered a hero. She had died doing her job. She had set out to find information and had had the misfortune of getting herself killed. It was the stuff that journalistic legends are made of: intrepid reporter fighting to get the story, martyr for the public's right to know.

But Tisha had apparently died after breaking into another reporter's home. According to the sole eyewitness, she was stark naked when last seen. And the legs found in the quahogger's skiff had the appearance of being tied up. Authorities made this conclusion because they were still firmly lashed together at the ankles. All in all, the story was a bit too kinky to qualify for a laurel in the *Columbia Journalism Review*.

The fact that Sol Herskowitz had initially backed away from the saloon where he'd seen Tisha hog-tied probably saved his life. The blast drove him nearly straight up, then out, about twenty to thirty feet in the air, depending on which witness the police consulted. He landed on the foredeck of a commercial fishing boat, broke an ankle, and pitched over the side. Two men in a Cigarette boat had pulled him from the water as he babbled about his leg and a nude woman. He was still babbling as paramedics checked him over, then loaded him into a rescue van for the trip to Rhode Island Hospital.

"Know him?" a cop asked Michael Carolina. The reporter sat on the edge of a pier, legs dangling down toward the water, with a blanket over his shoulders.

"Never seen him. He hurt bad?"

"Busted ankle, I hear. First, no, probably second-degree burns on his face. Know why he was on your boat?"

"I haven't got a clue."

A white Ford Crown Victoria with radio aerial pulled up. Detective Corvese of Providence climbed out, ambled over to a crew of officers, and began to chat. Two officers, fresh out of a police boat, came over and handed Corvese a thin parcel wrapped in plastic. After a few minutes, he went over to Carolina.

"Aren't you out of your jurisdiction?"

"I got special dispensation when I heard you were involved," Corvese said.

"I'm not involved. I just happened to be here."

"Was that your boat?" the detective asked, gesturing at some pieces of wood floating nearby.

Carolina nodded glumly.

"Then I'd say you were involved."

Corvese looked around. Most of the firefighters and rescue personnel were packing up. A few boaters drifted by, gawking at the remains and at the people on the marina piers. Overhead, the sky had turned an ominous shade of gray. The rain promised by the forecasters was on its way.

"Uh, Mike, I know this may seem like a bad time, but would you have any idea how a woman came to be tied up naked inside your boat?"

"Who told you that?"

"This guy Herskowitz says that's the last thing he saw before the boom."

"Really. Did he say why he was in my boat?"

"How 'bout you let me ask the questions for now, okay?"

Carolina looked at the hulk smoldering on the water. It was all that was left of the finest possession he had ever owned. "In all honesty, Sergeant, I have no idea why anyone was aboard."

"What were you doing down here in the middle of the day?"

For an answer, Carolina looked up at the sky.

A Warwick cop came up and pulled Corvese away. They went and talked to the kid who'd worked at the guard shack. The place was starting to swarm with reporters. Carolina could see officers starting to push them back toward the edge of the parking lot. A few photographers who'd gotten there early scrambled along the piers, hoping for a good shot of what was left of *Maeve*. Carolina remembered the last time that he'd seen a crowd like this—waiting for pictures of him and of the dead body being rolled down a pier, wrapped in a plastic bag. There wouldn't be any body this time.

Carolina felt sick. His home was gone. If Corvese was to be believed, another woman was dead. The nausea he felt seemed familiar, almost comforting.

Corvese returned. "Kid says he saw someone else on the pier this morning. Doesn't think he's a boat owner. We're going to show him some photos."

"You have a suspect?"

"Not yet. But this was a professional job. Your boat went just like an M-eighty."

"You don't need to tell me. I caught the show."

Corvese awkwardly put a hand on Carolina's shoulder.

"Where are you going to stay?"

"I'm not sure."

"Let me know. We'll want to stay in touch. You'll probably be hearing something from the feds—FBI, ATF. Maybe both."

"Don't you people work together?"

"You're a reporter. You know better. Oh, this yours?"
Corvese held out the parcel, a tattered Ziploc bag.

"Yeah, it's my passport."

"Well," Corvese said, "at least you salvaged something."

Accent didn't know whether Carolina was alive or dead, and
didn't wait around to find out. Instead, he parked in a garage
in Providence's downtown and slipped quietly into Tommy
Flannery's law office. The speaker of the Rhode Island
House of Representatives was holding his temples with his
fingers, elbows resting on his broad cherry-wood desk. A
small television set was on behind him, the sound turned
down.

"There were complications," Accent said.

"You missed him."

"I saw a man go down into the boat. He would have seen
a woman there, tied up. I had no choice."

"You missed him," Flannery said again, the anger in him
beginning to show.

"I told you why."

"Who was the woman?"

"Dunno. Think it may be some woman he worked with."

"Why was she tied up?"

"She saw me. Came in as I finished the wiring. Not too
smart, I think, but I couldn't let her go. I had no choice."

Flannery continued to rub his temples. He nodded absently.

"Tasty thing, she was." Accent smiled at the memory.

Flannery wanted to shoot him.

"Were you followed?" The speaker asked.

"No. And I was a long ways off when she blew."

"Don't come to the office again. It's too dangerous."

"I can still get him. He doesn't know who I am." Accent
was irritated at the failure. But he had enjoyed the work
nonetheless. He looked forward to a chance to try again.

"I think you had better not. There's too much going on. Lay low."

"Is that the club's position?" Accent asked, disappointed.

"The majority. Now get out."

Ron Davis covered the explosion. A fisherman described watching it from about a hundred yards out on the water, how it nearly capsized his boat. Out of courtesy to the station, Carolina gave a brief interview, saying, no, he did not know why a woman who appeared to be Tisha Billings had been confined inside the yacht's cabin, no, she had not been invited, and no, he didn't know why Sol Herskowitz, aka the Reverend Rasmus, was aboard, either. In his stand-up, Davis restated the obvious, that authorities were investigating the explosion but had no suspects.

Billy Guano called the station at 6:30, looking to talk with Carolina. Instead, Michael walked out of the building and went for a drive—through downtown Providence, up College Hill, then back down Benefit Street. He saw a sign for Wickenden and turned right, then drove slowly down to the South Side. He cruised the low-income housing projects and the boarded-up homes, then turned north and kept going, past stoplights and signs, auto-body shops and small businesses, until he arrived back on Federal Hill. He drove slowly down Atwells Avenue, past the restaurants and a tattoo parlor, a laundry and a few delicatessens. Then he braked, and came to a stop outside Amerigo Vespucci Loan and Investment, all closed up, with the signs that said it would not reopen per the order of Governor Dunleavy.

He stared for an hour, then fired his engine and drove off.

10

Even without a quote from the bomb's intended target, Billy Guano had plenty of ammunition for his column.

Tisha Billings learned the hard way.

Learned how dangerous it is to work with Michael Carolina. Even to work at the same station as Michael Carolina.

But Tisha Billings is not the first. The first was a woman named Roberta Glaser.

Glaser was a news photographer at a station in the Midwest. The same station where Carolina worked. He went on assignments with her. Covered stories with her. Used her pictures to build and tell those stories.

And what happened to Roberta Glaser? Not much.

Until a man slit her throat. A man Carolina had previously identified as a murderer on live television. Identified him without any confirmation from authorities.

I'll bet Roberta Glaser had a pretty good life before she met Michael Carolina. I'll bet Tisha Billings did, too.

And while I'm only a critic, it seems to me that Mr. Carolina has a nasty habit of getting women killed. Who's next, Mike? An anchor? Perhaps your news director? Why not try for Connie Chung?

"I'm really sorry about this," Shirley said. They were sitting in her office drinking coffee.

"Well, we both knew he liked Tisha."

"It's a lousy way to show it."

"He may just have a point."

"Bullshit. What happened to Tisha was horrible. But it doesn't change the fact that she had no business being aboard your boat. The truth is, she was probably spying on you or trying to steal something. Why else would she be there?"

"Hot sex?" Ron Davis said. He had slipped into the room unannounced.

"You're a pig, Ron," Shirley said.

"Well, she was nude and tied up," Davis said thoughtfully, picturing it in his mind.

"This is a private conversation."

"Okay, okay. Did you want me to follow this today?"

"Yes. Now. Out." Shirley waved her hand dismissively.

"Glad you came out okay," Davis said to Carolina as he glided out the office door. Carolina smiled wanly.

"Did you sleep last night?" Shirley asked.

"Sure."

"Hotel okay?"

"Fine." He was staying at a Days Inn just outside of Providence. Clean. Quiet. Cheap.

"You can stay a week. Like we do when someone moves to the area without their own houseboat."

"Gee, thanks."

"You know I've already had twenty calls from people asking about Tisha's job?"

"This is a cold fucking business."

"Indeed. Look, I could really use you, what with Tisha gone. But I think you'd better take a day."

"I'll work, if you need me."

"We'll get along. Take the day. Want a vitamin?" Shirley shook the big jar of C for him.

"No thanks," he said.

"Mike?" she said as he hit the door. Carolina did a 180 and looked at her.

"It really wasn't your fault."

"I know," he said. "It just feels like it is."

Carolina didn't get far. Two men in charcoal gray suits and black mirrored sunglasses were waiting as he emerged from the Channel 3 building.

"Michael Carolina?" one said as he reached his car.

"Yes, sir, that's me. By any chance are you federal agents?"

One man looked annoyed, the other disappointed as they showed their badges. ATF—Alcohol, Tobacco, and Firearms. The job just wasn't as much fun when people guessed before you flashed them your ID.

"We need to talk with you," the annoyed one said. He was about twenty pounds overweight, with a flattop haircut right out of a sixties high school yearbook. The other wore his hair slightly longer, but still short enough to meet with bureaucratic approval. He was slender and the suit he wore seemed too big.

"So what's up?" Carolina said as they drove the few blocks into downtown. Neither one answered him.

"Gee, those Red Sox are having a great season, eh, guys?" Not a word.

"You know, I bet your mothers are very proud of you." Still no answer.

"Of course, that Waco thing probably hasn't done much for the organization. Imagewise, I mean."

"Shut your sore," the heavier agent said as they pulled into a parking space at a building off Kennedy Plaza. They climbed out and held the door, then led him down a hall and into an elevator. Carolina didn't count the floors up. The agents unlocked an office door and took him down another hall that ended with a large office. From there, the three went into a smaller side office with a table and chairs.

Carolina was getting more and more angry. The two agents were treating him like a suspect. What's worse, they wouldn't tell him a thing. "Why don't you turn down the lights and then shine a big spot on me?" he asked. "You know I just love that third-degree stuff."

"You're not under arrest," the heavier agent said. On closer examination, Carolina could see that he was older than his colleague.

"But you could be." The younger one sounded like he'd been dying to get a word in.

"Shut up, Ernie. I said he wasn't a suspect," the older agent said.

"Then why are you treating me like one? And why am I here?"

"Because we're trying to find out who blew up your boat yesterday. And who kidnapped that girl, while we're at it. As to why we're acting this way, well"—the older man leaned in close—"we don't really like reporters."

"What a surprise," Carolina said, averting his head. He didn't know if the agent had bad breath, but he didn't want to find out.

"Why would someone want to kill you?" the older agent asked.

"I don't know that anyone does," Carolina said.

"Humor me."

Carolina looked the man over. He was in no mood to trust anyone. But if I don't give them something, he thought, I could be here all day.

"I've been working this story on Amerigo Vespucci's failure, the connection between the state and Frankie Falcone."

The older agent took notes.

"Anyone threaten you?"

"No."

"Get any nasty mail or phone calls?"

"Not so far. Except . . ."

"Yeah?"

"Tisha Billings wasn't exactly thrilled that I was on the story."

"No?"

"She wanted to cover it. She was looking for her big break."

The two agents exchanged glances.

"What was she doing on your boat?"

"You are one in a long line of people who have asked me that."

"And?"

"I truly don't know."

The older agent stopped writing and looked up again. Carolina caught a glimmer of sympathy in his eye.

"So there was nothing between you two?"

"A little spite maybe."

"You ever do her?" the skinny one asked.

"You ever do a Branch Davidian?" Carolina shot back. The skinny agent's face turned red.

"In response to your colleague's question," Carolina said, turning to the older agent again, "no. I never went out with her. I only met her last week."

"What about this guy Herskowitz?"

Carolina gave him a blank look.

"You know, the radio guy."

"The Reverend Rasmus? Don't know him, either."

"How soon before the explosion did you get to the marina?"

"Four, maybe five minutes. I saw someone climb aboard. I went and talked to the guard, told him I was going out to my boat and to call the cops if there was a problem."

"And then?"

"Then I walked down the dock and saw my boat get blown to smithereens."

The older agent left the room. Carolina sat and smiled at Ernie, who stood against the wall and stared, probably stewing about Waco and the Branch Davidians. In a few minutes, the other agent came back, holding a large brown book stuffed with photographs. He slid the book across the table.

"Have a look."

The pages were loaded with black and whites, mugs—head shots and profiles.

"What am I looking for?"

"Anybody you might have seen around the docks," the older agent said. "Anybody you've seen in the last few days, for that matter."

"I didn't see anyone yesterday that I haven't told you about."

"Try anyway. Even if it's been in the last few days."

Carolina spent twenty minutes going through the pages. They were filled with all kinds of heinous-looking individuals. Busted noses. A few with one eye. One with a scar that ran from his forehead diagonally across his face to his jaw. Another who looked like he could have been cast for an alien guest shot on *Star Trek*.

"I'm sure I was in the same fraternity with some of these guys," Carolina said finally, "but none of them was around the dock when *Maeve* blew."

The older agent started to open his mouth.

"And I haven't seen any of them in the last few days, either."

The heavy agent held a manila envelope. He carefully removed an eight-by-ten black-and-white photo.

"Ever see this man?"

The photo was different from the others. It was not a mug shot, but some sort of surveillance photograph. The camera's subject was a short man wearing a brown leather jacket, with dark hair and eyes. He was crossing a street, his hands stuffed in his pockets.

"Who is he?" Carolina asked.

"You ever seen him?" the agent prodded.

"No."

The skinny agent looked disappointed again.

"Sorry, Ernie," Carolina said. "Who is this guy?"

Neither agent said a word. The older one slid the photo back into the envelope.

"Sit tight, Mr. Carolina. We'll be right back." The two agents left the room, closing the door behind them.

Carolina looked around. The room had no mirrors or windows, no cameras. He was alone. The envelope lay in front of him.

Two minutes later, the agents came back.

"That's all for now. Thanks for coming in," the older agent said.

"That's it? You're not going to tell me what you've got?"

"No, we're not. I told you, we don't like reporters."

"How about a ride back to my car?"

"We'll call you a cab. Will you take care of that, Ernie?"

"With pleasure, Bert," the young agent said with a grin. Then his face fell, as if he had realized he'd made an enormous mistake.

"I told you never to—" Bert said, sputtering. But it was too late.

"Bert. Ernie," Carolina said with obvious delight. "How fitting. On second thought, I'll get my own cab. Better yet, I'll walk. By the way, can you tell me how to get—"

"Don't," Bert said.

Carolina smiled. "Yeah. You're right. It's too easy. But hey, give my regards to Big Bird."

Bert Schumacher often wondered what he'd done to get saddled with a partner like Ernie O'Mara. He'd spent most of his career in the New England region and had a record for good solid arrests. Now he was stuck with this rookie. It wasn't that his new partner was a bad guy. But Ernie acted liked he'd seen every FBI film and TV show ever made. Which, in fact, he had.

Ernie had passed all the exams for entrance into the FBI but had failed somewhere during the interview process. Too much Hollywood had been the consensus of the interviewers. ATF hadn't been quite so stringent. So now Bert was forced to put up with Ernie's shtick. Both criminals and witnesses saw through it, which was bad enough. But when they heard the two agents call each other by their first names, it became unbearable.

"I told you never to say my name if I say yours first."

Ernie looked sheepish. "Sorry, Bert."

"That guy's a real smart-ass. He could make a running joke of us on TV."

"I didn't think of that."

"I know."

"Bert . . ."

"What?"

"What about the picture?"

"What about it?"

"Why didn't you tell him?"

Bert hitched up his pants and let go a long, heavy sigh.

"Three reasons. First, we don't know for sure if we've got the right guy. Though I'll admit, it sure looks like his kind of work. Second, we're not dealing with your average crime victim. This Carolina is pretty smart. If he wasn't, he wouldn't have nailed down so much stuff about the Vespucci bank so fast. Third, and worst thing of all, he's a reporter. He'll be out there trying to find this character, or putting his name on TV."

"Well, what if he is the bomber and he's still going after Carolina?"

"That's why we're going to get some overtime this week. I think we need to tail this guy."

Thomas Patrick Flannery hadn't always wanted to be the speaker of the Rhode Island House of Representatives. He first wanted to be a soldier.

It wasn't the uniforms soldiers wore. It was their power. Their guns. Cannon. If someone got in a soldier's way, he killed them. That much was apparent to a boy growing up. Little Tommy loved to play war. He played it with sticks and, sometimes, a few stones. Played it with his older brother, Jimmy, and the other neighbor kids. It didn't matter which side. He was equally adept at Germans or Japs or Indians, as well as GIs and cowboys.

But as he grew, Tommy realized he not only liked power; he liked money, too. Liked the fine clothes it could buy, and the cars and the homes like those of the well-to-do people who lived on Providence's East Side, where his mother and then his older sister went to work as domestic help.

Later, he realized that the power of a soldier was more limited than it had first appeared. As he read volume upon volume of military history, he discovered that men with guns were only powerful when they had someone to lead them—and not just generals, but men who had the cash to pay for the costs of war, men with their hands on a gigantic purse. Slowly, Tommy Flannery's heroes began to change, from Audie Murphy, to George Patton, to Ike. LBJ. And Nixon. Their personal politics didn't matter so much. What mattered was what they had. That power. The ability to get things done. To humiliate, crush, and toss aside those who stood in the way. Tommy loved the story of Johnson chewing out a subordinate while he defecated in a White House bathroom, of Nixon and the dirty tricks. Someone had to drive the world, and these men held the wheel.

In some other place with some other background, Flannery

would have completed his education at an Ivy League university or Amherst or Williams. If he had lived in California, he might have gone to Stanford or Berkeley or Pomona. But Tommy grew up in the west end of Providence. The money his father made as a deputy sheriff at the courthouse barely fed the wife and four children.

His sisters didn't want school, or if they did, knew it was useless to say so. His brother Jimmy didn't seem to know what he wanted. Jimmy fell in with some other tough Irish kids and started staying out at night. Once he got arrested driving a stolen car and went away for a few months to reform school.

Tommy's mother said Jimmy was bad seed.

When Tommy Flannery was thirteen, he won a half scholarship to a private Catholic high school. His mother and sister did domestic work to pay the rest of the tuition. Flannery worked, too. He could remember coming home at night after helping lift boxes off trucks and watching his mother make dinner after a day of working in someone else's home. She always looked withered, like a plant beaten down by the wind.

When he graduated with honors, there was another scholarship waiting, this time with full tuition to Providence College. Flannery went from unloading trucks to bussing tables to pay for clothes and spending money. He studied politics and history with other poor and middle-class Catholic boys who didn't stray far from home. There were basketball games and morning Mass and extracurricular activities like the club that occupied all his spare time.

The club.

Early on at meetings of the Business Club, he saw another kid with dark hair and olive skin. Handsome, in the way that Italian men were. And knowledgeable. He knew which people to schmooze at the registrar's to get the courses he wanted. Knew where term papers could be purchased and for what price. And to Tommy Flannery, Frank Falcone seemed to know a hell of a lot about business.

The two of them became fast friends. And between them they made another. Another young man with an interest in how to make a buck and how to be in charge. They were all the same and all very different, each one's strengths complimenting the others. By senior year, they were the leaders of the Business Club. President. Vice President. Treasurer. They made plans, invited members of the community to come in and speak. They invited captains of industry: jewelry manufacturers, the owners of textile mills, attorneys, and bankers.

More often than not, the Business Club was turned down. Many of their invited guests reasoned that they were too busy for poor Catholic kids from PC. The captains of industry spoke at Brown or up in Cambridge. They didn't have time for the sons of micks and wops.

The Business Club accepted it all with grace. But its members did not forget. And they persevered.

One night, the club's officers all went out. They dipped into club funds and went to a good restaurant, ordered big meals and drinks.

"To the club," Tommy said, holding a glass of whiskey.

"To the club and to us," Frank agreed, raising a glass filled with a dry martini.

"To business," the third one said, and lifted a snifter filled with cognac. "Someday, we'll do business together."

When they graduated, the three men each went their own way. Tommy's dreams of soldiering had long since died; with the war in Southeast Asia raging, the thought of a military career had lost much of its appeal. Flannery's father knew a fellow who handled clerical work at the draft board. The cost of corruption was cheap. For a hundred dollars, his service file was lost for the duration of the conflict.

Instead of boot camp, he went to night law at Suffolk in Boston. He finished in four years, near the top of his class, and hung out his own shingle. He practiced storefront law: divorces and drunk-driving cases, simple wills and a few house closings. Easy money that required little thought and offered less challenge.

Then there was an election. A local hack who'd served ten years in the general assembly and always voted the way the leadership told him was calling it quits. Tommy had been to the fund-raisers, the meetings, the political caucuses. He saw a way to build his practice and increase his stature at the same time. His mother and father helped. So did his sisters. Every home in the district got a visit. If no one answered the door on the first try, a second attempt was made. Vote for Tommy. Tommy the lawyer. Tommy your friend. He'll get you what you deserve, what you got coming. No crime. A better job. A cleaner street. Tommy's your man.

Flannery got help from another relative, too. Jimmy had just finished a six-year stretch in Leavenworth for bank robbery. Now he was back in the neighborhood, building his own career. Word got out on the street and in the voting precincts that Jimmy was *sure* his little brother would win. One opponent dropped out. Another watched his support quietly fade away to fewer than two hundred votes. Tommy Flannery won in a walk.

It didn't take long for the young representative to be noticed. He quickly learned what it took to get a popular bill through a committee and, more importantly, what it took to keep a dangerous or unpopular one from getting to the floor. Tommy Flannery rose fast, from whip, to committee chair, to majority leader, and, finally, to speaker.

Over the years, he kept track of his classmates. Frank Falcone had taken over his father's bank. He was hard to miss, wearing shiny suits and driving a Mustang, then a Caddy, then a Benz. Frank was at all the fund-raisers, always smiling, always shaking hands. Frank was always good for a few hundred, sometimes a thousand-dollar donation for the reelection bid.

Their friend was there, too. He'd made his own way up

the ladder of political and business success. Always moving in the same circles.

The three of them never worked together directly after college. But they never forgot where they began. Sometimes, at a cocktail party or a dinner, they would spot one another, almost as if by some prearranged signal. In a bizarre ritual of male bonding, the three would nod but never speak. And each would smile.

The members of the Business Club understood one another.

Time had, of course, moved forward. Frankie became a pillar of the Federal Hill financial community. His bank appeared prosperous, and rock-solid. When it came to loans or any other kind of financial transaction, it seemed like Frankie had a piece of just about everything.

Now, nearly everyone on the Hill wanted a piece of Frankie Falcone.

It would never happen, Tommy knew. Frankie had made it clear that he wanted out, and the other members of the Business Club had agreed. It was the only natural thing for a bank president to do once his bank had been looted.

Of course, there was that one ugly piece of business. Simmons had been recruited because his public persona was so clean. The white-knight image he showed during the bank-insurance hearings a year earlier was to everyone's advantage; it made it harder to quibble with the way the man ran the department. And it didn't hurt that Simmons was thoroughly Ivy League. That kept the editors over at the *Herald* satisfied. But in the end, Simmons was a liability. He wanted an equal cut—15 million split four ways instead of three. To the original members of the club, that was unacceptable. Flannery found some pleasant irony in the fact that the poor kids from PC would snub the rich WASP from the East Side.

That knife in the gut had been one hell of a snub.

The man with the accent had been an enormous help

there, and it was all because of Tommy's brother. Hardly anyone ever mentioned the fact that Tommy Flannery was related to one of the most notorious gangsters in New England. Not the pols, not the civil-service types, and certainly not the flunkies who did the lawmaker's bidding. Every once in a while, a reporter with a bug up his ass would come around and try to do a story about the two brothers. Tommy would never comment. And those who wished to get anywhere within the sordid field of State House politics had sense enough keep their mouths shut.

So far, no reporter had been brazen enough or stupid enough to approach Jimmy directly. But now Tommy was wondering whether Carolina would be the first to try.

He rolled the thought around in his mind as he sat in a tenement's kitchen in the west end. The apartment was inside a nondescript building, but it was clean and comfortable. Jimmy had half a dozen of these places around town, places to stay for a few days or at the most a few weeks. Tommy's brother always liked to keep moving. It was too easy for the feds to bug a place if you stayed too long.

Jimmy was taller than his brother by an inch and twenty pounds heavier. In his younger days, it had all been rock muscle, but now his belly was just beginning to grow soft from too much food and alcohol and too little exercise. Still, he was a good-looking man, with black hair beginning to show flecks of gray and deep blue eyes. And Jimmy was cool, with nerves like iron rods. It was the biggest reason why the bank-robbery stretch in his youth represented the only serious time he'd ever done.

"So, little brother," he said softly, "did anyone follow you here?"

"I need to talk to you," Tommy answered.

"You know it's dangerous coming in daylight." Jimmy glanced out the apartment window, checking the sidewalks and looking for parked cars.

"It's important that we discuss this."

"Was there anyone on the street?"

"This man of yours, he did some good work."

"Snitches are everywhere. Wouldn't surprise me if you had a tail."

"Are you listening to me?" Tommy said sharply. His brother turned and gave that hard, penetrating stare that had made dozens of criminals want to follow Jimmy Flannery on any kind of job. It was the kind of stare that left Tommy feeling small, insignificant. Finally, Tommy looked away.

"I can't do you any good if I'm pinched," Jimmy said.

"I'm very careful," Tommy replied. "Almost too careful."

"There's no such thing," Jimmy said. He eased away from the window and pulled out a chair at the apartment's kitchen table. Apparently, he was satisfied that Tommy had not been followed.

"You didn't come here to compliment me on my employees."

"No. He's a good man, but he screwed up."

"I read the papers," Jimmy replied.

"So what are you gonna do?"

"Careful, now, Tommy. You don't want to start talkin' like you still live in the west end. Mustn't put all those fine diction lessons to waste."

Tommy stiffened. He hated it when his brother mocked him, made fun of him for how he had risen. But he needed Jimmy's help. The kind of help that only Jimmy could provide.

"What are you . . . going to . . . do?"

"About what?" Jimmy asked.

"About this reporter, Carolina."

"Nothing."

"Nothing?"

"What do you want me to do? He's very high-profile right now. If someone takes another crack at him, it'll bring the wrath of God down on all of us."

"I'm aware of that. But there's still a problem. He's still out there, still digging around. And if he digs too hard, he could bring me into it. And if that happens, he could bring you into it."

Jimmy didn't flinch. He had handled all kinds of threats in his life. From other crooks. From cops and prosecutors. Even from politicians.

"Well, little brother," he said, "I guess I am glad that you came by after all. If this is how you feel, then you're right. It's important that we talk."

Jimmy stood up from the table and walked around the kitchen. Tommy felt smug. He had never been able to show Jimmy up before. It was a first.

Jimmy slipped behind his brother, opened the door to a refrigerator, examined its contents, and closed it again.

"And yes, Tommy, I agree with you on something else. This man Carolina is dangerous. He's a plugger. He could find out more and that would be a very bad thing." Jimmy patted his brother's shoulder. His hand was firm. Calmly, Jimmy slid his hand to his brother's collar. To his starched white linen shirt with the tightly knotted red paisley on the front.

"Where I disagree with you, brother, is that I am somehow exposed on this matter." Deftly, Jimmy slipped two fingers under Tommy's collar and grabbed the tie. With his free hand, he grabbed the front of the tie so the knot wouldn't give. Then Jimmy twisted his right wrist. Tommy's eyes bulged.

"No, baby brother, I have no exposure at all. None. I subcontracted a man to you. For free. I am getting nothing from this. And I want nothing from you and your pissant little partners. I am not involved. I am not going to be involved."

Tommy's face was beet red. He was unable to breathe in or out. He reached up to claw at his brother's fingers. But Jimmy held tight.

"You can talk to my man. You can even advise him.

Maybe you'll want to rough this reporter up. Put him out of commission temporarily."

Now Tommy's face was almost blue.

"But I am not . . . I am truly not involved. Right, little brother?"

Tommy Flannery gave the barest of nods.

"Good," Jimmy said, letting his fingers slip away from the collar and the knot. Tommy Flannery gasped heavily for air.

"Sorry if I mussed your nice clothes," Jimmy said, and sat down again at the kitchen table. "Now, do us both a favor and get the hell out of here."

rospect Park is located near the crest of College Hill. It is a patch of green grass with a few benches and an iron fence running along the edge and it looks out over the city's downtown. The houses that sit across from it to the south and the east are old and well made. The condos erected to the north look new and cheaply built.

Michael Carolina didn't look at the houses. He gazed out at the city. These people have homes, he thought. Some were princely, stately, with little plaques that announced to the world their age and heritage. Some were little more than a few pieces of siding thrown around a frame. But they were places to go, to return to at the end of a day.

My home is gone.

Maeve had been a beautiful yacht. Carolina had spent hours working with sandpaper and tack cloths, getting the mahogany ready to drink in eight, nine, sometimes twelve coats of varnish. He'd polished the brass and bronze until his hands were black and green and the metal shone like pieces of the sun. The coamings and cabin tops, the masts . . . now nothing more than waterlogged kindling.

I've lost my boat. I've lost a piece of my soul.

The image lead once again to the question that had plagued him since the moment of the explosion. Who was trying to kill him?

He fingered the manila envelope lying on the park bench, thought about the picture inside it. Who was the man in the leather jacket? Why were the feds interested in him? And if he had blown up Carolina's boat, why had he done it?

And what was Tisha Billings doing in the saloon of *Maeve,* tied up and without a stitch on?

His thoughts drifted to Guano's morning column. Logically, what had happened to Tisha had nothing to do with Carolina. He hadn't provoked her, hadn't asked her aboard *Maeve.* Just the same, another person had died. If I hadn't been around, she'd still be alive.

"Do you know who that is?"

The voice made him jump. Carolina turned, to see Lilly Simmons standing behind him, a bemused look on her face.

"You startled me."

"And you surprised me. What are you doing here, looking for a place to live?"

"I should be. I was just taking in the view."

She nodded in understanding. "So, do you know who that is?"

"Who?"

"Him." She pointed a long, slender arm toward a statue. It stood in the middle of a concrete monument at the center of the park. The statue of a man, watching over the city. His hair was long, and his hand was raised as if he were holding something out to some unseen person.

"He looks like a cigar store Indian without the cigar," Carolina said.

Lilly smiled and pushed a piece of hair away from her face, the same way she had when Carolina had first seen her in the newsroom.

"That's Roger Williams. He founded Providence. The Puritans threw him out of Massachusetts, so he came down here in the seventeenth century."

"Did he," Carolina said. Somewhere in the recesses of his memory, a long-lost history lesson stirred; an image of a man fleeing in the middle of snowstorm, trying to escape a band of people who had fled from religious intolerance in the Old World and now were intolerant themselves.

"Do you think Roger Williams had any idea what a cesspool this state would turn out to be?" Carolina asked.

"This is not a cesspool!" Lilly was genuinely angry. "This is a great state. It's just that people get carried away with their own power. And bad people do bad things. I think Roger Williams knew a lot about that."

It was probably not a good topic, Carolina realized, considering what had happened to Frederick Simmons. It occurred to him that he had not seen her since that first day in Shirley's office.

"I'm really sorry about what happened to your father," he said.

"Thank you."

"And about the way you found out."

"You couldn't have known."

She wore jeans and sneakers and a Brown University sweatshirt. He noticed how pale her face was, that she had rings under her eyes. Lilly Simmons seemed very delicate, almost childlike.

"Want to sit?"

"Sure." She took the edge of the bench.

"Do you live around here?"

"A few blocks away. I like to walk around here. The houses are pretty."

"They are."

They seemed to have run out of conversation. For a moment, Lilly kept looking at the statue of Roger Williams.

"You know, he does look like a cigar store Indian."

They both laughed a little.

"When you're from out of town, sometimes things look a little different," Carolina said.

"I guess. I, uh, read about the explosion."

"Yes. Made great copy."

"Was it insured?"

"The boat? Yes, but not for replacement value. I couldn't get half that boat with what the insurance policy pays."

"So you're searching for a place to stay?"

"So it seems. This is a good neighborhood."

"It is. It's close to town, but the streets are quiet. And you're near the university. Near Thayer Street."

"Thayer Street?"

"It's kind of like Greenwich Village, but on one street that runs a couple of blocks."

"Really?"

"Want a little tour?"

Thayer Street was crowded with youth in the late afternoon. Preppy kids, grunge kids, and many who fit somewhere in between. All of them moving up and down the street, in and out of the record shops and ethnic restaurants and bookstores like ants over a ripe piece of fruit. A saxophone player stood on the corner of Thayer and Meeting, wailing away for dimes and quarters. Across the street, a huge man with a heavy black beard and tattoos that filled both arms held two pit bulls. He held them by heavy leashes with one hand, and their eyes bulged as they strained at the leather. The man chatted amiably with a shopkeeper and casually slapped an ax handle with his free hand.

"Charming," Carolina said as they stepped around the trio of animals.

"They don't hurt anyone," Lilly said. "Just part of the scenery. Besides, they're cute."

"So the wood he's carrying is just for show," Carolina said.

"This whole street is just for show," she said.

Carolina was feeling better. For a few minutes, at least, his mind was off the loss of *Maeve*. Lilly moved easily along the street, with the grace and comfort of someone who knew it well. People waved to her. Some said hello.

"Hungry?" she asked.

Carolina realized he hadn't eaten all day.

They went to a Greek restaurant and ordered beers and lamb sandwiches wrapped in pita. The food came loaded down with black olives and onions and yogurt dressing.

"This isn't bad," Carolina said. Lilly looked pleased.

"Mind if I ask you something?"

"Go ahead," Lilly said.

"Why are you doing this? I did the story that said your father worked with Frankie Falcone. That's not exactly a compliment."

"No, it isn't." She ate a little more, taking small bites.

"So?" he said after a minute.

"The way I see it," she said finally, "you did a great job of digging up what happened at Vespucci. And you did a great job making the connection between the bank and my dad."

He watched her carefully. She didn't show the slightest sign of embarrassment or self-consciousness.

"And now someone actually went after you," she said, "so you have a personal stake in this whole mess. So"—she sipped her beer—"I figure that you're my best shot at finding who killed my father."

"Very pragmatic of you."

"Thank you." She smiled, then ate another bite. "I was sorry to see what happened to your boat."

"It's not as hard on me as it was on Tisha."

"True." Lilly had a sad smile, and she showed it now. "It's strange, though."

"What?"

"Not that I want to speak ill of the dead . . . but Tisha wasn't exactly a patron saint for reporters."

"Maybe for burglars," Carolina said.

"You're sick."

"So I've heard."

"But funny."

"Thanks."

They ate a few bites.

"So do you plan on finding out who did it?"

"I may already know."

"Really?"

Carolina picked up the manila envelope, pried the metal clasps open, and slid the eight-by-ten glossy photo out and across the table.

"Ever see this guy before?"

"No," Lilly said after studying it. "Who is he?"

"Someone the ATF thinks might be involved in the bombing."

"And they just gave this to you?"

"Not exactly."

"You're trying to find out who this is."

"You're very quick. Ever think of getting into journalism?"

Carolina took the picture back, placed it in the envelope, and stretched. "This place is pretty good."

"I'm glad you like it. So do you mind if I ask you something?"

"Turnabout is fair play."

"Who was Roberta Glaser?"

Carolina carefully examined the label on his beer.

"You read the column in the *Herald.*"

"I don't mean to pry."

"Yes you do. People always say that when they're really digging."

"I'm sorry."

"It's okay. She was a news photographer and a good friend. We worked together at my last station."

"Were you involved with her?"

"You could say that."

"What made you so close?"

"We worked on a story about a child molester."

"No shit."

"Yeah. His name was Larry Traynor. He was the anchorman at my station."

"My."

Carolina laughed. " 'My' is right."

"What did you do?"

"I told the news director."

"And?"

"Roberta and I got suspended."

"Was that the end of it?"

"No. We still managed to do the story."

"Did you go to another station? To the papers?"

Carolina shook his head. "We kind of invaded our own station's broadcast tower."

"You what?"

"Went to the tower, flipped a switch, and did our own live shot. I told the whole story with Larry Traynor watching, right there on the set during the six o'clock broadcast."

"Oh my God. Did you get fired?"

"That and a lot more."

"What happened to Traynor?"

"He went nuts. Took off. Cops looked all over town for him. Then–" Carolina stopped. He could see himself aboard *Maeve* again. Could feel R. J. Glaser kissing him, then climbing down into the cabin. . . .

"What? What?" Lilly said.

"You must not have seen Guano's first story about me coming to town," Carolina said.

"Just the one this morning," Lilly said. "So what happened?"

"He jumped the two of us inside my boat. He cut Roberta's throat. Tried to kill me." It was amazing how calm he felt. How matter-of-fact his voice sounded. He hadn't talked about this since Traynor's trial.

Lilly said nothing. She apparently had no more questions.

"Maeve," Carolina said, "brought me a lot of joy. And a lot of pain."

"Maybe we should go," Lilly said.

When they got back out on the street, she tried to slide her arm through his. But he shrugged her off.

"Michael, I'd like to help you with that photo."

"It's not a good idea."

"I have a stake in this. That man may have something to do with my father's death."

"Maybe. But right now, I don't think that's a terribly good idea." As you've just heard, he thought, women who hang around me tend to have short life expectancies.

He made his way up the street. "Do you want a ride home?"

"No, I can walk," she said. "I'm going to do this, you know. I'm going to find the man who killed my father."

He stopped and looked at her.

"You'd be really stupid to try," he said. "Take a look at me. I went hunting for a criminal once. And I found him. What did I get for it? I lost my job. Someone I loved got butchered. I was blackballed from my profession. Now I'm thirty-four years old. I have no home, no family. And someone just tried to blow me to kingdom come. Don't be an idiot. Go home and wait for this to sort itself out."

He turned and walked away.

"What about you?" she called. "You're still looking. Why should you be different?"

"Because I'm beyond redemption," he muttered to himself, and kept walking.

Detective Sergeant Donald Corvese stared at the steaming plate of diet lasagna, fresh from the squad room microwave. Just 225 calories, the box said. The smiling woman with big hair and capped teeth on the cover said it was simply delicious.

He took a small saltshaker and a miniature pepper grinder from his desk drawer. Three shakes of salt. Five grinds of pepper. Then, gingerly, he picked up a plastic fork, cut a bite.

He chewed. Swallowed. The noodles were like rubber. The sauce had the consistency of watered-down catsup. The cheese had no taste at all.

"I fuckin' hate diets," Corvese muttered, tossing the red-white-and-yellow mass into the wastebasket by his desk.

"Someone to see you, Sergeant." The blue uniform who brought the visitor had already done a 180 and was heading back to the front desk.

"Hey, Sergeant," Michael Carolina said.

"Hey, sailor man," Corvese said, arching an eyebrow. "How's the search for the new home?"

"Slow. Got a minute?"

"For you, anything."

"Know who this is?" Carolina slid the photograph toward the cop. Corvese looked it over. Now both eyebrows arched. Then furrowed, squinting.

"Where'd you get this?"

"You know who it is?" Carolina said.

"I didn't say that."

"Well, do you?"

Corvese slid the photo back. "Never seen him."

Just like a cop, Carolina thought.

"Excuse me," he said. "Maybe you don't remember who I am. I'm the guy who nearly got his ass blown up two days ago."

"I remember."

"It's my understanding that this guy may have been involved."

Corvese looked at him and said nothing.

"Sergeant, since no one has been arrested, I'm a little worried. And to ease my worry, I'd like to know who this gentleman is."

"It ain't gonna ease your worry," Corvese said.

"Humor me."

"What a nice set of brass balls you have."

"Thanks. I acquired them after dealing with members of the law-enforcement community such as yourself."

A smirk crossed Corvese's face.

"You eaten lately?"

"Yes." He could still taste the Greek sandwich.

"Well, I haven't. Come on."

Corvese took him to a place called Junkyard Dawgs, down on Westminster. It was a hole-in-the-wall wedged between a bar and a porno bookstore.

"Gimme a bulldawg," the sergeant said, walking in the door.

A T-shirted man behind the counter nodded.

"Make it two. One for my friend here."

"What's a bulldawg?" Carolina asked.

"Kraut, onion, mustard, chili, hot peppers."

"Sounds like dinner in a sewer."

"You'll love it," Corvese said, offended.

"When's the last time this place was inspected?"

"Probably before you were born. What are you, a wuss?"

"Just careful where I get my grease."

Corvese wolfed his hot dog down with huge bites, breathing heavily, occasionally whistling through his nose. Carolina tried to time his questions for the moments when Corvese was about to swallow.

"So are you going to tell me who this guy is, or did you just want to buy me dinner?"

"I said I didn't know," Corvese said, and took another bite.

"That was after you asked where I got the photo."

Corvese glanced over at the counterman, who, with no one else in the restaurant, seemed to be listening in. The stare from the detective sent him into the back of the kitchen, outside of hearing range.

"Not too many folks know about him. I figure you got that picture from ATF."

"Maybe I did."

"Only I can't figure out why they'd just give it to you."

Now it was Carolina's turn to say nothing.

"Well, well, you ain't as clean-cut as I thought."

"I can't stand being in the dark."

"So I see. Liam O'Shea."

"Lee-em Oh—what?"

"Liam O'Shea." Corvese tapped a pudgy, chili-stained finger on the print. "He is not a nice man."

"I already gathered that. Why does ATF think he blew up my boat?"

"Because what was done to your boat is his kind of work. At least it was when he worked in Ulster."

Carolina forgot all about the smell of his uneaten hot dog.

"He's IRA?"

"No, he runs a tourism office for Buckingham Palace. Of course he's fucking IRA."

"What do I have to do with the Irish Republican Army?"

"Nothing, unless there's something you haven't told me. But Liam's in semiretirement now. Or what's that word you TV people use? Hiatus. He's on hiatus."

"I don't follow."

"He's believed to be on this side of the water. We've had reports on him come through the NCIC. Interpol. He's wanted for bombing two kids in Londonderry two years ago. He was trying to assassinate a prosecutor and he fucked up. Then he went underground. Scotland Yard can't find him. They think he came here. Feds think he may be connected with some Irish-American mobsters."

"Irish mobsters."

"Sure, you don't think us guineas keep it all to ourselves, do you? Not even in Providence. You want the rest of that?" Corvese pointed at the bulldawg.

"No."

The detective polished it off in two bites. Then he wiped the grease and chili from his hands with a paper napkin.

"Ever hear of Jimmy Flannery?"

"I've heard of Tommy Flannery, the House speaker."

"Tommy's Jimmy's brother."

Carolina's face was blank. He was still digesting the fact that an international terrorist might have tried to blow him to bits. But the news about Flannery grabbed his attention again. He listened as Corvese filled him in on Jimmy Flannery's exploits as a member of New England organized crime. How his reach extended through Rhode Island, up into southern Massachusetts, even to the docks on Boston Harbor.

"Feds have circulated flyers and bulletins for months about Liam. They figure he may be freelancing for Jimmy. That's not unheard-of, you know. You catch a little heat over on the old sod, as they say, you come over here till it cools off. Guy like Jimmy, he offers plenty of protection. Only be natural for Liam to want to pay him back."

"So how come I haven't been bothered by FBI?"

"I don't know. I don't work for them. But explosives are what ATF is all about. This one is a natural for them."

"I don't think they have anything."

"Probably not. If they did, they'd have made a bust by now. But that kid who works at the marina gave them something. Otherwise, they wouldn't have shown that picture to you."

"So if I was going to look for this Jimmy, where should I start?"

Corvese burst out laughing.

"You are definitely not from Rhode Island," he said, holding one side. He stopped for a moment, looked at Carolina, then started laughing again.

"You sound like a truck with no muffler," Carolina said. He didn't smile.

"I'm sorry," Corvese said. He grabbed another napkin to wipe tears and blow his nose. "It's just that"—he paused to stifle another wave of guffaw—"you don't go looking for Jimmy Flannery. Not if you're a reporter."

"Corvese . . ."

"And most definitely not if you're a reporter one of his boys just tried to kill."

"Corvese."

"What?"

"Where do I find him?"

"You are really fucking crazy, you know that?" Corvese was genuinely irritated. But then, so was Carolina.

"Okay, Detective. I'm crazy. I'm a nutcase. Psycho. A dingbat. One slice short of a loaf. Two cards shy of a full deck. Now, where do I find Jimmy Flannery?"

The sarcasm achieved its intended effect, cooling Corvese's laughter. The detective was sizing the reporter up once again, trying to figure out where he got the onions to talk to a police officer this way.

"I'm not going to be responsible for your death," the cop said.

"You're not. And you won't be. I am just trying to figure a few things out."

"Such as?"

Carolina shook his head. "Newsman's privilege."

"What's that, some kind of First Amendment bullshit? Lemme tell you somethin'. It ain't gonna be any privilege to get your head caved in by one of Jimmy's goons."

"Look at it this way, Sergeant. If you don't tell me, I'll go off looking on my own. And you know from experience that I'm pretty good at finding things. Sooner or later, I'll figure out where Jimmy Flannery can be found."

Carolina leaned close to the officer, until his face was just a few inches away. "Of course, if I do that, I might run into trouble. There might be another problem like the one down at the marina."

"Yeah, that ought to be a lesson to you."

"Sergeant, they took my home. It's the only thing I had. I can't walk away. It's just not in me."

Corvese looked at him again. Without a word, he turned and walked out of Junkyard Dawgs. Carolina followed. When he caught up, Corvese spoke.

"I'm only saying this once. There's an entertainment company in town. It's registered with the secretary of state. Very profitable. You never would imagine that it could bring in this kind of cash. You'd almost believe that it was used for some other purpose, you know? Like taking dirty money and washing it clean."

"What's it called?"

"The Rose Tattoo. Go check it out at the secretary of state's. You'd be intrigued by who owns it."

"Sergeant . . ."

"What? Don't ask anything more, 'cause I done my service to the press today."

"Thanks for the dog."

Corvese stopped and scuffed a shoe on the pavement. Then he held a hand up and pointed a finger at the reporter.

"These guys . . . These guys'll fuckin' kill you, you don't watch out. Don't ever say I didn't warn you."

Corvese watched as Carolina dodged a car and made his way down the street.

"Be careful, kid," he called.

The Rose Tattoo was Providence's strip joint of record. It was located in a cement-block building just a mile from downtown, near Providence College. The headline acts that made the most money were usually women who worked a series of clubs between New York and Boston. The Tattoo was the stop after New London and before Brockton or the Cape.

Detective Sergeant Donald Corvese was correct. The Rose Tattoo did make a lot of money. He was also correct, although he knew it would be impossible to prove, that the club was a laundromat for Jimmy Flannery, providing a quasi-legitimate source of income that helped to mask more illegitimate sources of revenue like gambling and drug sales.

None of this was really of much concern to Michael Carolina as he parked near the edge of the Tattoo's massive lot early in the evening. Indeed, Carolina wasn't quite sure why he was stopping there. But he felt drawn to the place, half-expecting to be greeted by a burly Irishman in a leather jacket.

Instead, he found two blow-dried bouncer/valets dressed in boots, T-shirts, and tight black pants at the door. He paid the five-dollar cover and was immediately overwhelmed by the mixed scents of alcohol, smoke, and feminine perspiration. Two women wearing G-strings, cossack riding boots, and nothing else were dancing in tandem on a runway for an audience of businessmen and hard hats. The crowd showed mild interest.

A bartender approached. He was built like a linebacker and had long, oily hair pulled back in a tight ponytail.

"What'll ya have, chief?"

"Heineken," Carolina said, looking the room over.

"Five bucks," Ponytail said, handing over the bottle. Carolina gave him ten.

"Need change?"

"No."

"Thanks, chief." The bartender looked surprised but pleased. "Let me know if you need something else."

"Since you ask, tell me how to find Liam."

The bartender's pleasant expression faded.

"Who?"

"Liam."

"Don't know anyone with that name, chief." The bartender turned to walk away.

"What about Jimmy?"

Ponytail turned again. His hair gleamed, reflecting the bright lights coming from the stage.

"Don't know anyone by that name, either. You a cop?"

"No."

Carolina drank his beer. The bartender busied himself cleaning glasses. Carolina turned back to the stage, where the tandem cossacks were finishing up, grabbing dollar bills that were strewn about the stage. A couple of topless waitresses who looked like they had retired from dancing worked through the room, hitting up the customers to buy more drinks. Carolina looked back down the bar and saw the ponytailed bartender on the phone. When he realized Carolina was looking at him, he averted his eyes and turned away.

Carolina looked back out across the dimly lit club. The chairs were an odd blend of metal and plastic, with vinyl upholstery. The tables were tiny, just big enough to hold perhaps half a dozen drinks, no food. Presumably, Carolina thought, that left room for dancing beside, instead of on, them. The club was filling up with more businessmen and hard hats, with the occasional group of lawyers thrown in—an early-evening crowd, off to see a few breasts before going home to the wife and kids.

Overhead, there were dozens of Frezzi stage lights aimed in a wide variety of angles. In the middle of the club hung a mirrored globe—the kind commonly seen in dance halls—that would give the impression hundreds of little stars were flying around the room when the lights were turned low. And on the wall over the entrance to the runway was a large piece of glass.

It took several seconds before Carolina realized he could not see through; the glass was also mirrored. Probably a one-way mirror, Carolina thought. Just as he did, he was seized by the feeling that he was being watched.

The recorded sound of a trumpet flourish grabbed his attention. It came from the speakers next to the stage. From high above, two cords dropped down over the runway, a steel bar running between them, joining them together, a trapeze.

There was a flash of light, a bang, and bright red smoke shot up from the runway floor. As it cleared, a tall figure wearing a red cape and hood appeared. The figure moved forward with a comfortable stride as a nasal-sounding male voice emerged from the speakers.

"Good evening and welcome to the Rose Tattoo! Tonight, we are proud to present, direct from engagements in New York and Hollywood, the star of clubs and video screens across the land, a lady who has it all. And I do mean all! Measuring a mind-boggling sixty-four–twenty-six–thirty-four, the Rose Tattoo takes pleasure in introducing a lady who isn't afraid of the big bad wolf, the one and only Sunburst!"

The cape was off, revealing a tall, buxom woman with a gorgeous mane of red hair. She wore spiked black patent-leather heels at least six inches long, orange sequined shorts, and a bright yellow halter that barely restrained two massive breasts. She stood with a hand resting on a cocked right hip, her left foot keeping time to the beat of a bass drum. The pulsing sound of a guitar joined in and the woman strode confidently onto the runway. As she did, her breasts swayed, defying gravity.

"Look at dem," an older man sitting next to Carolina said, jabbing him in the ribs, "Dose definitely ain't fuel-injected, you know. Dey's the real thing."

The dancer called Sunburst began to sway, her pelvis twitching to every drumbeat.

"I am woman, hear me roar. . . ."

It was an old Helen Reddy tune, recut, remixed, and rerecorded with a disco beat. Sunburst grabbed the trapeze and hoisted her ample frame aboard, singing lustily.

"Jesus," Carolina muttered, and took a slug of beer. The perversion *was* mind-boggling and the crowd loved it, hooting and clapping and offering suggestions as to which article of Sunburst's scanty clothing should come off first. The music and shouts were deafening. It was so loud, it was hard to concentrate on anything else, so Carolina almost missed the movement to his right. When he did turn his head, he saw that the two bouncer/valets were now inside the club. Looking at him.

"What do you suppose he's doing in there, Bert?"

Bert Schumacher shifted his weight in the front seat of the LTD Crown Vic. They were parked perhaps fifty feet away from Carolina's blue Toyota outside the Rose Tattoo. Schumacher had a mild case of hemmorhoids flaring up and Ernie's question made him all the more irritable.

"No doubt he's drinking diet Coke and pondering what hymns they'll be singing in church this Sunday."

Ernie was stung by the response and quietly sulked for a moment. The two ATF agents had tailed Carolina for the better part of two days. Watched him up at Prospect Park, then with that young Simmons woman on Thayer Street. Somehow, the two of them missed his showing of the photograph to Lilly. But they did not miss that he had eaten lunch with a Providence detective or that he was now inside the club owned by Jimmy Flannery.

"Think Flannery's inside?" Ernie asked.

"Maybe."

"We oughta go inside," Ernie said.

"They'd make us as soon as we walked in the door."

Ernie was quiet for half a minute.

"You ever been in there?"

"Yeah," Bert said.

"What's it like?"

"Like a strip joint. Jeez, what a stupid question." He looked at his partner. "You ever been in a strip joint?"

"Oh. Sure." Ernie's face was red and he looked out the window. Bert didn't know whether to laugh or feel sorry for him.

"They're all pretty much the same," the fat agent said. "Lots of smoke, booze, women running around with everything hanging out. Where'd those two guys go?"

Bert had kept an eye on the two bouncer/valets outside the building's entrance. Now they were gone, even though a few cars were pulling in every few minutes. The two goons were missing valuable tip money.

"I don't like this," Bert said as he watched more customers walk inside.

Carolina had never before considered the difficulty associated with removing clothing on a trapeze. But Sunburst did it with considerable skill, displaying a fabulous body and a remarkable amount of gymnastic ability. She was now down to a G-string and the halter top. The trapeze swung in a fifteen-foot arc, the full length of the runway.

"Ohh, yes I'll pay the price, but look how much I'll gain. If I have to, I can do anything."

Now Sunburst had hoisted herself into a seated position on the bar, as if she was riding on a swing set. The crowd whooped it up, shouting encouragement.

"I am strong. I am invincible."

Sunburst leaned back, catching the bar with the backs of her knees. At the same time, her hand fluttered at the front of the halter top.

"I am wooomaaaaaan!!!"

Her breasts sprang free as she flew, back and forth, back and forth as the tune came to a crashing end. Her chest heaved and her body stretched, like some mammoth, obscene hood ornament. The crowd went wild.

Carolina was halfway through his beer. The bar and tables were now almost full. He looked around and noticed that the bouncer/valets were no longer near the door. Then he saw one at the end of the bar, on his left. Carolina looked some more. The other was about ten feet away, to his right. From time to time, both of them appeared to glance his way.

Sunburst had pulled herself up onto the trapeze bar again. A new tune spilled out from the speakers: "Disco Inferno" by the Trammps. Vintage seventies sound. Carolina wanted to gag. But Sunburst seemed to love it.

She left the stage and began to dance her way through the crowd, working for tips. She grabbed the hard hat off a construction worker, put it on, then grabbed the man by his ears and buried him between her breasts. His buddies roared and threw dollar bills on the table. She released the man and scooped up the cash as he gasped for air.

Sunburst moved closer to the bar. There were three men in business suits, collars open, ties askew, a round of manhattans on the table they shared. The one in the middle wore glasses. Sunburst reached out to his face and grabbed them, placing them on her right breast, the nipple popping out from under the bridge between the two lenses. The man in the suit turned twenty shades of pink and red while his friends screamed in laughter and threw a pair of five-dollar bills on the table.

Now she was just a few feet away. Carolina tried to look around, to see if anyone matching Liam O'Shea's description was about.

Sunburst bounced. The music pounded. The customers sang the chorus.

"Burn, baby, burn. Burn, baby, burn, Burnin' that motha down."

She was right in front of him. Sunburst reached out and put both arms around him, lacing her fingers behind his head, pushing him down, down, into the warm, sweaty place between her breasts. Carolina tried to pull away.

And he heard Sunburst scream.

The crowd jumped back. Before Carolina could look up, the two bouncers were on him, pinning his arms, hauling him up and off the bar stool.

"He grabbed me," she said.

"The hell I did," Carolina said.

"Hey, asswipe, can't you read?" one of the bouncers said, pointing to a sign that said NO TOUCHING.

"I didn't touch her."

"He's lying. I saw him," said the ponytailed bartender. He spoke loudly, as if he was addressing the crowd, not the bouncers, who were already dragging Carolina away—but not toward the front. They pulled him to an exit at the back of the club and threw him out the door.

He couldn't see the cars. They must be parked around front, he thought. "It's all right, guys. I'm leaving."

"Not just yet," one blow-dried thug said as he hit him.

The punch landed squarely in Carolina's stomach, just below the ribs. The force would have knocked him down, but for the other thug holding him up. He felt his wind take leave, felt the pain sink in through his chest and stomach, and wondered whether his heart had stopped.

"Little message for you, fuckwad." The guy who had punched him was talking. "We don't have no answers to your questions. Got it?"

"What questions?" Carolina gasped. The thug hit him again. This time, Carolina doubled over, but the pain wasn't quite as severe. He let his body sag a little, relax. The grip of the man who was holding him loosened.

With everything he had, Carolina picked up his right foot and drove it into the instep of the thug standing behind him. He heard a small snap, and the man cried out and released him. For an instant, the thug in front of him showed mild surprise. Carolina wound up and punched straight at the man's face. It landed on the bridge of the thug's nose.

And nothing happened.

The thug just stood there. There was no reaction, no blood—nothing. Then the thug fired a right at Carolina, catching him full on the side of his head, just below the left eye. The blow rocked him. Blood rushed from a two-inch cut. The thug launched a combination of punches to the body and face, and Carolina dropped to his knees.

The bouncer with the crushed instep was still clutching his leg, but the other was not yet finished. He took a step back, then forward, and slammed a booted foot into Carolina's chest, like a field-goal kicker attempting one from thirty-five yards. Carolina heard something else snap, and he fell back, his legs sliding out beneath him. He felt his head strike something, hard, then bounce onto the concrete surface they had all been standing on. There was blood inside his mouth, salty and sticky and dripping out and onto his chin.

Carolina was slipping out of consciousness, but he could still hear a voice somewhere above him.

"Don't fucking kill him. There's cops outside."

"Hooray," Carolina mumbled, then blacked out.

All he could see was gray.

Maybe it was the shadows, the way the light from the window was cut off by a shade. The sheets seemed dark, and the walls and sink in the corner. He felt as if he was in a movie, shot in monochrome.

"So you're awake," Shirley Templeton said. He rolled his head and saw her sitting on a chair in the corner. "The doctor said you'd come around this afternoon."

The room was cool. He took a breath, smelled antiseptic.

"Where am I?"

"Rhode Island Hospital. Private room. The station has pretty good health insurance." She looked at her watch. "Visiting hours started ten minutes ago."

He sat up and rubbed his eyes. The black-and-white world dissolved into a more familiar one with color. Shirley wore a pink dress that seemed too cool for the room. She unsuccessfully attempted to suppress a smile.

"You look so cute."

Carolina unconsciously clutched at the hospital johnny, pulling it closer.

"Is that the kind with no back? Why don't you turn around and let me see? . . ."

"Some news director you are."

"Best you've ever had."

"Uh-huh."

"Any complaints?"

"No."

"Good."

150

"What happened to me?"

"You have two cracked ribs and you suffered a mild concussion. You've been kept overnight and you'll probably be staying one more day. Oh yes," she said as he touched the left side of his face, "you also have a nasty cut below your eye. It took six stitches to close. Another inch and you could have lost it."

"Who found me?"

"A couple of ATF agents. I believe they think the bouncers did this to you; no one saw it. I'm not even sure why the agents were there."

"I have an inkling."

"Bar fights aren't really the kind of thing ATF investigates."

"That's very true," Carolina said, touching his face and thinking back on what had happened the night before. He remembered the dancer and the first punch from the bouncer. Everything else blurred together.

"I didn't know you liked those places," Shirley said, her tone mildly reproachful. "Good thing it wasn't in a station car. I had to fire someone for doing that once."

"I was trying to run down a lead."

"Is that right?"

"I was, Shirley. Jimmy Flannery runs that club. And I think he employs a guy who may have had something to do with Tisha's death.

"How did you find out he runs the club?"

"A tip. And some records at the secretary of state's."

"What makes you think he was involved with the explosion?"

"Another tip. Not yet confirmed."

"How are you feeling?"

"Like somebody used me for dropkick practice."

He told her about Sunburst, omitting a detailed description of her act. Shirley listened, then nodded.

"You shouldn't have gone in alone."

"At least no one else got hurt."

A nurse came in to check his pulse and an IV bottle that ran fluid into his arm.

"Could I have something to drink, please?"

"That's what got you here in the first place," the nurse said, smirking. She'd heard about where he'd been found.

"If I wasn't in bed, I'd double up with laughter. Some water? Ginger ale?"

"I'll see what we have." She went out.

"Very friendly here," Carolina said. He picked at the bandages on his left arm and peeled the adhesive tape that held the IV. Then he pulled the catheter out. Shirley was aghast.

"Why are you doing that?"

"I don't need it."

"You're not a doctor."

"No, but for two cracked ribs and a headache, I think I can manage. Who do I see about getting out of here?"

"Michael . . ."

"What?"

"I think you should lay off this story for a while."

"And why do you say that?"

"Don't be an idiot. It's obvious that the people involved are dangerous. And I don't believe your life is worth any story."

"My life's not in danger," he said, and instantly realized how dumb it sounded. "Sorry."

"Look, I know I hired you to do investigative reporting. And I never expected you to do as good a job as you have. But I think it's time to let the police do their job. When they come up with something, you can report it. Otherwise, I think we should lay off."

"Ordinarily, I'd agree with you," Carolina said. "But this really goes beyond the police, don't you think? This is a whole system. I mean, think how fucking crazy this situation is. I do a couple of stories . . . a couple of TV news stories on the lowest-rated station in town, and what happens? Tisha Billings gets blown to kingdom come. That loony talk-show host almost joins her. My boat gets destroyed. I walk into a nightclub, ask two lousy questions, and get my head handed to me. I'd say that this is more than the police can handle. "Besides, we made a deal, remember? All the way. No backing off."

"I remember," Shirley said, "but I wasn't expecting a boat explosion and my reporter getting beaten up in a strip joint." She looked at him as her words hung in the air. He watched as she absently dangled a shoe off the toes on her right foot.

"You really do look just like a little boy who had his tonsils out," she said, smiling.

"Well, my throat isn't sore. And I'm not looking for ice cream."

"My, we have no sense of humor."

" 'We' didn't just get the shit beaten out of us. I did."

"That's why I want you to ease off."

"Bargains can be tough to live with," Carolina said. "Thanks for coming to see me."

The nurse returned and handed him a white plastic cup with a jointed straw so he could sip while lying down.

"Ginger ale," she said.

"My favorite," Carolina replied.

She spotted the IV bag, now dripping on the floor.

"Did that fall out?"

"I didn't notice," Carolina said.

"It's supposed to be in until morning."

"Forget it."

The nurse frowned and muttered to herself as she scribbled something on his chart and turned to leave.

"I'll have to tell the doctor," she said.

"Give him my regards," Carolina replied.

"He must be hard to love," the nurse said to Shirley.

Shirley said, "More than you know."

* * *

Shirley left, after warning three more times that she wanted to lay off the Falcone story. That night, Carolina had four more visitors.

First, Bert and Ernie dropped in.

"Guys! How are ya?"

Neither smiled.

"Uh-oh. Looks like it's time to be serious," Carolina said. "Do your wives know what you're doing out at this hour?"

"You look better than the last time we saw you," Bert said.

"Thanks for getting me here."

"It's our job," Ernie said.

"I know. And you do it so well."

Ernie nodded gravely. Bert rolled his eyes.

"So what can I do for you?" Carolina said.

"How about answering a few questions?" Bert asked.

"Depends on what they are."

"Let's give it a try. What were you doing at the Rose Tattoo?"

"Watching the show."

"Who kicked the crap out of you?"

Carolina shrugged. "Two big, strapping gentlemen with beautiful hair. They chose not to introduce themselves."

"Why'd they do it?" Bert was getting aggravated.

"I must have upset them."

Ernie leaned in. "Look, Carolina, we want to nail these guys. But we can't do it without your help. You gonna play ball or what?"

"Ernie, that's really very good. Love the delivery. Real Efrem Zimbalist, Jr., with just a hint of Scott Glenn in *The Silence of the Lambs*."

"You aren't making this easy," Bert said.

"Tell you what," Carolina said. "I'll answer yours if you'll answer mine."

"What?"

"Why were you there?"

Neither agent said a word.

"Were you following me?"

Nothing.

"Gee, there doesn't seem to be a lot of give-and-take here, fellas."

Ernie looked helpless. He was clearly taking his cues from Bert. Bert's eyebrows arched and his lips pursed, like he was thinking, like he wanted to say something but couldn't.

"Thanks for your time," he said, and got up to leave.

"Hope you feel better," Ernie said, closing the door.

"You too," Carolina said.

Twenty minutes later, Lilly Simmons walked in.

"Hey, Brown University. See what happens to those who go digging?"

"You seem to be in good spirits." She touched his forearm lightly and, it seemed, with some affection.

"Nice of you to come by," he said.

"I was in the neighborhood," she said.

"Oh?"

"Yes."

"You make a habit of hanging around hospitals?"

"There was someone I had to see."

"Who?"

"Weeelll . . ." She looked down. Her hands were thrust in the pockets of her jeans, and she rocked back on the heels of the blue flats she wore. "Can you stand another visitor?"

"You mean it's not going to be just the two of us anymore?"

She grinned and reached over to open the door. A bandaged man was sitting in a wheelchair. He pushed himself into the room, banging the door with one wheel.

"I'm still gettin' the hang of this," he apologized, then extended a hand. "Sol Herskowitz. Pleasure to meet ya."

Carolina took the hand and looked quizzically at Lilly.

'You may know Sol from the radio. He goes by the name Reverend Rasmus."

"How ah ya?" Sol said.

"All right." Carolina forgot his own aches at the sight of the man. He wore a set of red pajamas that covered mounds of white gauze poking out of the sleeves and neck. The skin on his face was blistered in places, peeling in others. His eyebrows were gone, apparently burned away. And his head looked scorched and naked, like a monk with a bad tonsure job.

"Maybe a better question," Carolina said, "is, how are you?"

"Me? I'm fine. But I *was* a hurtin' guy, lemme tell ya. They're takin' me off the pain pills—I was gettin' codeine. Great stuff. Stare at a wall all day and never get bored. But I gotta get back to reality, I guess, or I'll turn into a drug addict." Sol caught the look on Carolina's face. "Hey, it ain't that bad, Mike. I can walk. I just use the chair to get around until the burns heal up a little more. Just a broken ankle, that's all."

"How bad are the burns?"

"Mostly second-degree. No third. Some first. It's only in the front, 'cause the blast threw me clear. I guess the concussion drove me straight up and out the door of your boat."

"Hatch."

"Whatever. Anyway, it's a lucky thing. If I'd been any closer, it mighta drove me through the roof."

"The overhead."

"Right." Sol seemed uninterested in nautical jargon. "Anyway, I'm okay."

"I don't know whether to thank you or ask what the hell you were doing on my boat."

"He was looking for you," Lilly said. "He's interested in the Falcone case, too."

"The door—I mean hatch—on the boat was open," Sol said. "I just wanted to see if anyone was home. When I seen that naked broad—er, when I saw that naked woman, I got startled. I backed up. Figured whoever was in there probably didn't need my company. Looked pretty kinky, y'know? Then"—he raised his arms in a small arc—"bang."

They all were quiet for a moment, imagining the scene. Finally, Carolina spoke.

"Did you see anyone else around that day?"

"No one special. Some federal agents came around, showed me a picture."

"Guy in a leather jacket? Heavyset?"

"Yeah. But I don't know him."

"Is that the same one you showed me?" Lilly asked.

"It is," Carolina said.

"Looks like a tough guy," Herskowitz said. "But I didn't see him. So, Mike, how'd you wind up in here?"

"I had a disagreement with some gentlemen."

"Looks like they disagreed all over you." Sol chuckled, shaking his head. "Whaddaya gonna do about it?"

"Is that how you speak on the radio?" Carolina asked.

"Wha—Brooklyn? Nah." Sol laughed. Then he stopped and boomed, "Brothers and sisters, we gather here today to pay out respects to the forces of God and do battle with the forces of EEEvil!"

Lilly cracked up.

"Pretty good, huh?" Sol said.

"It's Jimmy Swaggart on steroids," Carolina said.

"Thanks. But you ain't answered my question."

"It's hard to say," Carolina said, looking at Lilly. "Shirley wants me to drop Falcone for a while. For health reasons."

"Who's Shirley?" Sol asked.

"Our boss," Lilly said.

"Fuck bosses. Whadda they know," Sol said. "What do *you* want to do?"

"Same as always," Carolina said, wriggling to get more comfortable. "I want to find Frankie Falcone."

"We wanna help," Sol said, gesturing at Lilly.

"I've been through this once," Carolina said. "For obvious reasons, that is not a good idea."

"But three people are better than one," Sol responded, his hairless eyebrows furrowing. "You cover a lot more turf, get more done in a shorter period of time—"

"And run three times the risk of someone getting hurt." Carolina cut him off. "Look what's already happened. I get the crap beaten out of me. You turned into one of those half-cooked wieners from Seven-Eleven. And Lilly—" He stopped before saying what was obvious.

"My father died because he got involved with some bad people," Lilly said. Her voice was soft, but Carolina could hear the pain, and the dignity. "He lived a Rhode Island life, I guess. Lots of friends, lots of family. He worked hard and he trusted people. And he made a deal that probably cost him his life. He did some bad things. Illegal things."

She got up from the chair she'd been sitting in near the bed and moved even closer to Carolina. "I think I have the right to know why. I think I have the right to know who killed him, and the reasons for his death. He may have done some things that are wrong. But he didn't deserve to die like some animal in a stockyard.

"So, Michael, you can tell me it's dangerous. You can say that I don't know what I'm doing. But I am not listening to you. I want to help you. But with or without you, I'm going to find out what happened."

"I'm with her," Sol said.

A nurse poked her head in the door.

"Time's up," she said. "Visiting hours are over."

Lilly Simmons was still looking hard into Carolina's eyes. Then she leaned over and kissed him lightly on the forehead.

"Get some more rest," she said. "It's not always easy to come by."

"See ya around, Mike," Sol Herskowitz said, wheeling himself out the door.

He kept looking at the gray walls and the sheets when they were gone. They weren't really that color at all. The light just made it seem that way.

Carolina realized that his initial estimation of his surroundings had been incorrect.

And so had his estimation of Lilly Simmons.

14

The scar was pink and healthy and small when the stitches came out.

"In another month, you'll hardly notice it," the doctor said.

"Darn. I was hoping I could use it to pick up girls," Carolina said.

The physician either wasn't listening or didn't think the remark terribly amusing. "I'm signing your discharge. But you need to rest at least another day."

"I'll keep that in mind."

He got back to his hotel room in time for a call from Shirley.

"I spoke with your doctor," she said. "Just take your time. *Then* hurry up and get better."

"I am better," Carolina said.

"Well, when you get back to work, I want you to take it easy. Maybe some political stories. The state's been in an uproar over how to pay for a cross-bay water pipeline. . . ."

"You know what I want to do."

"Michael, you're no good to me if you're not alive. It would really help the quality of our news product if you remained in one piece."

"News product? What's that, some kind of breakfast cereal?"

She ignored the jab. "Where are you going to stay after the hotel? Did you find an apartment?"

"I don't like apartments. I like boats. I'm going to find another one." Indeed, he had hated the three apartments he had seen before his visit to the Rose Tattoo.

"Okay. Want to move in with me while you look?"

He had been waiting for the question. Shirley was a good boss. Tough but friendly. She had good news judgment and she knew how to put a story together. And she was fun. Like a big sister.

Not someone he wanted to live with.

"Uh, let me think about it. I'm not really sure what I want to do."

"Whatever," she said, too fast. Too casually.

"Shirley, it's nothing personal. I appreciate the offer," he said, hoping he hadn't hurt her feelings and knowing he probably had.

"Forget about it."

"I'm not an easy person to live with."

"I said forget about it." Her voice was stronger. She sounded like a boss again. "Just try and get some rest," she said, and hung up.

But he couldn't. He'd slept all night at the hospital, and he couldn't stand watching daytime TV. He ordered a sandwich from room service and looked at the paper. Nothing new about Frankie Falcone or Frederick Simmons. Nothing about the investigation into Tisha Billings's death. Billy Guano had written a column about a television movie that night based on a murder in California. At the end were a series of short clips about local television, bits of gossip, and news from the past week.

> Seems Channel 3's favorite new reporter can't stay out of trouble. Michael Carolina was taken to Rhode Island Hospital yesterday morning with broken ribs and a sore head. Police reports say he was assaulted in a bar fight outside the Rose

Tattoo, a Providence nightclub featuring nude dancing. Hey, Mikey, what kind of example does this set for your viewers, eh?

"Who needs rest?" Carolina mumbled, then tossed the paper aside. He grabbed his jacket and was out the door before the pages had settled on the hotel room's floor.

The Rose Tattoo looked different in the daylight. Not better, but different. It was still a concrete-block building. But without the neon lights, it looked forbidding and austere. More like a prison than a strip joint.

Carolina parked at the edge of the lot again but didn't get out of his car. It was early afternoon, and a lunchtime crowd was moving in and out. Cars came and went, but security was apparently not the problem it was in the evening. No one paid any attention to Carolina's car.

He sat for fifteen, perhaps twenty minutes, trying to decide whether he should venture another trip inside. He decided it would not be a wise move, even in daylight, with his ribs still tender and Guano's column fresh in his mind. He tried to imagine what the greasy little TV critic would do with two stories about a reporter in a strip club.

He was beginning to think the trip would yield nothing when a white Chevy Blazer zipped into the lot and parked in the space next to him. He saw a woman hop out and walk toward the club entrance, swinging a set of keys. When she was almost to the club, she stopped and turned, then punched an electronic device that locked the Blazer's doors and activated an alarm with a chirping sound. The woman had a blaze of red hair and dark sunglasses. She wore tight jeans and high-top sneakers, the laces half untied, and a black leather jacket. In a moment, she disappeared inside the club door.

Carolina checked his watch: 12:30. Too early for a headline act to be coming to work. And she hadn't been carrying a bag that might hold makeup or a costume.

He debated whether to go into the club. But in a moment, the woman was back outside, walking toward the truck. Carolina remembered the key chain. He saw her pull it from her front jeans pocket and, with a push from a bright red fingernail, deactivate the car alarm and unlock the doors. She climbed inside the Blazer and started it up.

Carolina jumped out of his car and shut the door. In almost the same motion, he grabbed the handle on the passenger-side door of the Blazer, pulled it open, and climbed inside. The redhead was startled.

"Hi, Sunburst, remember me?"

"What the—what are you doing?"

"I saw your show just the other night."

The redhead was eyeing him up and down, frightened, deciding whether he was another harmless creep or someone who could really be dangerous.

"I'm not going to hurt you."

"Goddamn right," she said, "but I'm going to hurt you if you don't get out of my car right now."

"You don't remember me?" he said.

"No, I don't remember you. Out." She had arched her back against the car door and pulled a leg back, as if she was getting ready to kick him.

"I'm the guy they told you to grab the other night. The one at the bar."

It took a moment for her to remember.

"Oh yeah."

"They rushed me out after you yelled." He said it softly, with no hint of anger or accusation. Her face began to soften.

"You pissed off about that . . . still?" she said.

"No. Not at all. Hell, you were just doing your job, right?"

She nodded, seemed to smile. All part of a day's work.

"I got broken ribs and a concussion out of it," he said.

The redhead's eyes widened, surprised. "They said they were only going to throw you out. You know, for trying to cut in on the competition."

"Cut in?"

"Yeah, you know. You bein' from that other club and all."

She thinks I own another strip club, Carolina realized. He shrugged his shoulders. "Well, it's all over. Business is business. But I still want to talk to you."

"Okay," she said, actually sounding pleasant. "Truth is, I did want to talk to you, too."

"Why don't we go somewhere besides this parking lot?" he asked, looking around to make sure no one was watching.

"Sure."

He followed her in his car. She took him to the Marlex Hotel, just outside downtown, up to a sixth-floor suite—two rooms and a bath, with a view of the Rhode Island State House.

"This is where I always stay in town," she said gaily. Her voice had the flat accent of the Midwest. Definitely not from New England, Carolina thought.

Sunburst was still talking about the hotel. "They got real good food and a pool that's cleaned every day. I like to swim," she said, throwing herself into a chair. "Helps me to stay in shape."

"I'll bet," Carolina replied. "That's quite an act you've worked up. How'd you get the idea for the trapeze, uh–" He stopped, realizing he didn't know her real name.

"I was a gymnast in high school. And my name is Emily," she said. "Emily Carter."

"Michael Carolina," he said. They shook hands.

"So, Emily. You said that you wanted to talk to me?"

"Sure. Ever since they said you were looking to hire me away. I mean, like you said, business is business. I'd like to hear what you have to say. But, you know . . . I work for them. And when I'm in their club, well . . . I have to take orders, you know?"

"Oh yeah," Carolina agreed. "So who's 'they'?"

"Billy and Jimmy. I thought you knew that."

"Billy and Jimmy," Carolina repeated.

"Yeah. Jimmy's the owner, but he's not always around. Billy's the guy that's been running the place during this engagement that I have. I guess you'd call him the manager." She crossed her legs and reached into a small white leather purse and pulled out a pack of long, thin brown cigarettes.

"How long you in town for?" Carolina asked while she lit up.

"A week this time. Then I head up to Boston and the North Shore. Then I drive back down to Washington and work my way back up the coast. Whole circuit takes about ten weeks." She held the cigarette carefully, with three fingers, as though it were some kind of magic wand. She took little puffs, then blew tiny rings into the air. An experienced smoker.

"How come you don't have an agent?"

"I did. But I figured I could do pretty much everything he did on my own, and I don't have to worry about being ripped off for fifty percent of whatever I bring in."

"You don't worry about getting hurt?"

She took another drag and smiled, shaking her head and blowing smoke through her teeth.

"I can take care of myself. If you hadn't explained so fast back there in my car, you'd have another broken rib by now."

"Thank heaven for small favors."

"So are we gonna talk business here? I get two hundred a day for my act at the Rose Tattoo. That doesn't include tips. Now if you can beat that—"

"Before we get into that, I need to find out a little more about Jimmy and Billy. That okay?"

She looked at him for a long moment, took one last drag, then snuffed out the cigarette.

"Are you really from another club?" she asked.

"No."

"You a cop?"

"No."

"I didn't think so," she said. "They wouldn't be stupid enough to beat up a cop. Why'd you tell me you were from another club?"

"I didn't. You assumed."

"Yeah, I guess I did. Well, nice talking with you."

She stood up and hooked her head toward the door.

"I just want to find out why someone beat me up."

"Well, I don't know. I already told you why I thought you were thrown out. But even if I did know why, I wouldn't say—not without knowing who you are."

"I'm a reporter."

She wasn't looking at him anymore. But for the first time, he detected that she was nervous. The redhead who flew a trapeze and felt she could take care of herself was worried.

"Emily," he said, "a woman I worked with is dead. The father of someone else I work with was murdered just a few days ago. And I've been burned out of my home and beaten up. I'm just trying to find out who did it and why. I'm just trying to take care of myself. You can understand that."

"I don't have any answers for you," she said, still not looking at him. "I'm sorry about what happened to you, but it's none of my business. And I've got my own problems."

"Does Billy have an accent?" Carolina asked.

"Yes. He's English, I think."

"Could it be Irish?"

"I wouldn't know the difference."

"Ever hear the name Liam?"

"Lee-um?"

"It's Gaelic. Irish for Bill, or William."

Her eyes told him she had heard the name before.

"Who asked you to grab me the other night?"

"I'm not kidding. You better go."

"Who asked?"

There was real fear on her face now. The kind battered women showed during interviews. The fear of pain, and undeserved punishment.

"Billy," she said. "He got a call upstairs from the bartender. Billy watched you from a one-way mirror. He called me to his office and told me what to do. I'm real sorry it happened. I don't want anyone else to get hurt. Now, would you please get out of my hotel room?"

"Thanks, Emily." Carolina walked toward the door and dropped a business card on her lap. "Here's something if you ever want to talk again."

When he looked back, just before he closed the door, he thought he saw her crying.

Wilbur Dunleavy didn't cover his balls when he met with Lilly Simmons. Indeed, he was solicitous.

"So good to see you again, my dear," he said with a gracious tone. "How are you bearing up?"

"I'm bearing up just fine, Governor. I'd like you to meet my associate, Mr. Herskowitz."

"How do you do," Dunleavy said.

"S'up, Guv?" Herskowitz said. With his scorched head and eyebrows, Sol's face had a strange, babylike quality. Wilbur flinched but managed to shake once, firmly, then drop Herskowitz's skinny hand.

They were alone in Dunleavy's private office, the one where he actually worked, instead of holding ceremonies or press conferences or any other matter deemed fit for public consumption. The room had red wallpaper with gilt edges, large velvet curtains, and heavy wood furniture. Lilly figured the decorator had first worked in a law office and then a whorehouse.

"You know, my dear, we still miss your father up here. So terrible the way things ended. I have the state police working very hard to find the killer." Dunleavy's voice had a hoarse quality, similar to a saw in need of sharpening. "And of course, off the record"—he winked, as if he was about to share something important with her—"we're going to get to the bottom of this banking mess."

"That's very reassuring, Governor," Lilly Simmons said. "How long do you think it will take?"

"Oh, that's hard to say. Can't rush this sort of thing."

"It's already been two weeks."

"Not much time for this sort of business, I'm afraid," Dunleavy said, shaking his head. "Would you like me to send for some coffee? A soda perhaps?"

Lilly shook her head. Sol watched her, then shook his head, too.

"Governor, what have you and your investigators learned about Frankie Falcone and his whereabouts?"

"Why do you ask, my dear?" Dunleavy's voice was faint.

"Because I want to know, sir."

"Well, I'm afraid not very much at this point. We understand what he did, of course. That new man of yours, Carolina, has already reported that. But as for whereabouts . . . I'm afraid we are at a loss."

"Why do I find that hard to believe, Governor?" Lilly said. "Are you telling us that after two weeks of work you have no clues whatsoever?"

"Is this meeting on the record?" a voice said behind them. John Rollins had entered through the office's back door.

"Because if it is, you really should apologize. The governor only agreed to meet with you out of concern for your personal loss. He's not doing interviews while the investigation continues. You know that."

"Who's this guy?" Herskowitz hooked a thumb in Rollins's direction.

"The governor's chief flack," Lilly said, loudly enough for Rollins to hear.

"I guess I'd expect that from the daughter of an apparent felon," Rollins said without hesitation. Dunleavy continued to smile, ignoring the tension.

"My dear, we will, of course, let you know as soon as we hear anything. But at this point, my hands are really tied."

"The governor has other appointments today," Rollins said impatiently, opening a door.

"I was told we would have a half hour," Lilly said.

"The schedule has changed."

"Governor, before we go . . ." Lilly said, standing up. "I just wanted to acquaint you with Mr. Herskowitz's new line of programming at WAIL. When he gets back on the air in the next day or so, he's going to focus all his attention on the Vespucci story. Three and a half hours a day, five days a week."

"It's gonna be great, Governor," Sol piped in. "You know, how it happened, why it happened, the lack of regulatory supervision, crisis in government. People are gonna eat it up. We'll do call-ins for the whole three and a half hours. I think we'll call it 'The Vespucci Crisis: Did the Governor Screw Up?' "

"Maybe you can do on-air polls," Lilly said.

"Sure. And a count, day by day, till the depositors get paid back. You know, like *Nightline* did during the '79 hostage crisis. It's gonna be a beautiful fuckin' thing."

"Just a moment," Dunleavy said, panic growing on his face. Lilly and Sol ignored him.

"Maybe you can devote a day to the personal angle. You know, little old ladies and retirees who worked all their lives, only to lose it all when Vespucci collapsed?"

"Of course," Sol said. "We can call that 'Money Held Hostage.' "

"Naturally, you'll want to get the official perspective," Lilly said.

"Oh, absolutely. Gotta be fair to the gov." Sol turned to Dunleavy. "Uh, Wilbur, my good man, we will need some cannon fod–er, someone from your office to tell the public what you're doing to clean up this mess. Maybe you'd like to do it yourself?"

"I'll tell my news director. I'm sure we'll cover it," Lilly said.

"The *Herald,* too." Sol's eyes lit up like a pinball machine at the thought of all the publicity.

"So, thanks for seeing us, Governor," Lilly said.

"I'll say a prayer for you on the radio," Sol said, taking Lilly's arm.

Governor Dunleavy had sunk into a chair. He began a slow curl into a fetal position. His hand reached for his crotch.

Rollins grabbed Dunleavy's hand. "This is just a cheap threat," he sputtered. "Media extortion."

The governor's face had now transformed into a tight-lipped smile, but he looked as happy as a man having a heart attack. His complexion took on the pallor of old wax. Rollins had seen this happen once before, just before a final campaign debate in the last election.

The governor looked up into Rollins's eyes.

"Erp," he said.

"What are your terms?" Rollins asked, looking at the two visitors.

"A taste of what you've got, where you're going, what you've found about Frank Falcone," Lilly said.

"And if we have nothing?"

"You've got something," Lilly said.

The governor slid lower in his chair; Rollins was having a hard time holding on.

"What else?" Rollins asked.

"That's it for now. We're not looking for miracles."

"Will you air it?"

"Maybe," Lilly said. "Depends what it is."

"It can't come from this office."

"No attribution," Lilly said.

"And in exchange, there's no radio show, no press releases, right?"

"Not this week, anyway," Sol said. Rollins's head snapped toward him. "Just kidding." Sol chuckled.

"Something will be messengered to your offices this afternoon," Rollins said. "Now, if you please. The governor is very busy this morning, and we must prepare for his next meeting."

"Better change him first," Lilly said. "It looks like he had an accident."

"Not again," Rollins exclaimed as Lilly and Sol closed the office door.

"You did what?"

"Just jacked him around a little," Lilly said. They were standing near Michael Carolina's desk back in the newsroom.

"I tell ya, Mike, it was a fuckin' beautiful thing," Sol said, fingering his newsroom guest pass.

"You kiss your mother with that mouth?" Carolina asked.

"No, I kiss your mother's," Sol said, smiling.

"How long has the governor had this little incontinence problem?"

"I'd heard rumors of it before," Lilly said. "People say it's brought on by stress. And God knows how much he hates bad press."

The three of them broke up at the thought of Dunleavy in such a state. Carolina was amazed. Lilly was proving tenacious in her efforts to learn what had happened at Amerigo Vespucci Loan and Investment.

"What's so funny?"

Shirley Templeton had come up behind them as they talked. "We were just chatting," Lilly said.

"About a story for tonight?"

"Maybe," Carolina said. He looked at Lilly. They both knew the chances of another story turning on Frankie Falcone and his friends were slim at best.

"Who's this?" Shirley asked, looking at Sol.

"Reverend Rasmus, say hello to Shirley Templeton. The rev has been talking to us about a story," Lilly said.

"Nice to meet ya," Sol said, extending a hand.

"I'm glad to see you're on your feet again. How are you feeling?"

"Better, thanks." He noticed Shirley staring at the bare skin above his eyes.

"I don't know when they're growing back in."

"Sorry." Shirley flushed. "I didn't mean to stare. Michael, can I speak to you in my office?"

He followed her to her office. "I get the impression you're pissed."

"You have good impressions. I told you in the hospital that I want you to back off on this banking story. Now you've got that talk-show host in here and you're chatting up my assignment editor."

"I didn't bring him in here, and they came over to my desk."

"You're not even supposed to be here."

"I didn't feel like staying in bed."

"Why don't you go look for a boat? Isn't that what you said you wanted to do?"

"We've come across some leads."

"Like what?"

He told her about his conversation with Emily.

"Doesn't sound like much."

"I know the guy is working there."

"Even if he is, you can't do anything about it. It's something for the police to handle."

"They haven't handled it yet."

They both stared hard, each waiting for the other to blink. Neither one did.

"Why is this so important to you?" Shirley said finally.

"It's just the way I am," he answered. "The way I was back in the Midwest. I've got to do it myself."

"Michael, this story isn't worth your life."

"I seem to have heard that somewhere before."

"You didn't listen."

"Yes I did. But it's my decision to make. We've already been through this. You didn't hire me to go cover the next press conference or do feature stories about Newport or Westerly. You hired me because you want someone to go out and find stories that people don't want told, stories that mean something. That might boost this station's image and its ratings. And maybe, just maybe, make this state a better place to live.

"Now, the way I see it," he said, "I've been trying to do that. And you're starting to get in my way."

"I could fire you," she said quietly.

"Maybe you should. It might make your life easier."

The frown on Shirley's face deepened. She looked sad, almost frightened. "Is there something happening between you and Lilly?"

"Why do you ask?"

"I saw the way she looked at you out there, and the way you looked at her. Do me a favor, please. Keep her out of this thing that you're doing?"

"I tried," Carolina said. "I had about as much luck as you did."

The report from the governor's office arrived that afternoon. It was a week old, its thirty single-spaced pages laser-printed on thick office stationery. Inside were memoranda from bank examiners, police investigators, Vespucci depositors, and relatives of the fugitive Frankie Falcone.

Yet it said almost nothing.

Most of the information had already been published or broadcast in the week since Vespucci failed. There were even quotes from the paper and attributions to local news broadcasts, including Channel 3. The investigators were actually relying on the media. Or so it appeared.

"This is basically bullshit," Carolina said.

"I know," Lilly agreed. "I've got half a mind to call up Sol and have him start preparing that radio show."

"Don't," Carolina said. "A promise is a promise."

"We could do a piece about how little progress they've made."

"We could," he said, "but it won't get us any new information."

He looked at the report again, then at the notes he'd been taking, then at the taped stories that had already aired, including Tisha's piece with the elderly depositor. Then he took a legal pad and made a list of all that he knew about Amerigo Vespucci and Frankie Falcone and Frederick Simmons. Nothing new emerged.

He showed his work to Lilly. After ten minutes of review, she agreed there was nothing newsworthy that had not already been published or broadcast by Channel 3 or a competitor.

"What about the assault at the Tattoo? That's new."

"But it doesn't show any connection to Falcone or Vespucci. If we do another story, we need to show some kind of connection. All Jimmy Flannery has to do is deny any involvement with Falcone or Vespucci."

"But you've already said you know there's something there."

"Sure. Feds show me a picture of a guy they're looking at

in connection with the explosion on *Maeve*. Cop confirms the guy is an IRA hood who's rumored to work for Flannery. I go looking for the guy and get slapped around. I go back and find someone who helped set me up, and she says a guy named Billy with a British accent told her to do it. British accents can be confused with Irish. Liam is the Irish name for William."

"It all fits," Lilly said.

"Yeah, but it doesn't bring us closer to Frankie Falcone and the cash."

"Are we missing something?" Lilly asked.

"Probably," Carolina said. "Let's narrow it down. Tell me—did your Dad ever talk about Frankie Falcone?"

"No."

"Did you ever meet him?"

"Never."

"Did you ever see him?"

Lilly thought for a moment. "I haven't been on this job all that long. But I remember him at a press conference once—Sons of Italy or something like that."

"What was it about?" Carolina asked.

"Some kind of charity fund-raiser for children, I think. We did a VO about it."

"Do we have the tape?"

Lilly went to the station archives. Michael Carolina scratched absently at one of the cuts on his face. It was healing well but itched constantly.

Lilly was back. "Here it is," she said, taking a cassette and popping it into a deck. "It's from last winter."

The video was just twenty seconds in length, with the sound turned low so that an anchor could provide narration in the background. A group of men stood around a podium with a red-green-and-white banner behind them. Most of the men had dark hair and complexions, like those of southern Italian immigrants.

Frankie Falcone was speaking into a microphone, his eyes shining, his face deeply tanned, his suit elegant. The handsome businessman doing something for his community.

"I could kick myself," Lilly said. "I forgot we had this."

"I guess everyone else forgot, too. Haven't seen this on any other stations. There's something wrong with this picture."

"What? It looks okay to me," Lilly said.

"Look how tan Falcone is. The others are all dark-skinned, but not like Frankie. When was this story done?"

She checked the date on the tape box. "December third."

"Christmas season. Too late for him to have a tan from the summer."

"So maybe he'd just come back from the islands."

"Isn't that a strange time of year to be in the tropics? People who work usually don't go until the holidays or February."

"It's a little unusual. But the guy had money. Maybe he likes being in the sun."

"Maybe," Carolina said. He stopped the tape and rewound, then watched it again. When it ended, he popped the cassette.

"Was he active in any other civic groups?"

"I don't know," Lilly said.

"I just thought of something," Carolina said, the faint memory in the back of his head finally coming to the surface. "I remember being in Falcone's office. There were a few decorations from the Italo-American organizations, but there was something else."

"What?"

"A bottle of booze."

"So? What was it? Chianti? Frangelico?"

"Poitin. It's a kind of Irish moonshine. Potato whiskey. Really horrible stuff. Powerful as hell."

"Just because you're Italian doesn't mean you can't drink rotten Irish alcohol," Lilly said.

"That's true. But it's strange. Why would he want to? How would he even know about it?"

"There could be a million reasons. I think you're grasping at straws."

Carolina wanted to say something more, but just then Shirley started yelling to get over to the Marlex, where a woman had just fallen out of a sixth-story window.

15

Emily Lane Carter, also known as Sunburst, was lying on a brick sidewalk outside the Marlex Hotel. Her flaming red hair was caught in the rough texture of the brick, matted down by dark, rich blood that seeped out from beneath her head. A Providence cop, slouching, his collar open, was pulling on a cigarette next to her, waiting for backup and cleaners from the ME's office.

"Oh Christ," Carolina said as soon as he was close enough to recognize her.

"Back it up," the cop said. "And don't touch anything."

Carolina stopped. "Don't I know you? You were at the Simmons homicide."

"Yeah. But I brought my own cigarettes today." The officer turned his back.

It was early evening. A crowd of guests and patrons of the hotel's restaurant and bar poured out to gawk and whisper about who the dead woman was and whether it was an accident. A concierge and three conscripted bellmen were trying to move the crowd away from the scene and back into the building. The bellmen looked like they were hoping for tips. The concierge looked as if he'd rather be making someone's dinner reservations.

Lilly arrived with Earl in tow.

"No peectures." The concierge spoke with a thick Spanish accent. He reached up to put a hand on Earl's lens. The photographer's free arm swept him away like a gnat.

"No touch, José. Public sidewalk."

With a molten look and a few muttered words, the concierge went to tend to some other gawkers. In the distance, the whine of a siren pierced the air. More police.

"If it's a suicide, we won't run it," Lilly said.

"It's no suicide," Carolina said, looking at Earl. "Grab what you can before the cops move you back."

"I know the drill," Earl said, moving a few steps to get a better angle.

"Run some interference for him, will you?" Carolina said to Lilly.

"I'll look around for some witnesses." She went off after the photographer.

Carolina walked inside, trying to act like a guest. The staff's attention was focused outside, but a man wearing a blue blazer, tie, and gray slacks was standing by the elevators, asking everyone who approached for a room key. Hotel security.

Carolina slipped into the gift shop and picked up a magazine, pretending to look at it. Out the window, he could see more police arriving. A minute later, Sergeant Corvese entered the hotel and went to the front desk. A manager pointed to the elevators. Corvese nodded, walked over, and flashed his badge at the security man. The door to one elevator opened just as Corvese arrived, and the passengers quickly emptied out.

Carolina stepped out of the gift shop and started for the elevator. He looked to the hotel entrance. The security man watched him. The doors to Corvese's elevator car began to close.

"Hey, you stop!" Carolina shouted, pointing toward the entrance. The security man shifted his attention back over his shoulder, toward the hotel doors.

Carolina jumped in the car. The security man looked around and swore as the elevator closed.

Corvese was only mildly surprised.

"What the hell are you doing here?"

"I'm a guest. Got a room on the sixth floor."

"The hell you do," the cop said. "Don't you ever quit? I heard about how your face was rearranged."

"Thank you for caring. The get-well card was nice, not too drippy." The elevator stopped. Sixth floor.

"So what the fuck do you want now?" Corvese said as they stepped into the hall.

"A look in the room."

"I don't think so. Besides, this is probably a suicide. You're not gonna do a story about a jumper, are you?"

"She didn't jump," Carolina said.

"How do you know?"

"She worked at the Tattoo."

The detective's eyebrows arched.

"I met her. She was smart. Somebody used her to set me up."

Corvese walked down the hall as the reporter recounted his conversation with the now-dead stripper. They reached her room. Another blue-blazered security man with gray slacks and radio was there.

"I see him," the man said into the radio.

Corvese flashed his badge. The security man grabbed Carolina by the arm.

"Can I help you, sir?" he asked.

"He's with me," Corvese said. The security man held on, uncertain.

"My guy downstairs said—"

"Trust me on this," the cop said. Grudgingly, the man let Carolina go.

"Thanks."

"Don't thank me yet," the cop replied. "Tell me some more about this woman."

Carolina did as they looked around the suite. The sitting room was in order, just as it had been when Carolina was there earlier in the afternoon. Corvese walked over to the small balcony. The sliding glass door that led to it was open, and he stepped out and looked down.

"See anything?" Carolina said.

"One dead lady," Corvese muttered. "But nothing up here. Anybody else been in?" he asked the security man.

"Not since she hit the sidewalk," the man replied.

The bedroom looked trashed, with clothes and underwear on the unmade bed, shoes strewn on the floor, and an unfinished paperback, upside down and open halfway, sitting on the nightstand. "A romance," Corvese said. He lifted the cover on the bed. "Come stain."

Carolina went into the bathroom. The tub, toilet, and towels were all clean and neat. The sink and counter contained makeup articles, combs, and a toothbrush, along with a small box of tampons. A pair of white plastic slippers were by the tub, one of them straight, the other tipped over, so the heel stuck out to the side.

"Get out of there," Corvese growled. Carolina stepped out while the Sergeant looked around. "I'm trusting you were smart enough not to touch anything."

"I try not to disappoint," Carolina said. Corvese gave him a funny look. "Honest, Sergeant, I didn't."

"I think you've seen enough," the cop said, hooking a thumb toward the door.

"Wait a second," Carolina said. "Tell me what you think. Do you still think she jumped?"

"I don't know. Don't know enough about her," Corvese said.

"When I talked to her, she didn't sound like a woman who'd want to check out."

Corvese mused. "As my wife always says, it's a woman's prerogative to change her mind. And I don't see any signs of a struggle."

"Yeah, but if she was going to jump, don't you think she'd

do more to put her affairs in order? I mean, look around this place. It's lived in. She isn't packed. The bed's unmade. She's got that paperback on the nightstand. Shit, her toothbrush is out and the toothpaste cap is off."

"I've seen weirder things," Corvese said.

"Is there a note?"

There wasn't. Not that the detective or the reporter could find.

"I don't know too many strippers," Corvese said, "with a great deal of writing skill."

"Come on, Sergeant."

"All right, all right. I know you just want me to say something so you can report it. For a background quote from a source, I'll call it unusual. Suspicious. Yeah, that's a good word. I'm not calling it a suicide, and I'm not calling it a homicide, either." Corvese grabbed Carolina's arm and started prodding him toward the door. "Forensics will be here soon. We'll check some more. In about thirty seconds, a captain is probably gonna come in here, and if he sees you, there won't be a sling big enough to hold my ass."

"Let me know if anything turns up," Carolina said as the detective pushed him out the door.

"Fuck you," the cop said, half-smiling at the arrogance. Then Corvese turned to the security man. "This gentleman is no longer with me and I don't believe he is a guest of your hotel. Feel free to throw him out."

"After all we've been through together?" Carolina said as the guard hustled him back toward the elevator.

"Love stinks," Corvese called after him.

The guard pushed Carolina out the hotel door and threatened him with a trespass complaint if he reentered. Before he could say anything, Lilly took his arm.

"There's someone you should talk to," she said.

She led him down the street to a plain white van with a

microwave transmitter on top and a license plate that said TV3-#2. Reporters from the other two station were walking past, checking out Carolina as he walked away from the hotel.

"Hear anything?" one of them called, with the anxious, paranoid tone of a competitor who fears he may be scooped.

"Sorry," Carolina said. "Shit," he heard the reporter mutter as Lilly opened the van door and practically shoved him inside.

A middle-aged woman in a pink uniform was sitting in the swivel-back seat, the chair used to edit and feed videotape back to the station. She had dark hair that was just beginning to gray and deep lines that creased the sides of her face. Her skin was brown and looked as though it had spent years in the sun. The woman looked frightened.

"This lady is a chambermaid," Lilly said. "The day shift ended fifteen minutes ago. I found her walking out the back door."

The woman's eyes were stone black, nervous, and darting between Lilly and Carolina.

"My name is Michael," Carolina said, extending a hand. The woman took it gingerly. She said nothing.

"Her name is Sandra. She doesn't speak English. She's from the Dominican Republic," Lilly said. "And she worked on the sixth floor this afternoon."

"I don't speak Spanish," Carolina said.

"I do," Lilly answered.

"¿Es la migra?" the woman said to Lilly, still frightened.

"No es la migra, señora. No es la policía. Es periodista."

"¿Periodista?"

"Sí, no tenga miedo, señora." Lilly patted the woman's arm.

"She thinks you want to deport her."

"Tell her we just want to know if she knows what happened on the sixth floor this afternoon," Carolina said. "Promise her we won't use her name."

Lilly spoke to the woman again. The fear was still there, but it was beginning to ebb. She spoke rapidly to Lilly.

"She says she was up there about an hour ago. Says the woman there likes the room done late."

"The lady on the sidewalk?"

Lilly asked the chambermaid. She nodded, a tear forming in one eye.

"Was the woman there? Was anyone else?" While Lilly translated, Carolina dug into the folder he had carried from the station and pulled out a paper.

"La señorita? Sí, sí, y un hombre gordo . . ." The woman gestured with her hands, as if she was demonstrating the size of a large fish.

"She says the woman with the red hair was in the room, and a man showed up. A big man. Just as she was leaving," Lilly said.

Carolina handed the woman the photograph of Liam. The woman studied it for a moment. A look of recognition swept her face.

"Sí, sí, es el hombre gordo," she said.

"She says yes, that's the man."

"I got that," Carolina said. "Is this woman going to talk to the police?" Carolina asked Lilly. At the word *police,* the woman jumped.

"No policía. No policía." She grabbed Carolina's arm as tears welled.

"There's your answer," Lilly said.

"Okay." He looked at Sandra in the eyes. "Tell her that no one will identify her in our story. And no one from our station will talk to the police about her unless she agrees."

Lilly spoke to the woman.

"Muchas gracias, señor," she said as Earl opened the van to let the woman out. The reporters from the other stations were all at the front of the hotel, and they never saw the woman in the pink uniform scurrying down the street.

"How much money do you figure this hotel saves by using illegals?" Carolina asked Lilly as she closed the van door.

"I don't know, but I bet it would make a good story."

"Some other time."

Carolina did a live shot at six, his first since his release from the hospital. He gave the basics about Emily Carter's death: that she worked at the Rose Tattoo; that police were investigating the death as a possible homicide; that there was no suicide note. At the end, he threw in one last line.

"Channel Three has learned that this man"—a picture of O'Shea appeared on the screen—"was seen inside the Marlex on the sixth floor late this afternoon. Police sources identify the man as Liam O'Shea, a suspected IRA terrorist currently living in the United States. The person who identified O'Shea has asked to remain anonymous out of fear for personal safety."

"Nice job," Earl said when the producer cleared them.

"Thanks," Carolina said. He looked at Lilly. "And thanks for checking on the guests. You know someone in the hotel?"

"I went to high school with a girl who works the front desk," she said. "What's next?"

"I have an errand to run, and I better do it fast. The cops should be out any second to ask about O'Shea. Can you get a ride back with Earl?"

"I want to go with you," she said.

"I'll call you if something turns up."

He jumped into the Toyota and pulled into traffic. Lilly watched him go as Earl broke down his equipment and began to pack up. "Is there some connection on all this to the Falcone story?" he asked.

"Maybe," Lilly said.

"You know," Earl said as he loaded a tripod into the van, "there is something I've been meaning to tell you. . . ."

* * *

Liam O'Shea, the man with the accent, the man who wore a leather jacket, enjoyed working out of the Rose Tattoo. Jimmy Flannery had told him he could use the office anytime Jimmy wasn't there. Which was often. He also told O'Shea he could use the strippers. Which he did.

Flannery had maintained ties with members of the provisional Irish Republican Army for more than a decade. When Liam had arrived at the Port of Providence after nearly two months in the hold of a freighter, Flannery had met him, fed him, and found him work.

O'Shea had done significant work of late for the Business Club, the partnership that included Jimmy's brother. He'd done other odd jobs, collecting cuts from rackets Jimmy controlled, offering a little muscle on a shylock operation in North Providence and Central Falls.

But what Liam liked best was managing the Tattoo, from behind the big one-way mirror that offered a view of the bar and the stage. He would park himself in one of the dark velour chairs and catch the action down on the club's floor. Sometimes he'd watch movies or CNN or even the local news on the office's wide-screen TV. When one of the girls caught his fancy, he'd invite her up for a drink.

The one called Sunburst was the one he had liked the most.

O'Shea was amazed at the things American women would do for money. And he was amazed at the clubs in which they chose to do it. There was nothing like the Rose Tattoo in Belfast or Derry. He doubted there was anything like it in Dublin. He had watched, spellbound, the first time that Sunburst performed. The flaming red hair reminded him of a woman he'd once seen at home. Only that woman had been pushing a stroller with two kids through a dirty run-down Falls Road neighborhood, not swinging from a trapeze as she unbuckled a sequined brassiere.

He'd called Sunburst in and plied her with alcohol.

"You talk funny," she said, taking a sip of vodka.

"I'm English." He chuckled, amused at his own lie.

"What do they call you?"

"Billy. Bad Boy Billy."

"Why do they call you that?"

"There's only one way to find out," he said, pointing at his pants.

The girls who worked the Tattoo understood the concept of managerial privilege. Sunburst obliged him, as she had those in many other clubs where the money was good.

When Liam had gone to her hotel that afternoon, he knew she'd be leaving soon for another club on her circuit. He didn't know when he would see her again, and he wanted to exercise a bit more managerial privilege.

"What's your real name?" she asked. He was lying, naked, eyes closed, on the soiled hotel bed.

"I told you already."

"No, I mean your real name. I told you mine. Tell me yours," she said, getting dressed.

"What d'ye mean?" he asked.

"Isn't your real name Liam? Isn't that Irish for Billy?"

"Who said I was Irish?"

"No one. I just guessed," she said quickly.

"What's in a name? And why are you talking so loud?"

"I'm not," she said. "It's the way I always talk, Liam."

There was a loud clicking sound. They both heard it. Emily flushed, her face nearly as red as her hair.

"What was that?" O'Shea said. He was up now, stark naked, looking around the room.

"I didn't hear anything," Emily said, her face still red. Now she spoke in barely a whisper. O'Shea looked at the lamp next to the bed, then at the cable box on top of the television. His eyes searched the room. There were clothes on the floor, a suitcase lying open on a bureau table, a towel piled on the end table at the other side of the bed. . . .

She had put the towel there before he got undressed. He figured she'd use it when they were through. She had not.

"I thought I heard a noise," he said. In two steps, he moved around the bed and snatched the towel off the night-stand.

The palm-sized recorder was the kind used to give dictation, with a built-in microphone on the top. Liam picked it up. "Looks like your tape run out, lass," he said.

"Oh, Billy. I was just kidding," she said, trying to laugh. "I just wanted to play a joke. And I wanted to have a recording of your voice so I could practice that accent. I'm saving to take acting lessons, you know—"

He had grabbed a fistful of her hair.

"You're gonna have to do better than that," he said.

"You're hurting me. Don't hurt me."

He slapped her once, hard—not enough to draw blood, but enough that she knew he could if he wished. "Who's been talking about me?"

When she told him about the reporter, he wrapped a hand around her mouth and nose. He held them there until she passed out. Then he kicked the glass door to the balcony open.

She was so light, she cleared the railing. He didn't step out to see where she landed.

He thought he'd got out clean, down the back stairs. When she didn't show up for work, he'd send someone to find Jimmy and tell him. Jimmy wouldn't mind. There were plenty of other girls.

But now that fuckin' reporter had ID'd him and talked about a witness. And then he remembered: the spic chambermaid.

He switched the television off and picked up a special phone Jimmy kept, one that was checked every two days for a trace. The names and numbers of the club members were inside his jacket pocket. He called Flannery. No answer. He tried the second number. On the third ring, the phone picked up.

"Yes." The voice sounded irritable.

"I may be in a pinch. There may be some police lookin' for me."

"Imagine that. Do you suppose it has something to do with Carolina's report on Channel Three tonight? He described you beautifully."

"I need out."

"What's that to me?"

"Listen, fucker," Liam O'Shea said, "this ain't no Provo fight where I'm goin' down for the cause. This is just you, Flannery, Falcone, 'n that money. If y'don't think I won't put you all up for sale if I'm pinched, then you're dumber 'n a fuckin' sheep."

There was a pause on the other end of the line. When the man spoke, he was calm and decisive.

"Go to Logan. Buy a ticket for the island. You know where to get the cash?"

"I'll have to dip the till."

"Then do it. And one more thing . . ."

"Yeah."

"I don't care who you are or what you have done for us. If you ever threaten me again, I'll have your balls cut off with a dull knife. And I'll make sure that you watch while someone feeds them to a fish."

The line clicked loudly as the caller hung up. Liam O'Shea looked at the receiver for only a minute before he went looking for the till.

t didn't take a genius, in Michael Carolina's estimation, to know where to look for Liam O'Shea. Emily's information told him that he'd been right to go to the Tattoo. Carolina's still-tender ribs told him he'd been wrong to ask for Liam in person.

So on his third trip to the strip club, he stuck with the method that had served him well; he pulled in at the edge of the Rose Tattoo's vast parking lot and waited.

There were the usual several dozen cars parked, no doubt many of the drivers inside waiting to see Sunburst's show. It would be a long wait, Carolina thought.

A movement at the Tattoo's front door drew his attention. One of the valet/bouncer types had come out at a trot. Carolina recognized him as one of the men who had beaten him. The man headed to a blue BMW 320i, fired it up, and wheeled it around and into the alley that led to the back of the club. The car disappeared around the building's corner. Carolina started his own car's engine.

In a moment, the bouncer was trotting back down the alley. A few seconds later, the beamer appeared. It rolled out into the lot, right down the lane where Carolina was parked. The reporter hunched down, until he could just see over the dash. The blue car eased past, the driver not paying attention to the little Toyota.

Liam O'Shea apparently had other things on his mind.

Carolina saw him for only a second, but clearly enough to know he had the right man. The BMW accelerated rapidly as it left the lot and moved up the street. The little blue Toyota rolled after him.

O'Shea turned left, onto Chalkstone Avenue. Carolina waited at the stop sign just before the turn, until another car passed, then pulled out. He was at least a block behind the BMW, wondering what to do if a light turned red or if more traffic got between the cars. But the traffic lights were timed, and the BMW stayed within the speed limit.

At the Smith Street intersection, the beamer turned left. O'Shea was headed toward the State House or downtown. A few more cars had slipped in between them, but Carolina was still able to keep O'Shea in sight as he crossed the bridge over the interstate. Just before reaching the State House, the blue car turned right and down the sloped and curving road that bordered the State House lawn. At a stoplight, the car turned right again on the street that entered downtown. The car slipped into the right lane and flashed a blinker, then turned onto the highway entrance. Liam O'Shea was headed north.

Carolina followed. He dropped back nearly a quarter mile, keeping his eye on the car. It was close to seven in the evening, just starting to get dark. Carolina wondered whether he would be able to follow once night fell. O'Shea seemed to be in no hurry, cruising at five miles under the posted speed limit.

The car pressed on through Pawtucket, across the state line into southern Massachusetts, and up the thirty miles of interstate toward the 128 loop around Boston. The BMW made the Canton exchange in thirty-five minutes and went right, onto I-93.

Carolina kept the distance. The beamer cruised up, into the city. The Toyota sped up as they approached the Callahan Tunnel. Carolina watched as the car turned right, into the Callahan, headed toward Logan Airport.

The door opened just a crack in the twilight.

"What?" the elderly female voice demanded. In the background, the strains of *Wheel of Fortune* could be heard.

"Mrs. Bianchini?" Lilly asked.

"Who wants to know?"

"My name is Lilly Simmons. I work for Channel Three."

"I'm busy," the lady said. "Vanna's gonna turn another letter and I almost got the puzzle solved." She started to close the door, but Lilly reached out with her right hand to stop it.

"Please, Mrs. Bianchini, this will only take a minute."

"You find something out about my money?" The little old lady opened the door another six inches. Suddenly, she looked hungry.

"Not yet, ma'am. But we're getting closer."

"Yeah, and I'm your mother," Anna said.

"Please, Mrs. Bianchini. I came because Michael Carolina asked me to."

Anna Bianchini opened the door another inch.

"How do I know you're really from Channel Three?"

Lilly fumbled in her purse for a press ID. As she did, Earl stepped up behind her. "Hi, Mrs. Bianchini, remember me?"

"Yeah, Jethro, you're the cameraman had to throw his two cents in the last time you was here."

"How are you?" Earl said brightly.

"Lousy," she said. The sound of applause came from the background. "Ah shit, they solved the puzzle. See what you made me miss?"

Lilly found her ID and held it out to the woman. Anna squinted for a minute, then handed it back. "Okay, so come on in. Show's gonna be over soon, anyway." She waddled over to a chair and sat down. Lilly and Earl closed the door.

"Mrs. Bianchini, do you remember talking to Tisha Billings?"

Anna looked at Lilly. "How come I don't see you on TV?"

"I work behind the camera."

"You ain't replacing that Tisha girl?"

"No."

"I saw she got killed."

"That's right."

"I don't wanna be mean, but that girl was no great loss."

"I'm sorry you feel that way."

"She had no class."

"I understand your feelings."

"Probably got what she deserved."

"Mrs. Bianchini, was there something you wanted to tell Michael Carolina?"

"About what?"

"About Amerigo Vespucci."

Anna smiled.

"Forgive me, Mrs. Bianchini, but you look like the Cheshire cat."

"Yeah? Well, forgive me, but you don't look like Michael Carolina."

"Michael is working hard on the Vespucci story right now. He wanted me to come talk to you before we waste any more time."

Anna looked at the slender woman standing in front of her.

"I like youse," she said. "You show a little respect."

"Thank you," Lilly said.

"Not like that Billings girl. She was trash."

Lilly and Earl both looked uncomfortable.

"I know neither one of youse wants to be here," Anna said. "I'm just some little old Italian lady with a big mouth and an attitude, right? I even talk bad about the dead."

"You can say whatever you want," Lilly said softly.

"That's right, I can," Anna said. "But there ain't many people wanna listen. At least you listened a little. Even when you didn't like what I said." The old lady zapped her television off. "What I was gonna tell your boy Carolina there, it ain't about Vespucci."

"It wasn't?" Lilly said, disappointed.

"No. It's about Frankie."

Carolina parked the Toyota in the garage next to the American terminal, two rows back from where Liam O'Shea had left the BMW. He watched as O'Shea opened the car's trunk and pulled a satchel out, slammed the trunk shut, and headed for the ticket counters. Carolina removed his jacket and tie. He opened his collar and rolled up his sleeves, then looked around the Toyota's backseat. He found a green windbreaker.

Inside the terminal, he went straight to a souvenir counter and bought a Red Sox cap. As he approached the ticket counters, he looked completely different from the way he had when he appeared on television at six.

He checked the arrival and departures on the television monitors, then the people in line to purchase tickets. The line of passengers with bags was long. Liam O'Shea was nowhere to be seen. Carolina turned to check another airline counter.

And almost bumped into O'Shea coming out of a men's room.

The heavyset terrorist was moving fast. The satchel he carried grazed Carolina's leg. "Excuse me," Carolina said automatically. O'Shea said nothing, his attention on the ticket counters. Carolina grabbed a seat and watched as O'Shea went to the PURCHASE TICKETS line. The leather-jacketed man pulled a wad of cash from his pocket and peeled off a string of bills. The ticket agent handed him a set of travel documents and pointed. Liam O'Shea set off in the direction of an escalator leading to the departure gates.

At that moment, Carolina realized he had no passport. Then realized that he had. He'd been carrying it since the police had recovered a little of the wreckage from *Maeve*. He reached inside his pocket to check that the little blue book was still there, then looked once again for O'Shea.

"May I help you?" the agent said. She was the same one who had handled O'Shea.

"Yes, ma'am. I just got a call from my boss to meet him at the airport. We're supposed to catch a flight this evening, but I don't see him anywhere."

"I can page him for you," the agent said.

"That would be great," Carolina replied, his mind racing as she picked up the phone. "What's his name, sir?"

"You know, I was just wondering . . . " Carolina said. "I'm a little late, and he may have already bought his ticket. Did you see him? Heavyset man wearing a brown leather jacket? Irish accent?"

The agent brightened again. "He was here just five minutes ago. Mr. Jameson. I'll page him." She reached down to the phone with her free hand to dial.

"Wait!" Carolina said. The agent's face was no longer bright.

"I'm sorry," Carolina stammered. "Look, the truth is that I just started with this company yesterday. We do construction work all over the world. When my boss called, he told me which flight to purchase a ticket for. I wrote the number down, but I forgot to bring the paper with me. If you call him, it'll look like I'm disorganized." He shrugged, looking embarrassed.

The agent's face softened. Then she smiled again. "I understand," she said. "It was tough when I broke in here, too. And you know, your boss *did* seem a little irritable. Why don't I just book the flight for you?"

"That would be terrific," Carolina said. "You're so helpful."

She began typing into the flight computer. "That's one way to San Juan, first class. Sounds like you don't know when you're coming back, Mr. . . . ."

"Carolina," he said. "Listen, you better make my ticket for coach. I have to use my Visa card and I don't want to max it out."

"Okay," she said. "It sounds like your boss is a tough guy to work for."

"He's a real killer," Carolina said.

Ten minutes later, he had a ticket to Puerto Rico and a call in to the Channel Three newsroom. "Is Lilly around?" he asked.

"I'll check," an unfamiliar voice said. A minute later, Lilly came on the line.

"It's me," Carolina said.

"Oh, hi, John. Listen, I don't think I can make our date tonight."

"What?"

"I know, I'm sorry. It's just too busy around here. We had this woman who died at a hotel this afternoon. Did you see the news?"

"Are the cops there?"

"Yes, that's the story. So now the police are here. They think one of our reporters may have some information for them."

"Providence police?"

"That's right."

"ATF?"

"Oh, John," Lilly said, laughing, "you should have been a newsman. Why in the world are you going to law school?"

"So they're within earshot, right?"

"Saturday? That's great. Will you make the reservations?"

"I've only got a few minutes. I'm at Logan. This guy O'Shea bought a ticket for San Juan. I bought one, too. I'm going to follow him as far as I can."

"John, you're crazy!" she said. "I've never been skydiving. Do you really think that's a good idea?"

"If I don't, we lose him."

"Listen, John, can you call me later? There's something I want to talk to you about."

"The plane is boarding."

"Maybe later?"

"The plane reaches San Juan after midnight. I'll try to call you when it gets in. Tell Shirley."

He hung up and looked out of the phone booth. One hundred and fifty feet away, he saw Liam O'Shea hand his ticket to an agent and walk down a skyway to the L-1011 that would take them to Puerto Rico.

San Juan looked like a birthday cake lit with a million candles.

He saw them through the window as the jet broke through the clouds and circled before making its approach, the lights of the city beckoning to nighttime travelers. Carolina knew the waterfront hotels, the casinos, and the cabarets would be burning at this hour. And he knew he probably wouldn't see them.

The flight had been uneventful with the exception of boarding. As he walked on to the wide-body jet, he had tried to see where the IRA man was sitting. But a flight attendant grabbed his ticket. "Right down this aisle, sir," she directed, in a hurry to get the coach riffraff out of the high-priced section. Carolina nodded, held up the newspaper he had bought, and pretended to read his way down into coach. He walked right past the terrorist, who was scarfing down a complimentary glass of whiskey, straight up. If O'Shea had noticed him, he didn't let on.

Carolina spent the rest of the flight pondering why an IRA bomber would be flying to Puerto Rico. Would Liam O'Shea hide there? Did Jimmy Flannery have a private home tucked away on some mountainous hillside or at the edge of some fishing village? O'Shea's hasty departure suggested he was running from something. Or heading toward something. Or both.

The wheels touched down. One bump, two. Not a perfect landing. No one in the plane broke into applause. As the jet taxied toward the airport terminal, the passengers began unbuckling, reaching for bags in the overheads, readying themselves for the inevitable rush toward the exits. A flight attendant chattered in Spanish and English for everyone to please remain seated until the jet had come to a stop. The warning was generally ignored.

At last, the plane halted. Through his window, Carolina could see the skyway extending toward the front of the jet. First class would exit before anyone in coach. The crowd had now filled the aisles. He would have to hurry to catch up to O'Shea.

A fat Puerto Rican woman blocked the aisle in front of him. She was unloading a heavy canvas bag from the overhead at an alarmingly slow pace.

"May I help you with that?" Carolina asked, reaching for the bag.

The woman screamed and started beating him with a chubby balled-up fist, jabbering away in Spanish. Carolina let go.

With a look she probably reserved for rodents and flies, the woman went back to wrestling the bag by herself. Huffing and puffing, she heaved it onto the floor. It spilled open, revealing a massive larder of kosher salamis. At a snail's pace, the woman squatted and began gathering the huge sausages. She cursed loudly.

"Excuse me," Carolina said, and stepped over her. The woman yelled something after him as he made his way down the now-empty plane aisle.

"Thank you. Bye-bye," an attendant said as he stepped out the jet's door.

The airline terminal was nearly empty. The jet from

Boston had been the last flight of the evening. Passengers were ambling toward baggage claim, the taxi stand, and a bus stop to head into San Juan for the night.

Where was Liam O'Shea?

He kept looking for the leather jacket, for the dark hair and grizzled white face that he'd seen in the surveillance photo, the face he'd glimpsed just a few hours earlier outside the Rose Tattoo. There were several men in leather jackets, but none with the right hair or build. He looked at the concourse business stands, a newspaper kiosk, a gift shop. All were closed for the night, wire cages locked down tight in front of them. People kept streaming out into the tropical night.

He passed a men's room and stopped to look inside. An old man was spitting and zipping his fly. A younger one was washing his hands. There was no one else.

If he didn't pick O'Shea up soon, he'd lose him.

Carolina was almost at the concourse's end. He knew O'Shea had only one bag, and Carolina guessed he would most likely grab a taxi or have someone outside to meet him. Which way to go?

He was so lost in thought that he heard but did not think about the quick steps behind him. Not until after he felt the shove that slammed him against a door on his right. Not until the door gave way and he fell, hard, on the dirty white tile floor of a large closet. The door closed behind him. A bright, naked bulb popped on over his head.

"Y'made that fat lady spill her sausage, fokker," Liam O'Shea said.

17

The surveillance photo made O'Shea look heavy, and he was. But it didn't convey his strength. He was hard, solid like a fire hydrant or a mailbox bolted to the ground. At least that was how he felt, Carolina thought as he tried to pull himself together on the closet floor.

"I must say, lad, you're a pretty good tail. Didn't pick you up in Rhode Island or at the airport." O'Shea hitched up his pants and grinned, enjoying the moment.

"Not that I was tryin' too hard. Must be losin' me edge. If it weren't for that fat spic bitch's wailin', you'd be followin' me still. Heard her all the way up in first class. Can't be makin' a scene if you want to track someone, now."

"Thanks for the tip," Carolina said. His side hurt again. Pain shot through his still-healing ribs.

"Pity, though," O'Shea said, "you'll never get to make use of it."

He shook his right wrist. Carolina heard a piece of metal snap. O'Shea held a long, skinny piece of steel in his hand. A knife, with a smooth, glinting edge.

"People say this sort of thing is out of date," he said, hefting the knife in his hand, "when every nigger and spic's got an Uzi or a nine-millimeter in their pocket. But I'm an old-fashioned man."

He dropped to one knee, a foot away from Carolina, and grabbed him by the shirt. He leaned close enough for Carolina to smell whiskey. "This is what I used to gut Simmons. Remember him? They found dogs eating him."

The door rattled. It was locked. But Carolina could hear

someone fumbling for a key. The noise startled O'Shea. He let go of Carolina's shirt and, just for a moment, turned his head.

Carolina swung his leg and kicked up and in. He was off balance, lying on the floor, without traction to lend much force. But there was enough. His instep landed squarely in O'Shea's groin.

The terrorist grimaced and exhaled. He did not fall. But in a moment, the pain hit him, through his groin and up, deep into his kidneys. The door opened. Outside, an elderly Puerto Rican man dressed in dark green coveralls was preparing to push a cart into the closet. When he saw the two men standing there, he stopped and stared. Carolina stood quickly. He shoved the Irishman as hard as he could into the space between the door and the wall. Then he bolted out onto the concourse.

And ran smack into the fat lady with her bag of salami.

The woman screamed and sprawled on the concourse floor, her canvas bag open again, kosher sausages rolling everywhere. Carolina looked at her, then at the cleaning man, who stood there speechless. Then he saw O'Shea open the door.

Michael Carolina ran down the last thirty feet of the concourse and out to the sidewalk, looking desperately for a cop.

He rapidly concluded that San Juan's airport, much like those in the major cities of the continental United States, never had a police officer around when you needed one. It took him a full five minutes before he tracked down an officer near the baggage-claim area and got him back to the closet, where the cleaning man was still vainly attempting to calm the salami woman. She had gathered her sausages into her bag once more and was chattering away. The custodian nodded his head. When the woman saw Carolina, she screamed again.

"She say you tried to keel her," the young police officer said, his English heavily accented.

"There was someone here who was trying to kill me," Carolina said, and repeated again the story about Liam O'Shea. The officer spoke to the cleaning man. He nodded his head again and answered in a throaty, gutteral voice. After a minute, the officer turned to Carolina.

"He say yes, there was a man here with a leather jacket. He say you on the floor and keeck heem. Then you ran and heet the lady."

"Where did he go?" Carolina asked. The officer translated. The old man shrugged. The fat lady looked at Carolina with a frightened expression, clutching salamis close to her ample and pendulous breast.

"I'm sorry," Carolina said. "I didn't mean to hurt you. I thought that man"–he gestured toward the closet–"was going to hurt me."

The officer spoke with the woman again. Her tone remained hostile.

"She says you're lucky her son is not here, that he would break your leg."

"I guess I am lucky," Carolina said.

"I theenk you should come with me." The officer grabbed hold of Carolina's arm.

"What about that guy? He's still out there. He's dangerous."

The officer smiled. "You need some protection," the cop said.

As the officer led Carolina away, the old cleaning man laughed.

Michael Carolina spent the rest of the night in a six-by-four-foot concrete cell. The room stank of vomit and urine, the probable residue of uncooperative and inebriated travelers.

The officer cheerfully advised him that he could be held on any number of charges, including assault of the sausage woman, who, as it turned out, was the cousin of another airport officer.

"But it was an accident," Carolina said.

The officer chuckled and held his thumb together against the tips of his fingers and rubbed them together.

"There's a man out there who tried to kill me," Carolina said.

"Then we protect you," the officer said.

Carolina didn't sleep that night, just stared and thought about Liam O'Shea and what he'd said in the cleaning closet. In the morning, the arresting officer went off duty and another shift came to work. After an hour went by, a new policeman came in and opened his cell.

"Go." At the desk out front, another officer handed him his wallet and the passport he'd been carrying.

"There was a hundred dollars in here," the reporter said. "Now there's only five."

The officer who had released him shrugged. *"No se,"* he said, suddenly incapable of understanding English. He pushed Carolina out of the police station's office.

Standing in the shadow of the building, he couldn't see the sun. But he felt its warmth and knew the day would be hot. The smell of car and bus exhaust fumes blended with the noise of jets in the distance, over on the other side of the terminal building. Carolina felt tired and dirty and in need of a bath. He hadn't shaved. He was a little hungry. He was stuck in San Juan with almost no money.

And he had lost Liam O'Shea.

He checked his wallet again. At least the Visa card was still there. The cop had probably figured Carolina would cancel the card quickly, so decided to take only cash.

He began to walk over the airport terminal to find a telephone. It was before nine, but he knew it would be an hour earlier in Rhode Island. Lilly would be at work.

"Channel Three News."

"Collect call from Michael," the operator said. "Will you pay?"

"Sure! Michael?"

"Good morning," he said.

"Where are you? Where have you been? Why didn't you call last night? I told Shirley. She's really pissed, and worried."

"Well, as long as she's worried."

"So where are you?"

"Still in San Juan." She listened as Carolina told her what had happened, sighing or saying, "Oh no" in the right places, but cracking up when he told her about the salami lady. "What a story," she said when he was finished. "Too bad we can't tell it."

"No way. Guano would have an orgasm over this."

"Are you all right?"

"Sure. Just a little dirty, a little tired, a little poorer. My pride hurts."

She sighed again. "What are you going to do now?"

"Your guess is as good as mine," he said. "The guy could be anywhere in Puerto Rico. Or he could be somewhere else—Europe, back in Ireland. More likely, he's here, or somewhere in the Caribbean. There's a helluva lot of islands to choose from." He ran a hand through his hair, trying to think where he might look for the heavy man in the leather jacket. And he wondered whether it might just be better to fly home.

His mind raced back over the evening, from the moment he'd seen Emily lying dead on the sidewalk, to when he'd tailed O'Shea as he left the Rose Tattoo, to the trip north into Logan, to the moment at the ticket counter and the frantic call back to Lilly. . . .

"Hey, what's up with the cops?"

"Well, there's this Detective Corvese. He's kind of pissed at you about not filling him in on this witness. Said you could have told him in the hotel."

"We didn't find out until after I got tossed out. Besides, you know we can't."

"I know."

"Even so, I think he kinda likes you."

"How special."

"Better than those two federal guys."

"Bert and Ernie?"

"Yes. The older one is okay, but the young guy acts like he just saw *The Untouchables*. Anyway, they want very much to talk to you."

"They know where I am?"

"I don't think so."

"The thing is," Carolina said, "you know as much as I do."

"True. But they don't know that."

"And you didn't volunteer it."

"I wasn't born yesterday, bubba. But there is something I want to tell you."

"What?"

"I met this lady last night. Her name is Anna Bianchini. Earl told me that she had something she wanted to share with you."

"This the lady that Tisha interviewed?"

"That's her. That's where Earl met her."

"What's her story?"

"Well, she's not the most charming person you'd ever want to meet. She's angry and bitter and looking for cash."

Carolina snorted. "Sounds like a thousand other people Frankie screwed."

"But Anna talked about something the rest of them haven't mentioned."

"What?"

"Frankie's not Italian."

Foot traffic inside the airport terminal was beginning to pick up, and along with it, the ambient noise. Carolina pressed the receiver tight against his ear. "I'm not sure I heard you."

"I said, 'Frankie's not Italian.' "

"What do you mean?"

"His mother was Irish."

"But his father was Italian."

"In certain neighborhoods of certain towns of this fair state, that doesn't matter. Either you're full-blooded or you're nothing. And the way Mrs. Bianchini talked, you'd have thought the kid was a leper."

"How so?"

"We're talking about two ethnic groups that both had to fight to get established in the United States. Both suffered discrimination; both were treated like second-class citizens for years. And both competed against each other."

"Okay," Carolina said, still sounding unsure.

"The point is, Mike, that a kid with mixed heritage would have had some trouble getting along, even with an Italian surname. Other kids might tease him, maybe even beat him up. Others might shun him, exclude him. That's what Mrs. Bianchini suggested. None of the kids gave a damn that his father was a banker or that he was connected to the Patriarca family."

Carolina pondered the new information. It was certainly an indication of why Falcone would leave, of how he could steal from a community where he'd grown up, then disappear without thinking twice. But it still wasn't enough.

"Lilly, it's all very interesting. We might even be able to use some of it in a background piece on Frankie. But here I am in Puerto Rico. O'Shea is long gone. And this doesn't get us any closer to finding Mr. Falcone."

"You're very impatient," Lilly said.

"There's more?"

"Little Anna says Frankie's mom didn't really come from Ireland."

"Come again?"

"You heard me. Anna says she wasn't from Ireland."

"So she was born in America."

"I don't think she was. Anna kept referring to 'that island down south.' "

"Down south?"

"Yup."

"Did she say anything else?"

"Nope. But I figure O'Shea flies down south; Frankie has a tan at what you think is the wrong time of year. Maybe there's a connection."

Carolina tried to process all the information he had gathered in the past weeks. Nothing about the story was the way it had first appeared. Frederick Simmons didn't protect banks; he made it easy to steal from them. Liam O'Shea didn't work for a revolutionary cause, he worked for a mob. And Frankie Falcone, the Italian banker, wasn't Italian at all. His mother was Irish, but not from Ireland.

She was from an island.

Down south.

"Michael, are you there?" He heard Lilly's voice in a fog, in the distance.

Down south.

"I'll be damned," he said.

"Michael, what did you say? Michael?"

He could hear the buzz of the airport terminal behind him. In one ear, he heard someone speaking Spanish, calling the boarding of a plane over the public-address system.

"I know where Falcone is," he said.

"What?"

"I know where Frankie Falcone is."

"Where?"

"Let me call you back, okay?"

"Michael, tell me where!" she cried, but he was already hanging up. He wanted to kick himself, it was all so simple.

18

I n November 1493, Christopher Columbus saw it during his second voyage to the New World, rising up from the Caribbean Sea. A jewel, green and lush, crowned with a volcano.

But Columbus had just come from the neighboring island of Guadeloupe, where he and his men had found evidence of cannibalism among the Carib Indians. Native women aboard Columbus's ship said the green island had been depopulated by the Caribs. The great explorer and his men sailed on, but he gave the island a new name, Santa María de Montserrat, after a monastery on a hillside near Barcelona.

More than a century later, Oliver Cromwell used the island as a place to banish those whose politics and religion clashed with his own puritanical views. Many of those he banished came not from England but from the wild island to the northwest–the island of Gaels and Celts. The island where thousands of men and women were slaughtered by English swords in places like Boyne and Drogheda. The island that would for centuries rebel against the iron fist of English rule.

And so the Irish came to the Caribbean in the seventeenth century–to Montserrat, the emerald isle of the tropics, where to this day the natives speak with a brogue.

Michael Carolina had first seen it from the deck of *Maeve*. He sailed past it, and around it, and eventually anchored in its harbor at Plymouth, with a charter customer who'd grown tired of the crowds in Antigua and the flat whiteness of Barbuda. The tiny volcanic island, just thirty-nine square miles, was too small to sustain much agriculture or industry. It remained a crown colony, governed by a representative of the queen, dependent on the English for its economic survival.

As the tiny commuter plane settled in for its final approach, Carolina looked out the window, almost expecting to see Frankie Falcone waiting to greet him. He was irritated he hadn't thought of the island sooner. There was no way to be sure that this was where Falcone was hiding. But a man with an Irish mother, a mother who hailed from an island "down south"—there could be only one place to look.

Lilly had been wild for him to find out. "It's the best lead anyone's developed."

"And it could still be a dud," he said.

"You must think it's worth trying."

"I do. But I'm also looking at the negatives. I know Shirley will."

And she did.

"What if he's not there?" she wanted to know.

"Then at least we tried," he said. "I can't guarantee I'll find him. But I can guarantee I won't if I come home."

"I'm worried. You left without permission. And the odds are this will be a wild goose chase."

"That could happen," he admitted, "but Monserrat isn't that big. We're talking about fewer than fifteen thousand people. How many Americans are going to move there with fifteen million dollars and not be noticed?"

"This is costing a fortune," Shirley said. "I really ought to fire you for leaving without permission."

"I called the station before I got on the plane."

"That's not getting permission."

"Did you want me to interrupt your conversation with Sergeant Corvese and Agents Schumacher and O'Mara?"

Shirley didn't reply.

"At least if I go, we have a shot at a story," Carolina said. Shirley Templeton was a complex woman. Her style of dress was peculiar. She popped vitamins the way that ballplayers dip chew. But above all, she had good news judgment.

"Shit," she said, "you're almost there, anyway. What are you going to do for pictures?"

He bought a Hi-8 mm Palmcorder in the San Juan airport's duty-free shop. The tiny camera produced pictures that were almost as good as Beta. He purchased two T-shirts, shorts, and a pair of flip-flops to wear in the sun, charging it all. The perfect American tourist. The customs man barely looked at him as he stamped his passport.

A cabbie grabbed his hand and half-dragged him to a beat-up rust red Ford wagon. The man's hair matched the color of the car, an unusual sight on someone with skin as black as coal.

"Sure, and where would you be going this fine afternoon?"

"Let me guess," Carolina said, climbing into the front seat. "Dublin, right? Or is it County Kerry?"

"Now don't be makin' sport with me, Yank, 'less you're plannin' on droppin' an awful big tip in me hand."

"Sorry," Carolina said.

The man nodded. "Name's Fergus."

"Michael."

"Last name is O'Neill," Fergus said, "and somewhere in the years, I got some blood from Ireland. But I never been there. Don't want to go, either. Now, where d'ye want me to take you?"

Carolina looked the man over. His clothes were worn but clean. He had brown leather shoes, no socks, and a small gold cross around his neck. A hardworking man.

"You look like a stand-up guy, Mr. O'Neill."

"Call me Fergus."

"I came here to find someone, Fergus, and I'm not sure how I should do it."

Fergus looked at him expectantly.

"I don't think this person wants to be found."

"What's he done?"

"He stole a lot of money."

"What's a lot?"

"Fifteen million U.S. dollars."

The cabbie's orange eyebrows lifted.

" 'N I suppose you think he's tellin' every cabdriver he meets."

"Well," Carolina said, adjusting himself in the worn seat, "probably not. But I've spent some time down in these islands. The cabbies see and hear quite a bit. And if they haven't, then they usually know someone who has."

Fergus thought for a minute. "There might be someone, mon, there just might be. What ya gonna do if you find who you're lookin' for?"

"Take his picture."

"That's it?"

"That's it."

"You don't want his money?"

"That's for someone else to deal with," Carolina said.

"Why should I believe you?"

"No reason you should, but I'm telling you the truth."

The cabbie looked around the tiny airport lot for a moment. During their conversation, the rest of the plane's passengers had departed. He looked back at Carolina and sighed, then shifted the beat-up Ford into gear. The car took off with a jerk and began the trip down Mt. Chance into Plymouth.

"You know where he is?" Carolina asked.

"No, Yank, but I've got a friend who might."

Frankie was in the throes of computer passion.

The helmet was still heavy on his head, but his body felt light enough to fly, like a hang glider crossing a gorge. The electrode-covered diaper no longer existed. There was only the woman and the blending of loins.

"Ooooh," she said, her eyes lit like glowing coals.

He had worked his way through virtually every film actress from the island video store, at the rate of two or three a day, depending on how much time and effort he put into each one. But after Julia Roberts and Katharine Ross from *Butch Cassidy and the Sundance Kid,* there was a sameness to it all. Lauren Hutton seemed a lot like Doris Day. Susan Sarandon was strikingly similar to Jane Fonda.

Frankie grew bored.

This new one had come from an old photograph. He had placed it under an optical scanner and the image had been transferred electronically into the computer's memory. It was the girl he had met when he was in high school, the one who'd called him a half-breed.

Now he had her just where he wanted her: legs splayed in the back of an old Chevrolet.

But the eyes bothered him. The computer could not correct for the camera flash, hence the red eyes. It was like screwing Bathsheba, Queen of the Jaguar Devil Women. The thought distracted him. The distraction made him take longer than usual.

He gasped again, his chest heaving with the exertion. He could feel his heart pound, his body heat beginning to ebb and cool as beads of sweat broke on his head and became a flood.

"Looks like fuckin' great exercise," Liam O'Shea said, laughing at his play on words.

Frankie jumped, surprised, then angered.

"I told you not to come in here."

"You are one strange fuckin' wop," O'Shea replied. He made no move to leave.

Falcone unstrapped the helmet, carefully lifted it off his head, then placed it on a shelf next to the computer. O'Shea continued to stand in the room's shadows. Frankie felt strange, embarrassed. Like he'd been caught masturbating—which, in fact, he had.

"You were makin' enough noise to wake the volcano. Figured you were havin' a heart attack."

"Don't come in here again."

O'Shea ignored him and walked over and began to examine the computer, then the helmet. Then he noticed a CD-ROM drive and a plastic box filled with discs.

"What d'ye do with this, crank up U2 while you put it to one o' them starlets?"

"The CD-ROM holds film and video." Indeed, he'd used the device to call up the image of Jean Simmons from *Spartacus*, the recut version. Frankie had pretended he was a gladiator, taking her in his cell, while Kirk Douglas whined in the room next door.

"What a fuckin' lark," O'Shea said.

"You still haven't said why you came here," Frankie said.

"You don't need to know," O'Shea responded, fingering the helmet, peering inside it.

"I think I do," Falcone replied.

O'Shea reached into a pocket of his leather jacket and removed a dirty handkerchief. He wiped moisture from inside the helmet. Sweat. Then he began to examine the mirrors and wiring at the helmet's front.

"Well, guido, what you think ain't important to me. Your fellow club members, they said to come here. That's what matters. Majority rules, as they say."

Now O'Shea was trying on the helmet. Despite the wall unit that conditioned the room's air, it seemed stiflingly hot. *Why doesn't he take off that stupid jacket?* Falcone wondered.

"I'm gonna swab out that diaper there and give this thing a try," O'Shea said, buckling the chin strap. Falcone felt sick.

"That is truly disgusting," he said, picking up his towel. "Would you use someone else's condom?"

"I don't see anyone telling me I can't, guido."

"My mother was as Irish as you."

"Your mother," O'Shea said with a smile, "was a nigger slave's great-granddaughter. An your da was a guinea shit."

Other men would have reacted. Some would have struck anyone with gall enough to hurl such a crude and outrageous insult. Some would have found a gun, then threatened to use it. Some would at least have thrown the person who made such a remark into the street.

Frankie Falcone was not such a man. Frankie Falcone was scared shitless of Liam O'Shea. Unable to stop the terrorist from speaking or touching his belongings, Frankie left the room.

"Hey! Y'got a copy o' *The Quiet Man*?" O'Shea called after him. "I always wanted t'do Maureen O'Hara."

Fergus and Michael hit several of the fancier hotels, the ones still left after Hurricane Hugo smashed the island. Carolina sat in the car while Fergus got out and engaged in animated talk with other drivers. As a charter captain, Carolina had become accustomed to the rapid-fire West Indian English of most island natives. But this dialect was altogether different. The additional blend of Irish brogue made it difficult for him to follow the way the conversations were going.

After three stops, they arrived outside a hotel called Vue Pointe. "This may be m'last shot," Fergus said as he lifted himself out of the driver's seat.

Carolina watched him go up to another cabbie sitting outside the restaurant entrance. Like Fergus, the man had the coal black skin of Africa but wore a flaming crown of red hair. Unlike with the other cabbies, this time Fergus bent his head down and the two men spoke quietly to each other. After a minute, Fergus sauntered back to the cab, and the other man climbed into his own beat-up Ford.

"We can take a little trip," he said, "but it will cost you double fare."

"This guy knows where he is?"

"I didn't say that. All we have is your description. Not even a picture of the man."

Carolina thought about the photograph of O'Shea. He'd left it in the microwave truck in Providence. He cursed himself for forgetting to bring it along.

"Why are we going for a ride?"

"Because he thinks he might know."

"Why double fare?"

"Because I'm taking you and he's leading us. Business is business, mon."

"I guess I don't have much choice," Carolina said.

"Not if you want to find him," Fergus replied, flashing a smile. He gave a nod to the other cabbie, who flashed an equally brilliant smile as his car pulled out. Fergus wheeled around and the two cars left the Vue Pointe in a cloudburst of dust and flying gravel.

The other cabbie drove fast, shooting along the narrow Montserratian lanes like a race-car driver. Even so, winding along a black-topped road near the ocean's edge, the ride took longer than the trip from the airport. A few miles out of Plymouth, the road twisted left and up into more hilly terrain. Thick green vegetation sprouted up from the earth on both sides of the road. Carolina noticed a smattering of houses, some nothing more than shacks, a few with people sitting outside watching what little there was of the world going by. Farther uphill, he saw larger houses, with impressive views of the ocean. He touched Fergus on the shoulder and pointed.

"Who owns them?"

"The rich and famous," Fergus said.

Half a mile later, they reached a plateau of sorts, filled with green grass and some stone ruins. The cabbie up ahead of them pulled over and Fergus did the same. It was still daylight, but the sun was beginning its descent to the horizon.

"What's this?" Carolina asked.

"Galway's Plantation. They grew sugarcane here."

The other cabbie came up and joined them. "My ancestors cut the cane for this plantation in the eighteenth century."

"Quite a place," Carolina said, looking around.

"His name is Seamus," Fergus said, gesturing toward the other cabbie. "Seamus O'Neill."

"Brother?" Carolina asked.

"Cousin once removed," Seamus said.

"So," Carolina said after a moment, "where do I find this man?"

"Come along." Seamus said. He was off at a trot, his shoes slapping as they hit the dirt. Carolina and Fergus followed.

They went through the ruins of the old Galway Plantation, over the soil where cane once grew, tended by slaves imported from Africa. Montserrat had once aspired to being a major center of agriculture in the Caribbean. But the cane and limes grown on the island were generally only enough to sustain the inhabitants. When Great Britain abolished slavery, the island's hopes for agricultural prosperity died.

At the plantation's edge, the ruins were met by more vegetation, plants and trees, and as they reached them, Seamus slowed and then stopped. His eyes scanned the trees and heavy shrubs, as though he was looking for something. Finally, he took three steps forward, pushing his way through two bushy trees. Carolina followed, taking high steps to clear the leafy growths coming out of the ground. He lowered his eyes to watch his step, then looked up. Seamus was watching him, laughing.

In a moment, Carolina understood why. They were now on a path, a slender, snakelike trail camouflaged by leaves and shrubs. But it was still a path. Seamus did not pick up his feet, but instead walked with a normal gait, the greenery parting as his legs cut through. Carolina looked back. Fergus was behind him, keeping pace.

They followed the trail for what seemed like half a mile before reaching a small clearing that appeared to hang on some sort of ledge. Seamus had stopped again to wait for the other men to catch up. Despite the trip down the path, Carolina didn't feel hot or tired. The sea breeze kept the men cool as it gently swirled against the mountain slope.

"Are we there?" Carolina said, thinking that he sounded like a kid on a school trip. Seamus must have thought the same. He gazed at the reporter with the look of a bemused parent.

"Don't you know that we are," he said.

"Where is he?"

Seamus raised a thin arm and pointed down, off the edge of the ledge. Carolina stepped over and looked. One hundred, maybe one hundred and fifty yards below was a villa painted white with peach trim. A small gravel road led up to it, one that ended in a circle drive, where a Range Rover sat parked. The house had a magnificent view of the ocean in the distance. The front of the house would be a spectacular place to watch the sunset.

In back was a gourd-shaped swimming pool, with a few lounge chairs and tables scattered around the edge.

A back door opened. A man emerged, dressed in a white cotton robe. He strutted to a lounge chair. Michael Carolina watched, utterly amazed, as the man shed the robe and plunged into the pool.

Frankie Falcone began doing laps.

19

"T his is a dream." Michael Carolina said.

The island was absolutely still. Grass and plants around him did not move. Insects made no sound. In the distance, it was almost as if the sea had turned solid. Nothing moved—except in a pool one hundred yards away, where Francis Xavier Falcone, the most notorious embezzler in Rhode Island history, dog-paddled.

"Got a flabby butt," Seamus said.

"Needs a few more laps," Fergus agreed, "and a salad."

Carolina grabbed the Hi-8. Carefully, he switched it on, then rested the camera on a rock to keep it steady as he began to roll off tape.

Falcone looked well tanned as he lolled about in the deep end, swimming, then resting on his back, his arms out for balance in water the color of Windex. His hair was a bit longer. His mustache looked the same. In fact, it appeared he'd done almost nothing to hide his identity—nothing except to come to this tiny island in the Leeward chain.

Carolina's mind raced with questions. Who owned the villa? Was Falcone living alone? How long had he been here?

"How did you know where to find him?" he asked Seamus.

"Easy, mon. Saw him just a few weeks ago. Walkin' in town. Paid me to take him up to this place. Must've been before he got that fancy-lookin' truck there." Seamus gestured toward the Range Rover. "Gave me a good tip. Ten dollars American."

"And now you're helping me?"

"I ain't seen him since. 'N business is business."

Carolina thought for a moment about the meters running on both cabs—double fares. Then he looked back down the ledge and knew it was well worth the price. Frankie Falcone. Captured by the magic of videotape.

"Who owns the house?"

"Don't know, mon," Seamus said. "He does, looks to me."

"How about the car?"

"Same thing, I bet."

Carolina rolled tape for another five minutes as the fugitive banker swam, then climbed out of the pool and dried himself with a white towel before easing back into his robe. Falcone lay down on a lounge chair, catching the waning heat from the afternoon sun. Carolina clicked off the camera, snapped on the lens cap, and got up.

"I'm ready to go."

"Someone else," Fergus said.

Carolina turned to see. Fergus was right. A man had stepped out of the villa but remained hidden by the building's shadow. After a minute, he stepped into the light. He was barefoot but wore a leather jacket and a pair of dirty-looking shorts.

O'Shea.

"Shit," Carolina said, reaching for the camera again.

"Quite a little gadget y'got in there," Liam O'Shea said to Frankie Falcone. "It's uh—how you computer people say, user-friendly?"

"Stay away from it," the banker said. He knew there was little he could do to keep the man from the machine. O'Shea knew it, too.

"Oh, I'll be staying away from it, sir, now, yes, sir," O'Shea said. "Wouldn't want to be screwin' it up, sir, if you'll pardon the pun."

It occurred to Falcone that the authorities of a British

colony would be mightily pleased to arrest a known IRA terrorist. But O'Shea was too familiar with the activities of the club, too knowledgeable about the membership and the fact that Frankie Falcone's name could be found on any Interpol computer. And Falcone knew that O'Shea would not have arrived here if things were comfortable for him up north. For the moment, he had to be tolerated.

"There are drinks inside if you want one. Wine. Beer," he said, in an attempt to be friendly.

"Later," O'Shea said. "I'm still gettin' used to me new surroundin's."

O'Shea strutted around the pool's edge, examining the trees and careful landscaping around the villa. Paradise with a manicure, he thought to himself. He had been here just a day, slept awhile, eaten some, then enjoyed himself abusing Falcone, his reluctant host. But Liam O'Shea felt restless. He thought about what had happened in the airport, about the missed opportunity to stick that bastard reporter.

"Pity," he said out loud.

"What?" Falcone asked.

"Never mind," O'Shea muttered. "Just pondering life's simple pleasures."

"Oh, I can't believe this," Carolina said, rolling off more tape.

Fergus poked Seamus in the arm. "Who's that?"

"I don't know, and don' be pokin' me," Seamus said.

"Quiet," Carolina said. "He's a suspected IRA terrorist. He's also a suspect in several murders in the United States."

The two Montserratians looked at the man below them. O'Shea was now making a second walk around the perimeter of the pool.

"He's a fat one," Fergus said.

"Sure, but not like the other one, mon," Seamus said. "That one, he's rock-hard."

Carolina now had more than ten minutes of video. He

shot another minute, then rewound and checked the tape. It was fine. All he needed was a telephone and a satellite uplink to send the pictures back to the United States.

"I think it's time to go," he said to the two cabbies.

It would have been the sweetest moment of the trip, a quiet victory parade through tropical weeds, was it not for the remains of an ancient bottle of Red Stripe beer. The bottle's contents had long since been drunk, the bottle itself abandoned, broken into pieces. All three of the men had missed it on their excursion down the hill, but two steps up the tiny trail, Carolina's left flip-flop flopped. The reporter's bare foot crunched down through the green leaves, right on to the jagged bottle base. Glass pierced the thick skin of his heel.

"Oh!"

Pain shot through his foot, up his leg. He didn't realize how loud his shout had been until he saw the surprised look on Fergus's face.

"Bejesus, what's the matter?" he asked, then grabbed Carolina before he could topple over. Fergus saw the glass before Carolina could answer.

"Seamus, mon, look what happen to his foot."

But Seamus was looking elsewhere—down the slope toward the villa, at the man in the leather jacket. Who was looking right back.

Carolina steadied himself. He lifted his heel and saw the steady trickle of blood covering his foot. Then he looked up and saw Seamus. He followed the cabbie's eyes until he locked on Liam O'Shea.

"Bejesus, we better be walkin'," Fergus said, pushing the reporter up the trail.

Carolina looked back at the villa. "I wish we could fly."

"Holy sweet fuck," Liam O'Shea said, breaking for the house.

"What's going on?" Frankie called. He had missed the

commotion uphill, lost in thought about new women to bed with his sex machine.

"Come on." O'Shea yanked at the collar of the white terry-cloth robe and dragged Falcone from the chaise lounge. Falcone sprawled before recovering his balance. O'Shea held on and hauled the banker into the house.

"What are you doing? Take your hands off—" O'Shea slapped him hard across the face, drawing blood.

"You shut up," O'Shea said, "Don't talk unless I ask you a question. Where are the keys to that Range Rover?"

Falcone was shaking. He pointed a tanned finger to a table near the villa entrance.

"You have a gun?"

The banker nodded and let out a small whimper as he pointed to a closet. O'Shea dropped him like a piece of luggage and threw open the closet door. He found the gun on the top shelf, a nine-millimeter, tucked inside a calfskin holster. The terrorist checked the pistol's action, then ran his hand across the closet shelf until he located a full clip.

"Nice," O'Shea said out loud. "How the fuck did you get this into a bloody British colony?"

Falcone didn't reply. O'Shea stepped toward him.

"I paid a captain!" Falcone shouted, and raised his arms to protect himself. "Down in Plymouth."

O'Shea snickered, then grabbed the banker's collar again and strode to the door, Falcone half-scraping along behind him. The terrorist grabbed the keys from the table, pulled Falcone to the villa's front door, then out to the vehicle. He practically threw the man inside.

"What's up the road?"

Falcone whimpered again. O'Shea reached through the window of the passenger side and slapped him once more. Falcone shook even harder.

"Now, guido, I'm not goin' to ask you again. What's up the bloody road?"

Falcone was trying to use the robe's lapel to wipe his face. He was trying hard not to cry. "Galway's Plantation," he said. "An old sugar plantation. It's a landmark now. Ruins."

O'Shea ran around to the other side of the Rover and climbed in. He fired the engine and threw the clutch into first with almost the same motion. The heavy-duty vehicle lurched forward. As it did, the banker seemed to regain a bit of his composure. But just a bit.

"I can't go out like this," he whined.

"Listen, wop," O'Shea said as he turned into the left lane and headed up the plantation road, "there's a little bastard from your beloved hometown who found your merry hideaway. I don't care how you're dressed or what you think of my methods. You're helpin' me to catch the little bugger and his carrot-topped buddies. Because if you don't, you can kiss that villa 'n pool of yours good-bye. And you'll be havin' it up your sweet little guinea bum in Rhode Island jail 'stead of doin' it to some movie harlot on that fuckin' machine of yours."

With Fergus and Seamus to help, Carolina limped up the trail toward the plantation ruins. His foot was throbbing. Fergus had managed to pull the piece of glass from the foot, an ugly brown sliver about an inch and a half long. Seamus had passed him his flip-flop, which he stuck back on his foot in case it accidentally hit ground again. The rubber sandal was now sticky with blood.

"How much farther to the car?" Carolina asked.

"Another quarter mile," Seamus said.

The two men were practically carrying the reporter over the weeds. Little drops of blood smeared the leaves as they passed.

"Is there any way to get down to Plymouth besides taking that road?"

"No, mon," Fergus said. "Unless you want to walk, and I don't suspect that you do."

It took two more minutes to reach the first part of the ruins. The three men stopped, and Fergus and Seamus eased Carolina down so that his back rested against the side of a stone wall.

"You need a doctor," Seamus said, looking again at the wound on Carolina's heel.

"Know any who make house calls?" Carolina said.

"You look plenty pale," Fergus said.

Carolina looked at his foot. It was hard to see the heel without twisting his leg, and twisting brought more pain. "I'm losing a lot of blood. I think I may have cut a vein or an artery. Either of you wear a belt?"

Seamus stripped off a thin brown belt. The leather was cracked and stained with sweat, but it felt strong. Seamus wrapped the leather around Carolina's ankle and threaded the end through the metal buckle."

"You know to tug on this when you're feelin' faint?"

"I do. Thanks," Carolina said.

"We'll get you out of here, mon," Fergus said, offering the reporter an arm.

"Do I still pay double fare?" Carolina asked. Seamus gave him a dirty look.

"I was only kidding," Carolina said.

Together, the three of them made their way through the ruins of the old plantation. The few tourists who had been there earlier were all gone, probably home to private villas or island hotels, images of the old sugarcane farm firmly etched on videocassettes or rolls of film. The place was quiet except for the sounds of scattered insects and an occasional bird.

"Do you have a television station here?" Carolina asked.

"Sure, we got television. I get all the channels," Fergus replied.

"Does the station have an uplink?"

"What's that?" Seamus asked.

"A device to send pictures out of here, by satellite."

The two cabbies looked at each other.

"Never mind," Carolina said.

Seamus kicked a rock with his shoe, then tugged on Carolina's arm to get a better grip.

"Your best bet, mon, is you fly to Antigua, or back to San Juan. We just a little island, don't you know, trying to get by in the big bad world—"

His words stopped just before Carolina heard the crashing report. Suddenly, the grip on Carolina's left shoulder eased. He looked and saw Seamus slump to the ground, his face gone.

O'Shea had not fired a nine in months. His aim was poor. He missed Carolina by at least a foot and caught the orange-haired man by luck. I'm out of practice, he told himself.

Falcone was down on one knee. His body still shook, but less than before, now that the terrorist's wrath was directed toward someone else. They were at the edge of the ruins, the Range Rover parked a few hundred feet away. Falcone had wanted to stay by the vehicle. O'Shea once again dragged him along.

"I may need you," he said.

O'Shea had considered the possibility that the reporter and the two other men were armed. Then he saw the parked cabs, realized who the two other men probably were, and concluded that they were not. Out of caution, he decided his first shot should come from a distance. With no return fire, he felt confident of his assessment. It would be easy now to kill them all.

As the black cabdriver fell, O'Shea was already lining up his second shot. But Carolina and the other man were too fast. They bolted left and disappeared behind a broken-down wall before O'Shea could fire another round.

Falcone looked up. "Did you get him?"

"Bagged one o' the niggers," O'Shea said. "I'll get him, though."

"What will you do?"

O'Shea looked around, following the line of the broken-down wall. When he looked back at Falcone, his face showed profound glee.

"I'm goin' huntin', Frankie. An' you're gonna be my hound."

"Holy Mary, mother of God, pray for us sinners . . ." The rest of Fergus's words were lost on Carolina as the two men scrambled along through broken rocks and brush. When Carolina looked up, he saw that the cabdriver was wiping his face with the end of his shirt. Sweat perhaps; more likely, tears.

"Bless Seamus's soul. He was a hardworkin' man," Fergus said.

"You can let me go." Carolina said. He was bloody and tired and scared to death. But he looked at the man beside him and couldn't help feeling an enormous sense of guilt for getting the two cabbies involved. Now one was dead, and the other might soon follow. "Go on. Make your own path. And don't wait for me if you get to the car first."

"An' why should I do that?" Fergus said. "I'm not going to leave you. That fella there wit' the gun, he'll shoot us down like dogs 'less we find a way out of here. I say we stick together. You just do like me. You pray a little an' you walk wit' me."

Carolina prayed.

The wall hooked right and led them into the remains of a small building—a cottage, built with stones bleached white by the sun, but without a roof. They stopped again.

"Which way do you think he'll come?" Carolina asked.

"Don't know," Fergus said, his eyes scanning the rocks and plants that surrounded them.

The sun was below the horizon now and cast a strange blend of shadows and colors across the plantation ruins. It was hard to see, and getting harder. Carefully, Fergus stuck his head up over a rock and peered out, looking for signs of the man with the gun.

Another shot banged off a rock two feet from the cabbie's head. He ducked down again.

"Man sees pretty good for this bad light. We best be movin' or he'll know where to find us."

They slipped past the building and worked their way along the wall, limping, crawling, sometimes trying to run, always trying to be quiet. The Hi-8 camera slapped against Carolina's side. He didn't notice, thinking instead of Seamus's faceless corpse, and about Liam O'Shea, hunting them in the ruins. Are we going to get out of here alive? he wondered.

They reached the end of the wall and stopped. Fergus peered out around the corner and quickly pulled his head back.

"Oh, mon, you're not going to believe what's out there."

"What?"

"That silly white man with the robe and flabby butt."

Frankie Falcone was dangerously close to soiling the fabric of his cotton robe. He stepped gingerly across the ground, unaccustomed to walking in bare feet. The ruins around him grew dim in the fading light. And somewhere behind him, that Irish madman was waiting with the nine.

"What can I do?" he had wailed softly to O'Shea.

"You can be bait," the terrorist said, then whispered the things he wanted Falcone to recite. O'Shea held the pistol comfortably in his right hand, gesturing with it for emphasis every time he drove home a point during the brief lecture. Falcone couldn't take his eyes off the weapon. It was black and sleek. O'Shea was clearly more comfortable with it than Falcone ever would be.

And now the banker stood alone, trying to lure someone he had never met out into the open.

"Carolina?" he said weakly. There was no reply.

"Carolina? This is Frank Falcone. I know you want to talk to me," he said, slightly bolder. "Come on out."

There was no noise but the insects and a tiny breeze washing the leaves on some nearby trees.

"Come on out, Mike," Falcone said. O'Shea had said to stay out in the open. But what would happen if the reporter was stupid enough to come out? Would O'Shea kill them both? The man had just blown the head off one of the reporter's companions. Hadn't thought twice about it. But if I don't do what he says, Falcone thought, he might just shoot me, anyway.

"Michael Carolina? Isn't there something we should talk about?"

From the growing blackness, Frankie Falcone heard a voice.

"There is."

It was crazy, Carolina thought, when he first heard Falcone. What was the man doing up here? In a bathrobe? He sounded frightened. Was he really trying to run from O'Shea, too? Or were the two men working together?

Whatever the answer, someone, probably O'Shea, was still out there with a gun.

"Fergus, we've got to split up," Carolina whispered.

The cabbie emphatically shook his head.

"We've got to," Carolina said.

"Give me a good reason why."

Frankie Falcone learned something new about himself. Sounds in the darkness, any sounds, made him jump. His robe flapped around him as he tried to pull himself together and not sound afraid.

"Where are you?" he called to the voice, and heard his own words bouncing across the rocks before being lost in the brush and trees. Was Carolina on the right? The left? Straight in front? Frankie couldn't tell.

"Where I am isn't important," the voice said. "What's important is where all that money is."

Frankie still couldn't determine the location of the sound, but he knew that somewhere behind him Liam O'Shea was waiting.

"What money?"

"You know very well what money." Carolina's voice echoed again. "The guts of the bank your father gave you."

"He gave me nothing," Falcone shot back, for the first time sounding more angry than scared. "I earned it."

"Did you earn all the money that those people on Federal Hill deposited with you? All those widows and retirees?"

"Those people . . . those people never gave me a thing," Falcone shouted. "I was dirt to them. They'd let me hold their money because of my father. But I wasn't good enough to go play with their kids, or go to their parties, or take their daughters out to a dance. I was just that half-Irish kid with the mom who came from the islands. I'll tell you somethin', I don't owe those people a thing."

"Frankie, you're nothing but a thief."

The banker was outraged. Who was this guy, calling him names? What did he know about life on the Hill? And where the hell was he hiding?

"So what's everyone else then, angels? What about all those union chiefs who dip into the funds? Or the cops and firemen who collect disability pensions while they're workin' another job or goin' to school? Or the waiters and waitresses who skim drink and food money in the restaurants? And how 'bout all the people who cheat on their taxes?"

Frankie took a step forward and pulled his robe close again.

"Listen, one way or another, everybody gets paid back. Nobody really gets hurt. My bank's empty, but the state'll pay everybody off. They always do. The people will yell a little, but eventually the governor will raise taxes, and the legislature will approve it. So everyone'll be all right. Everything'll be fine."

"Think your partner will be fine?"

"What? Who?" Frankie was taken by surprise. The voice didn't answer.

"Tommy's dead?" Frankie asked. Still no answer.

"Who in the club died?" Frankie demanded.

"Liam didn't tell you about Fred Simmons?" the voice asked. "Cut him down in an alley, left him to be eaten by dogs."

Frankie was petrified. It occurred to him that he didn't know who was worse now, the voice out front or the man lurking behind him.

"Tell me about the club, Frankie," the voice said. "Tell me about the Rose Tattoo."

"Listen, I don't know nuttin' about that," Falcone said, slipping into the thick accent of Federal Hill once again. "I just lived a Rhode Island life. That's all. And I know what rule number one is: Deep down, we're all the same. The only difference is how many zeros you have in your account."

The sound of insects had increased in the darkness. Overhead, a half-moon began to slither into the night sky. Frankie Falcone looked around and around, wondering where O'Shea was, wondering where Carolina could be found. He was scared to death.

"I have to disagree," the voice said. "We're not all the same. We didn't all steal fifteen million dollars."

"Hey, it didn't all go to me!" Falcone shouted, but not as loudly as the shots that burst through the night.

20

Fergus O'Neill grew up poor in the town of Plymouth. His mother worked at raising four children. His father worked at whatever he could find.

From time to time, his father took Fergus to Galway's Plantation to show him what remained of the period when slaves worked cane for Irish and English settlers, turning the tough vegetation into sugar for cakes and tea. The little black boy with the flaming red hair listened, his eyes bright, as his father told the stories. The experience etched the image of the crumbling buildings and stones and cane fields in Fergus's mind.

In the darkness now, Fergus could remember each wall and stone. It was small comfort as he thought about the man with the gun, and the other man, dressed in nothing but a robe, uttering angry words in the night.

The robed man didn't seem to be moving much. Fergus decided to use him as a reference point. A compass rose. He did not feel brave. But he knew he needed to steer himself around the rocks and bushes and trees until he found the man with the weapon.

"I'll just keep talking," the reporter had said before Fergus left him in a grove of trees. "If you get behind Falcone, you may be able to see O'Shea." Fergus had agreed. At least it was better than sitting still, waiting to be hunted and shot.

He could hear the conversation between the two men in the darkness, but he didn't listen to the words. He tried to listen for any other sound that might tell him where the man with the gun was hiding. He crept, low to the ground, his hands in front of him for balance. Fergus searched the shadows but saw nothing.

After a minute, he was ninety degrees to Frankie's right, perhaps thirty feet away. The men were separated by a crumbling wall. But Falcone was standing up, and from his squatting position, Fergus could make out the side of his face. The man was trembling as he called out into the night.

Fergus moved a little farther, skittering sideways like a crab, still looking, but facing Falcone, working his way around the compass. Where was the other man? He stopped for a moment and held his breath.

If he had not, he would have missed the sound. It was delicate, like a whisper. But Fergus knew he wasn't wrong. Somewhere to the left, a man's foot had kicked a pebble.

The cabdriver was now almost directly behind Falcone. The grove of trees where Carolina was hidden lay somewhere in front and slightly to the left of Falcone, but the reporter's voice was bouncing off the rocky walls and stones. The sound from the pebble was much closer.

If the moon had not chosen that moment to slide into the sky, Fergus would never have seen Liam O'Shea. But there it was, a half pie rising to dimly illuminate the sea and islands of the Gulf Stream. And there in front of him was a man, the same man who had worn a leather jacket down by the villa's pool. He was chunky, hard-looking, and, like Frankie Falcone, his back was to Fergus. He was still, apparently listening to the voices.

"Listen, I don't know nuttin' about that," Falcone was saying.

The man in the jacket had a gun, held loosely in his right hand. Fergus could only see the dark shape in the dim light. Off in the blackness, he could hear the reporter speak.

"We're not all the same."

The man before him stretched out his arm, the gun searching, almost like radar. Then it stopped. The man had found a target.

Fergus had no weapon. He looked around wildly, searching for a stone or a stick or anything he could throw.

"Hey, it didn't all go to me!" Frankie shouted.

Fergus ran at the man and hit him in the right side with a hip check that took them both off their feet. They crashed down on each other as the nine-millimeter sent two shots crashing into the sky.

Carolina was already trying to keep low, hiding in the grove, but the shots made him drop flat to the ground. His leg was throbbing, and in the dark he couldn't tell how much blood he had lost.

He had rolled tape from the Hi-8 camera through the whole conversation with Falcone. Nothing could be seen, but at least the sound would be there—if he ever got off Montserrat alive.

There was no new pain after the shots were fired, so he assumed they had missed. Then he heard another noise: grunting, and heavy breathing.

The sounds of two men fighting.

Carolina picked himself up and tried to run forward. But the best he could manage was a quick limp. It was hard to see, but the moon helped a little. He pushed on through the clearing where Frankie Falcone had stood. The banker was gone. But the grunting sounds were straight ahead of him and he pressed on. Out of the blackness, he began to make out shapes: two men rolling on the ground. He moved closer, each step sending a shock of pain through his lower leg. Was there a weapon? Where?

Now he was on them, the fat man in the leather jacket and Fergus O'Neill. Where was the gun?

Carolina was weak from loss of blood. The night seemed

to grow darker, the moon no longer helping. It occurred to Carolina that he might pass out.

But you have to help Fergus, he told himself. If O'Shea finds the gun, he'll finish the job.

Where was the gun?

Fergus was tiring. The fat man was very strong, and in some ways more agile—and more skilled in the art of combat.

Fergus had not fought since he was a boy in grade school. Montserrat had almost no crime, no violence. He had relied on his own fear, using it to draw strength as he fought this man in the leather jacket. Rather than punching the man, Fergus chose to wrestle him, tying up his hands, kicking at his legs to keep him from getting to his feet. It was a good strategy in that it kept the man from doing any damage. But it wouldn't last forever.

The men rolled again, the fat man grunting and cursing, Fergus holding on for dear life. The cabdriver was also wondering where the man's weapon had gone. Somehow it had slipped away in the struggle and now lay hidden in the darkness.

Where is the fucking gun?

Carolina could not see it. Without it, he didn't see how he could help Fergus. The scene before him seemed to ripple, zooming in and out like some kind of weird dream or a bad music video. He had no weapon. The rocks around them were too heavy to lift, too cumbersome to be of any use. He was losing blood. He tugged again at the belt wrapped around his ankle. He would have to drop it and get into the fight.

The belt.

O'Shea and O'Neill rolled toward him again. The rippling effect of the scene seemed to get worse. Carolina pulled the belt free, felt the blood easing back into his foot and out of his heel. There was Fergus before him, trying to grab again at the terrorist's arms. There was Liam O'Shea, his eyes wide, almost snarling as he brushed O'Neill's hands away. Fergus was on top of him now, but the terrorist was reaching up, toward the cabdriver's neck. His fat fingers closed on the throat and squeezed.

Carolina looped the belt around O'Shea's neck and pulled as hard as he could.

Fergus had grabbed O'Shea's wrists. The fat man's hands were choking the life from him. But with the belt around his throat, the hands trembled. Then they dropped free.

"Hold on. Please hold on," the cabbie gasped to Carolina.

Liam O'Shea struggled to breathe at the bottom of the tangled pile of arms and legs. The strength of the cabdriver had surprised him.

The strap around his neck had surprised him even more.

Each time he reached up to pull it off, the cabbie drove his hands away. Each time he tried to roll away, the strap held him in place.

So this must be what it's like to be hanged, he thought.

O'Shea had never been all that patriotic. He admitted, at least to himself, that he'd joined the IRA for the pleasure of wreaking havoc, of inflicting pain. But at a moment like this, he couldn't help thinking of the patriots he'd heard of: Emmet, Parnell, Collins. Their lives had meant something; their deaths, as well.

And here I am, he thought, because these bastards saw a sex-crazed embezzler taking a dip in the pool.

The thought enraged him and he gave one last heave, thrusting his hands up, bucking his hips in an effort to throw the cabdriver off.

But the cabbie hung on. Liam O'Shea knew he had lost his chance at life.

And as he died, he thought, I should have stayed in Derry. It was safer there.

Frankie Falcone stumbled down the mountain road, his bare feet scraped and bruised, his robe flopping around him.

O'Shea had had the keys to the Range Rover. The nine-millimeter was missing, somewhere up on the grounds of the plantation.

And now the terrorist was dead, or at least he had appeared to be in the dim light of the half-moon. Falcone had watched as the coal black man with the red hair and the limping reporter struggled with O'Shea. When the IRA man stopped moving, Frankie broke for the villa.

He knew the police would soon arrive, summoned either by people who had heard gunshots or by the two men who had survived the battle with O'Shea. They would find the other cabdriver, shot dead, his face blown away. They would find the nine-millimeter. They would find Liam O'Shea. Then they would come to the villa that belonged to Frankie Falcone.

I'll be arrested and deported, Falcone thought. I'll go back to Rhode Island. I'll wind up doing time at the ACI.

He found his way through the darkness to the villa. There were no lights; O'Shea and Falcone had left before the sun went down. Frankie crept into the house, wanting to turn on a lamp. He decided not to for fear it would attract people too quickly.

I never should have come here, he told himself. It was the land of his mother's birth, the land where she grew up, before going to America and meeting his father so many years ago. It was remote and tranquil. But it was also a British colony subject to the extradition treaties of the United Kingdom. He would be returned to the United States in chains.

Frankie felt his way into the darkened bedroom. He found a large stachel and threw in a few clothes, a few objects that he had brought from Providence, including a tiny brown book that contained a set of numbers. With this, he could start a life somewhere else, somewhere without extradition laws. Maybe Brazil, or Paraguay, or some island in the South Pacific.

He moved back toward the closet, and his foot kicked a sheaf of papers on the floor—a computer magazine, with an article on virtual reality. He glanced at the subheading that said the potential for such technology was endless. Frankie stuffed the magazine in his bag for future reference.

The magazine triggered thoughts, thoughts he didn't have time to consider. But the images consumed him: the great actresses, the bad actresses with great bodies. He felt his way back into the hall of the villa, his eyes now adjusted to the dark. The door to the one enclosed room in the house, the one with no windows, was half-open. Inside the room were hundreds of thousands of dollars' worth of machines—unbelievable computer equipment that took images on paper and videotape and film and made them come alive, all pouting and hot and wanting *him,* equipment that was too large, too noticeable to take with him.

Frankie was in the mood for love.

Maybe one last time, he thought.

He closed the door, threw on the blue and pink lights that gave the room the right mood. Soon he would have to run. He would go to the harbor, find a charter captain who could take him off the island. But he couldn't resist. One last time.

Who should it be? Marilyn? Julia? A porno star?

He shucked off the clothes he had just thrown on. The synthetic diaper lay on the floor. That bastard O'Shea had messed with it, left it in a heap. He didn't understand how sensitive the tiny electrodes were, how they had been tuned to maximize pleasure. But O'Shea wouldn't do that again.

He slipped the diaper on and made a selection. A woman who called herself Laura Luscious, who starred in a film called *I Can't Get Enough.* In it, Laura had made it with at least thirty different men. Frankie had used the picture twenty-nine times, trying Laura in different positions, each encounter better than the one before.

Frankie placed the VR helmet on his head and adjusted the mirrors to see and hear everything Laura Luscious had to offer. He adjusted the vinyl belt on the diaper and cinched it tight.

He didn't notice the break in the porous diaper's interior. It was hard to see amid the room's blue and pink lights. So Frankie had no way of knowing that the diaper had developed a set of three tiny cracks when Liam O'Shea tried it on. The terrorist's ample waist had strained the material almost to the breaking point. Now six different electrodes were exposed. The electrical impulses that were supposed to conduct through the special fabric would now make direct contact with bare skin.

Frankie took no notice as Laura Luscious began to moan and shed clothing. The computer program was designed in such a way that the initial impulses were audiovisual only. The diaper electrodes would fire only when Frankie touched a button on the console, and he did this only as climax was achieved.

Laura was in peak form. She laughed, giggled, coaxed him into her, telling him he was the best, how she had been waiting for him. Frankie's excitement grew. His heart pounded as she called him by name.

He took longer than usual—at least ten minutes. Laura cried with ecstasy. But he knew he had to be going. The police would be here soon.

He felt himself at near peak and placed his hand over the console, his finger poised over the electrode button. The beauty of virtual reality, he thought, is convenience. It does what I want when I want.

He relaxed and let himself go, his hand dropping, his finger lightly pressing the switch.

"I'm . . . coming . . ." he gasped.

The diaper shot 220 volts through his groin and Frankie Falcone went at the same time.

The buzz inside the *Providence Herald*'s newsroom was beginning to wind down. But the editor of the lifestyles section was making life hell for Billy Guano.

"We haven't had a column from you all week."

"I haven't felt inspired."

"Well, I'd suggest you inspire yourself. We need a TV piece."

"What do you want me to write about?" Guano whined. He had flipped through all the evening's local broadcasts and seen nothing of interest. Now it was late and he wanted to go home.

"It's not my job to find stories on your beat. Our last deadline is in a half hour. You better gimme something. I've got a meeting with the managing editor in the morning."

The veiled threat angered the critic. He spun in his chair and stared at the blank screen of his word processor, absently squeezing a pimple on his neck. It wasn't his fault that there wasn't much to write about. There had been nothing since Tisha Billings's death and Carolina's visit to the Rose Tattoo. He smiled at the memory of how he'd crucified Carolina. The public always loved it when you beat up on an on-air personality. . . .

And where had Carolina been?

Guano punched a key on his keyboard, then another.

> Where has Carolina gone?
> Remember Channel 3's hot new reporter who was recently caught in a fight at a local strip joint?
> Seems to me that this so-called reporter's star has already fizzled, even faster than it rose. . . .

Guano chuckled to himself. It would be easy to squeeze off six inches of copy on Carolina in time for deadline.

21

This time, the hospital room was blue, not gray, and Michael Carolina stayed only one night. A doctor carefully sutured his foot and closed the wound. The broken glass had almost severed an artery. After two units of blood, the world stopped rippling. After a night's sleep, Carolina was out, walking with a large bandage and a slight limp.

The local Montserrat police force greeted him at the hospital's entrance. A captain had already spent the better part of the evening interviewing Fergus.

"We'd like a few questions, sir," the officer said politely.

"No problem," Carolina said. "May I make a phone call first?"

Shirley Templeton nearly went into shock when he called the newsroom.

"You found him?"

"Not only that, I taped him, and this guy Liam O'Shea."

"Hold on. I need a vitamin."

From two thousand miles away, he could hear her washing the pill down.

"You know, Shirl, a balanced diet could do everything those pills do."

"Who's got time for that? Now give me details."

He did.

"Are you feeling well enough to do a phoner for us?"

"Sure."

Ten minutes later, the station broke into regular programming. An anchor gave the lead that Frankie Falcone had been found on a Caribbean island and tossed to Carolina. He ad-libbed a report about the events of the previous evening.

Shirley promptly notified Channel 3's network. Carolina spent the rest of his morning being interviewed by the police. When it was over, the captain advised him that the investigation would likely determine that the death of Liam O'Shea was a justifiable act of self-defense. Carolina finished just in time to call Providence with another telephone report for the noon broadcast.

By midafternoon a crew, a producer, and a correspondent from the network's Miami bureau arrived by chartered jet with a portable satellite uplink and editing equipment. Carolina's Hi-8 tape was dubbed onto a Beta format and up-linked to the United States.

"The other stations are going crazy," Shirley told him. "Lilly already took three calls from people claiming they were with the network, trying to get our satellite coordinates."

"Did she tell them?"

"Of course not! The network called us and said which bird to use. And Lilly recognized the voice of one of Channel Nine's assignment editors."

After an initial delay, Montserratian authorities permitted him to enter the villa with the network photographer. Frankie Falcone's corpse had been removed, but police officers were still trying to figure out why he was wearing a helmet and synthetic diaper when his body was found. Their initial determination was that Falcone had committed some bizarre form of suicide.

When the officers discovered Falcone's movie and pornography collection, they immediately confiscated it as evidence. One ranking officer smiled broadly at Carolina as he loaded the material into his car.

"We must review this carefully, sir."

"Don't strain your eyes," Carolina said.

Carolina went back into the house and saw the satchel with Falcone's clothes in it. The captain who had questioned him was examining the contents. He removed the computer magazine, flipped through it, then dropped it on the floor. As he dumped the other items from the satchel, Carolina noticed a small notebook.

"What do you suppose this is?" the captain asked.

"Beats me," Carolina said, motioning the photographer to roll on it.

The pages of the book were loaded with numbers. On one back page, there was a list of names and a heading.

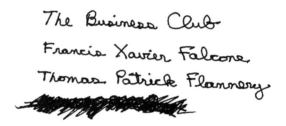

The Business Club
Francis Xavier Falcone
Thomas Patrick Flannery

"This last name is illegible," the captain said. He handed the book to Carolina. "And who is this Mr. Flannery?"

"A soon-to-be ex-politician," Carolina said.

Michael Carolina's piece for the station's six o'clock news had pictures of Falcone and Liam O'Shea, plus video of the villa and Galway's Plantation. The network also produced a report, relying almost exclusively on material from Carolina and Channel 3.

Carolina did live stand-ups, introducing and wrapping the story.

"And where did all the money go, Michael?" the anchor asked.

"That's still the big question. Authorities have found a series of numbers in a small book, but the only indication of where the money went comes at the back. The members of this so-called Business Club—Thomas Flannery among them—may be the ones who know the answer."

The anchor thanked him and went on to a Ron Davis live shot from the State House, where the governor had apparently run down a hall and ducked into a ladies' room to avoid being interviewed.

"So where do you think it went?" The voice was gravelly but familiar. Carolina turned.

"Sergeant Corvese. Nice to see you. Down here on vacation?"

Corvese was dressed in chinos and a short-sleeved shirt, but he still looked sweaty. He dragged a forearm across his brow.

"You know damn well why I'm here. To clean up the mess you helped make. Me and these two stiffs."

In contrast to Corvese, Bert and Ernie looked very out of place in their dark gray wool suits. "You're working together?" Carolina asked.

"We have a series of homicides to investigate up in Rhode Island," Bert said. He removed his jacket and revealed two massive wet spots, one under each arm. "The Sergeant here has his stripper and Mr. Simmons. We've got the guy who bombed your boat."

"Want to ask you some questions about Mr. O'Shea," Corvese said.

"I'll oblige," Carolina said.

"So do we," said Bert.

"Whatever I can do."

"Funny how you managed to put it all together," Ernie said, still trying to look tough.

"Ernie, if I didn't know better, I'd say behind that cool ATF persona, you're a little bit jealous." Ernie's face turned pink. He said nothing more.

"There's probably gonna be some FBI types down to talk to you, too," Bert said.

"Oh boy," Carolina said.

*   *   *

He did another live shot at eleven that night, along with a report for a station in Boston. Later, in his hotel, he called Channel 3 again.

"You were terrific," Shirley said. "The FBI got a warrant based on your six o'clock report. They're all over Flannery's office right now, going through his files. The competition is going nuts, trying to find a way to report the story without mentioning us. I hear they're flying people to Montserrat in the morning."

"They won't get much," Carolina said. "The house is being sealed. The bodies have all been removed. And Fergus promised me he won't do any interviews."

"That won't stop them. They'll just pretend they were there the whole time."

"The illusion of television," Carolina mused.

"I'd like to think there was a time when that didn't happen," Shirley said. "But there really wasn't. If you miss a story, you pretend that you didn't. Newspapers do that, too. If everything else fails, you go back to smoke and mirrors and hope nobody notices. But speaking of newspapers . . ." A touch of malice came into her voice, as if she was getting to the punch line of a joke.

"What?"

"Billy Guano had a column about you this morning. Talking about all your failures, hinting that I should can you if I hadn't done so already."

"Did he, now?"

"I heard the lifestyle editor and the managing editor had him on the carpet . . . right after your noon phoner. One of their reporters told Ron Davis you could hear the screaming all through the newsroom."

Carolina smiled. "Vengeance is mine, and it is sweet," he said, imagining the critic being dressed down. "So what happened?"

244

"He called about ten minutes after the six o'clock broadcast. He'll have a new column tomorrow—and I expect he'll be eating plenty of crow. There's one other thing."

"What?"

"He wants an interview."

"You're kidding."

"A profile for a Sunday magazine piece. Michael? What do you think?"

"I think hell just froze over."

"Well, while you're savoring that thought, there's someone who wants to talk to you." Shirley sounded a bit reluctant as she handed the phone away.

"So you did it."

"Only with your help. It's good to hear your voice, Lilly."

"Congratulations."

"Same to you."

"Thanks. I think I deserve some credit."

Carolina laughed, and she joined in. When they stopped, Carolina said, "There's something I need to tell you."

"Liam O'Shea killed my father, right?"

He paused for a moment. "I didn't put it in the story."

"I have good instincts, remember?" It was strange, he thought, how she sounded almost relieved. "I've been wondering about O'Shea ever since you showed me his picture up in Prospect Park."

"I'm really sorry, Lilly."

"I'm glad you took care of him."

It wasn't until that moment that Carolina stopped to think about what he had done the night before. I killed a man, he thought. He was a terrorist, a murderer, and he would have killed me. But I killed him first.

"Michael, are you all right?"

"I crossed the line."

"You had no choice."

"I still crossed the line."

"Well," Lilly said, "I, for one, am glad that you did."

They both were silent for a while.

"There's something still bothering me," Lilly said.

"What?"

"My father's name wasn't on that list. You know, the Business Club."

"Maybe his is the name that's illegible."

"I doubt it."

"Why?"

"Because he didn't have any money, at least not any large sums like Frankie did."

"Maybe it's in one of those hidden accounts in Frankie's book."

"Maybe. But nobody's found any record of that. Not in any of my father's things. You'd think he would have left it where we could find it."

"Maybe the police or the FBI will find it."

"There's another reason I don't think he's the third member."

"What?"

"My father didn't know these guys very well. He worked in a big bank before he went to work for the state. And he never talked about Falcone or Flannery. Besides, he was appointed by the governor."

"So? He could have been recruited after the appointment."

"Yes, except for one thing."

"What?"

"Remember that this was going on before Dunleavy was elected?"

Carolina thought for a moment. "I'd forgotten."

"When are you coming back?"

"Tomorrow."

"You did a great job, Michael."

They hung up. Carolina tried to sleep. But he couldn't stop thinking about Liam O'Shea. And the missing money. And the illegible name in a brown notebook. He got up several times and stood on his room's balcony, the images and their meanings playing over and over, like a cassette tape, as he stared into the ocean's waves.

Fifteen hundred miles north, in the house with the view of Narragansett Bay, another man stared at water.

He had long ago concluded that the world was filled with screwups and incompetents. That given too much freedom such people inevitably destroyed the work of those with ability. The evening news reassured him that his conclusions were correct.

That idiot terrorist had blown everything. First by missing Carolina when he blew up the boat, then by killing the stripper, and finally by permitting Carolina to follow him to the island. Now federal and state agents were ransacking Flannery's office, probably searching for account numbers that matched those found in Montserrat, along with clues as to where the accounts were located. And when the dust had settled just a bit more, the agents would begin another search: for the third member of the club.

Could Flannery be squeezed?

The man left the bay window and poured himself a cognac, wondering about the speaker of the house and whether he would cut a deal. Get some smart lawyer and strike while the metal was still rich and red and in the fire, give up one last person in exchange for a lighter sentence.

The man decided it would not happen. Tommy Flannery's brother wouldn't let it. He would expect his brother the politician to carry his secrets to the grave.

The man sipped more cognac and returned to his window. There were sailboats on the bay, their green and red running lights on, harnessing the nighttime breeze that would push them into Bristol Harbor. Even in darkness, the view was supremely beautiful. He had paid dearly to get this home. He wasn't about to let it slip away.

And that goddamned reporter was still around, he

thought. Still asking questions, still digging. He was worse than a fly. Buzzing and hovering, hard to destroy. A constant annoyance. The only way to get rid of a fly is to crush it, he thought.

Or let it fly away.

He sipped and pondered the idea. The work Carolina had done was bound to gain him national attention. It wasn't every day that a local television reporter tracked down a notorious criminal on a tropical island. Surely the networks would be calling, or one of those syndicated magazine shows. Perhaps Carolina would pick up and leave on his own. Perhaps the best thing is to let the little bastard buzz away, he thought.

If not, I'll have to kill him myself.

Lilly Simmons was also unable to sleep.

The death of Liam O'Shea gave her some measure of relief. But she couldn't escape the thought that someone else was responsible for the murder of her father. O'Shea didn't act randomly; she was sure of it. He was under someone's direction.

Was it Tommy Flannery? Possibly, but something didn't quite click. The speaker had been too careful through the years to stay clear of his brother's mob connections. And he was only in trouble now because of Frankie Falcone's notebook.

Was it Falcone? Again, it was possible. But the video of the man, paddling in a pool, the recording of his tangled explanation of his behavior . . . none of it made sense. He had sounded genuinely surprised to hear of Frederick Simmons's death. And in the end, Frankie Falcone was a weasel and a coward.

She put on a kettle to make tea, then looked at the kitchen table in her family's home. It was piled high with documents and papers, all of them related to Frank Falcone and

Vespucci Loan and Investment. Shirley was planning an hour-long special on the bank's failure.

Too bad he's not still alive, she thought. At least he could answer some questions.

She went through the papers, mostly reports about the missing money. The state's business regulators had taken only a few days to figure out how much money had been siphoned out of Amerigo Vespucci. In hindsight, Governor Dunleavy's office had moved very quickly.

She went through some personal items related to Frankie Falcone. There were pictures from his youth—a smiling senior portrait at LaSalle Academy, a more serious photo four years later at Providence College. Underneath each senior portrait was information about the graduate. Frankie Falcone had majored in business. He was a member of the Young Democrats and the Business Club.

The kettle whistle blew and Lilly poured a cup. While the tea steeped, she turned to the pages with the campus organization photos—groups of young men, all dressed in suits for the official photographs. The flower of Rhode Island youth. The best and brightest Providence College had to offer. There was Frankie again, smiling in the midst of the Young Democrats. There he was with the Business Club.

And there was Tommy Flannery. Had they known each other in school? Quite the coincidence, Lilly thought.

And there, behind the two young men, was another face.

It took a moment for her to recognize him. So young. He looked very serious, even then. His appearance gave the impression he did not enjoy being the center of attention. So he stood in the back, almost out of sight, his arms outstretched, touching the shoulders of his two pals. He was a part of the group, no doubt. But he seemed almost hidden.

Just as he was today.

Lilly's heart skipped. She felt adrenaline pouring through her as she grabbed the telephone, and it made her so nervous

249

that she stopped twice as she dialed and started over. As she heard the telephone ring, she looked at her teacup and saw that the tea was almost black. It would be strong enough to keep a horse awake.

"Hello?" a scratchy voice said after the eighth ring.

"Sol? It's Lilly."

"Don't you know what time I have to get up?"

"Get up now. I've got an idea and I need your help."

22

The Gregorian chant pinned the audio needles twice at WAIL as the Reverend Rasmus worked himself into an appropriate frenzy for the conclusion of the morning show.

"Brothers and sisters, I have said this to you before, but I shall now say it again: the Lord our God works in strange and mysterious ways. Ways we cannot always understand, but ways that always reveal His warmth and wisdom."

Rasmus hit the mute button to let fly a diet-cola belch. He swilled a little more and continued.

"Today, we have discussed and dissected the strange, tragic, yet wonderfully just happenings on the island of Montserrat." Rasmus thumbed a Birnbaum guidebook on the Caribbean until he found the chapter on Montserrat. "An island settled at the same time our ancestors settled this great state. An island once populated with outcasts and rogues. An island like our own.

"Today we have seen the evil that befalls men who rape and murder, the justice that awaits men who plunder, men who steal from their brothers and sisters, their mothers and fathers. God has brought His wrath upon those who have transgressed.

"For some, the price has been paid. But not for all. NO." The audio board needles pinned again. Rasmus's producer waved frantically from the control room, fearing Sol would damage the equipment. But Rasmus took no notice, engulfed as he was in evangelic fervor.

"And God above has His prophets. There is Mr. Carolina, the apostle of Channel 3, who has shown us all the light. Who has shown us where that great satan Falcone lay hiding. Who met the evil of a terrorist named O'Shea. Who at this very moment is returning home to our beloved state.

"But Michael Carolina cannot serve alone. No, he must be aided in his endeavors, and brothers and sisters, the Reverend Rasmus is here!"

Sol leaned into the mike. When he spoke again, his voice had dropped an octave.

"And brothers and sisters, Rasmus has had a vision. God has visited me, and spoken to me, and blessed me with knowledge. Brothers and sisters, God has told me that yet another satan is still among us. There is another demon present in this fine state, a disciple of Lucifer heretofore unknown. Rasmus knows who he is. And Rasmus knows what he's done. For Rasmus knows . . . about the Business Club."

Sol punched the button on the Gregorian chant cart once more. The music swelled. "And Rasmus will reveal all. Tomorrow. On this program. My brothers and sisters, may God be with you."

The general manager was swallowing Maalox directly from the bottle again.

"You really ought to use a spoon," Rasmus's producer said.

"What the hell is he talking about?" the GM asked, wincing as he gulped the liquid down.

"Beats the shit outta me. Listen, on second thought, could I get a slug of that?"

"You realize, of course, the incredible fucking risk I'm taking," Sol said. "I mean, what if things aren't like you figured?"

"Then you'll look stupid," Lilly said. "Which can't be too much worse than the way you've always looked. And who cares? The zealots in your audience will still listen. Look at Jimmy Swaggart and those other characters."

"But I promised I'd tell who the other club member is."

"So what? On your show, you could talk about Christ's second coming."

"Never." Sol bristled. "The show is strictly Old Testament. I'm still Jewish, you know."

"I forgot."

Logan Airport was busy with business travelers. The two of them walked through a herd of people before finding the arrival gate for the flight from San Juan. Carolina was almost the first off the plane.

"I could sleep a week," he said.

Lilly smiled, a happy, slightly malicious grin. "You better wake up. There's one more story out there . . . one you won't want to miss."

Sol lived in an apartment complex in Edgewood, a pleasant waterside neighborhood in Cranston, just over the Providence city line. The building was a cheap, ugly Tudor-style structure, built in haste by a developer in the mid-eighties, when choice Rhode Island real estate doubled in value every six months. Investors hoped to make a killing in condos near the water. But the market died, and dozens of developers went bankrupt. Sol's building was purchased by a doctor and two lawyers who hoped the market had bottomed out. They splashed a new coat of paint on the units and hung a sign out front that dubbed the place NORTH 'GANSETT FARM.

"Gives it a little class, don'tcha think?" Sol asked.

"Oh, certainly," Lilly said, rolling her eyes.

"Your linoleum is peeling," Carolina said as they crossed the building's lobby.

"For four hundred dollars a month, you think I'm gonna complain?" Sol responded.

They walked up two flights of stairs and down a hallway

to Sol's one-bedroom unit: apartment 3J. The J hung upside down.

"One of the nails fell off," Sol said as he opened the door and threw on a light switch.

The place was a mess, a gathering point for empty beer cans, pizza boxes, and old copies of *Radio and Records* piled high on a brown shag carpet.

"Do you subscribe?" Lilly asked, pointing at the magazines.

"Nah, just take 'em from the station." He settled down on a sofa cluttered with newspapers and a greasy Domino's box. "So what should I do? I've never been a target before."

"I've never coached one," Lilly said.

"Maybe I should move over there," Sol said, gesturing toward the window.

"I don't think so," Carolina said, looking onto the street, where lamps had just begun to come on. "It's bad enough that we're doing this. We don't want to make it too easy." He pulled a thin curtain across the picture window.

Lilly found a chair in the kitchen that looked clean and brought it in to sit down. "How long should we stay?" she asked, looking at Carolina.

"Not long. You and I ought to wait outside."

"What if Sol needs help?"

"We're not going far. We'll be right out on the street."

"By the way," Sol said, "I've been wondering when you plan on telling me who you think might be paying me a visit tonight."

"We're not sure," Lilly said.

"Yet," Carolina added.

Lilly had talked to Carolina while Sol went to fetch the car at Logan, explaining her theory on the mysterious third club member and the plan she had in mind.

"I like it," he said. "But it could be dangerous."

"Maybe. But Sol loves it."

"How much does he know?"

"Enough. I told him what to say this morning."

"But he doesn't know who the club member is?"

"Wadoyou think, I'm stooo-pid?" she said in her thickest Rhode Island accent. "That'd be like pouring gas on a fire."

"If I was going to stick my neck out, I'd want to know whom to expect," Carolina said.

"He's more concerned that no one will show up. But if that happens, he's covered. I'll show him the yearbook picture and he can rant and rave about it tomorrow. There's no libel, because they really were members of a club back in school."

"Yeah, but are they still?"

Her eyes twinkled. "You got a better theory?"

Carolina didn't. But now that they were in Sol's apartment, the idea seemed to take on strange, almost sinister dimensions. Each of them was wondering whether Lilly was right. If something went wrong, the Reverend Rasmus might end up dead.

Carolina grabbed the doorknob. "You sure you want to do this, Sol?"

"Hey, my reputation's on the line," Sol said in mock seriousness. "To tell you the truth, I feel like I'm onstage someplace saying, 'Kids, don't try this at home.' "

"You remember the plan?" Lilly asked, her brow wrinkled.

"I'll be okay," Sol said. "This is my chance to make a name."

As Lilly and Carolina stepped into the hall, Sol turned on his best Rasmus voice. "Bless you, my children."

"Same to you," Lilly said.

Lilly, Sol, and Michael Carolina were counting on the idea that the third club member would make some attempt to silence the talk-show host, probably before his next broadcast. They also assumed the attempt would come where Sol lived.

The initial plan was for Lilly and Carolina to leave, then double back and watch the building. Their car was equipped with a cellular phone, and Sol had the number in case someone tried to break in.

They had not considered the possibility that someone was already inside the building.

Across the hall from Sol's apartment stood unit 3L. As Carolina and Lilly walked down the hall, a man watched at 3L's peephole. Behind him, he could hear the ticking of a wall clock, counting off the minutes before a chime on the quarter hour.

He had heard the chimes eight times, waiting and watching for the talk-show host to come home. And he was not a patient man. But circumstance would force him to wait a little more.

The man looked back into the apartment's tiny living room. An older woman lay on a worn couch, her wrists, mouth, and ankles neatly bound with electrical tape. Quietly, he padded over to her.

"Your neighbor is back. It won't be long now, dear."

The woman's eyes stared at the pistol and silencer in front of her. It was an old .38, practically an antique. But the man held it as if it still worked perfectly.

"Remember, if you even begin to scream, I will bounce one through your brain. You trust me on that, don't you?" The man's tone was warm, almost friendly, like a doctor talking to a patient just before surgery. It made the woman shiver.

"Very good, dear. You're doing just fine."

He eased back in a chair and listened to the clock's tick.

Lilly and Carolina climbed into her car and drove off.

"How long do you think it will take?" she asked as she pressed a button to power up the car phone.

"It's your plan. I thought you knew," Carolina said. For

just a moment, Lilly looked cross, then broke into a 'tiny smile. The joke eased the tension. They drove two blocks before turning right, then down two more and turned right again. With every turn, Lilly glanced back in the mirror.

"Anybody?" Carolina asked.

"Not that I can see."

It was now almost dark, and Lilly doused her lights as she turned back onto the street that was home to North 'Gansett Farm. The Miata roadster crept along until it was less than a block from the house. Lilly parked between two cars.

"So. You think we should have called the police?"

"You said we didn't need to when you filled me in this afternoon," Carolina said. "And Sol didn't want them, anyway."

"You're not answering my question."

Carolina watched the apartment building. "Truth be told, it would have been safer. But you've got nine-one-one programmed into the phone. And we don't know if anything's going to happen." He yawned. "Probably nothing."

"That's what I thought when you went to Montserrat."

An hour went by, disturbed only by the chimes on the wall clock.

He fingered the .38 once more. The woman was still lying on the sofa, tears sliding down her face, wetting the upholstery.

"Show time, dear."

He stood the woman up, a difficult feat with her legs bound together, but they managed. Carefully, he peeled back the tape on her mouth. With little hops, he guided the woman over to the apartment's door and picked up the telephone hanging just outside the tiny kitchen.

"You're hurting me," she said faintly.

"Shut up, or I assure you it will hurt much, much more." He dialed the telephone.

Sol was not used to sitting home alone. The sound of the phone ringing startled him. But he was glad to hear it, thinking that Carolina or Lilly would be on the other end.

" 'Lo?"

There was no sound on the other end of the line. "Hello?" Before he could hang up, he heard the knock at the door. "Mr. Herskowitz? Mr. Herskowitz?"

The woman looked like she might faint. The man had to struggle to hold her up.

"Mr. Herskowitz?" she said again, and glanced to her left, where he stood just out of sight of the peephole.

"Yeah?"

"It's Rita Thompson. From across the hall. A package came for you this morning.

Sol checked the peephole. Mrs. Thompson stood in front of the door, looking miserable. But she always looked miserable, he thought. She had told him several times how much she hated his program. Blasphemy, she had called it. Now here she was, on what could be a very big night, to tell him that UPS had dropped in.

"What do you think he's doing in there?" Lilly asked, looking at the light in the apartment window.

"Probably daydreaming about working in a top-ten market."

They had seen a teenaged couple walk down the street, along with an elderly man and his dog. No one else. The streetlights played tricks on their eyes, twinkling and flickering, making them think someone was coming when no one was there.

"We could be here all night," Lilly said.

"I know. And I'm really wiped." The adrenaline had left Carolina that afternoon.

"Maybe I should check in," Lilly said, picking up the cellular phone. She dialed Sol's number, pressed the send button, listened, then dialed again. Carolina's eyelids fluttered.

"Must have pressed a wrong number," Lilly said.

"Line busy?"

"No, there's no answer. And I know he has Call Waiting."

The thought hit them both at the same time.

"We'd better check," Carolina said, pulling the door latch.

They began walking toward the building when the light in Sol's window fluttered. They both heard a shout.

Then the window broke.

"Call nine-one-one," Carolina said, pushing Lilly back toward her car. He turned and sprinted toward the building's entrance.

Sol Herskowitz was only human. Even on a night when he feared assassination, he could not resist the temptation presented by a neighbor waiting to hand him a package.

As he opened the door, Rita Thompson literally fell on him. He did not know whether she had jumped or been pushed. But there she was, knocking him over, crashing down on top of him, a mess of hair curlers, housedress, and electrical tape.

"Aaaagh!" Rita cried.

"Uuuuh," was all Sol could manage, as Rita's weight took his breath away. When he looked up, a man dressed in black and wearing a ski mask was standing over him. The man knelt quickly, shoving a revolver under Sol's chin.

"I am going to make this very simple, Mr. Rasmus. There are hollow-point bullets in this weapon, bullets that will splatter your head all over this room. If you don't answer me quickly and precisely, I am prepared to use one—on you. Do you understand?"

Sol, petrified, somehow managed to nod.

"Good. Now, who is the third member of the Business Club?"

"I honestly don't know," Sol gasped. "They won't tell me."

The man hit him once with the butt of the revolver. A tiny gash opened on Sol's forehead.

"Next time, I use the bullet."

"I really don't know!" Sol cried.

"Who's 'they'?"

"The people who told me to say it."

The ski-masked man pulled the .38's hammer back with his thumb.

"Who?" he demanded. Then he screamed to high heaven.

Sol grabbed at the gun just as it went off, driving a hollow point round through the window and shattering it.

Rita Thompson had never liked Sol Herskowitz. In fact, she hated him. She listened to his show each day in order to keep the hatred fresh in her mind.

But she hated even more that a masked man barged into her apartment while she had her hair in curlers and tied her up with sticky black tape. And that he then had the nerve to threaten her with a gun.

She cried with fright, but also with anger. The man forced her to her feet, forced her to call to Sol and get him to open his door. And now, with the man's back to her, Rita saw a way to get even.

Just that morning, Rita had returned from the dentist after a final fitting for a new set of dentures. The adhesive recommended by the hygienist was supposed to be extra-strong. Rita had planned to test it that night on an ear of corn.

But this man's heel will do just fine, she thought.

When she bit clean through to the Achilles tendon, she wasn't the least bit surprised. She wasn't even startled.

And she wasn't about to let go.

Michael Carolina took the stairs three at a time. He raced down the hall, wondering if Sol had been shot.

The door to 3J was locked. Carolina threw his weight

against it. Nothing gave. He backed up and tried again. His shoulder slammed against the cheap wood and he felt a stab of pain. But the door made a cracking sound. He backed up again. Someone inside was still screaming, and it sounded like a man. The sound mixed with another's voice.

"Let . . . go! Legoo mother . . . fuc—"

Michael Carolina slammed against the door once more, and it broke, sending splinters flying.

Sol Herskowitz was struggling with a ski-masked man who was screaming at the top of his lungs. Between them was a gun. But the strangest thing he saw was the woman in hair curlers, taped up like a Thanksgiving turkey, flopping around at the end of the masked man's leg. The woman reminded Carolina of a pit bull, one who would not let go until it was shot dead.

Carolina grabbed for the pistol, picked it up, and tossed it into the hall. Sol had managed to pull himself away, leaving the man flopping around on the floor.

"God! Please! *Let go!*"

"I canff," the woman seemed to say. "M'tef'r stu-uh."

"Oh Jesus! I'll do anything! *Please!*"

"M'tef-r stu-uhh!" the woman said again.

Carolina and Sol reached over and started pulling tape off the woman's legs and wrists, leaving patches of raw skin exposed. With every pull, the woman bit down harder and the man screamed again.

Lilly appeared from the hallway.

"Better grab that gun," Carolina said to her, then turned to Sol. "Think we should try to get them apart?"

Sol smirked. "No way. I haven't had a tetanus shot."

From outside, they heard a siren. The man in the ski mask didn't seem to hear. Instead, he moaned hysterically, clutching at the fabric on the foot of Sol's living room couch.

Displaying great poise and presence of mind, Sol reached over to a coffee table and grabbed a microcassette recorder.

He punched the play and record buttons. Then he reached down and ripped off the man's ski mask.

"I'll be damned," Michael Carolina said.

"Told you." Lilly grinned.

"Why, Mr. Jack Rollins," Sol said into the microphone, "so nice to see you again. Tell us a little about your club."

Joey Giovannetti didn't get to be mayor of Providence by sitting in the dark. He made it his business to stay in touch with the day's events, waiting for the right moment to make some political hay. You never knew when a good PR opportunity might come along.

Which, of course, was exactly what the arrest of the mysterious third member of the Business Club would be. When the news carried over his limousine's police radio, Joey dropped everything.

"Haul ass, Billy," he called to his police driver from the backseat of his limousine. "Gotta get on this mother and ride it."

"Yes, sir, Mr. Mayor!" the officer replied.

The brunette on the limo's floor was trying to put herself together.

"Thought you were gonna ride me, Joey," she said, her voice slurred with scotch. He'd picked her up from the coat checkroom at a Federal Hill restaurant. She thought he was really cute.

"Later. Just sit here and wait for me. Put your stockings back on. And some lipstick. Anyone asks, you're my sister."

"I wanna come!" the lady whined, reaching for the bottle in the wet bar. Joey deftly slid the bar door shut.

"Plenty of time for that later."

North 'Gansett Farms was awash in police strobe lights. A *Herald* photographer and reporter had arrived, along with a crew from Channel 3.

The mayor half-stumbled out of his car, but, to his good

fortune, the cameras were turned the other way. Their attention was diverted by the unusual sight of fire officials standing by with an unusual contraption known as the Jaws of Life as police officers carried John Rollins and an unidentified woman outside. Rollins was moaning softly. His leg appeared to be *attached* to the woman's mouth.

"Bring 'em on!" an officer barked to the fire crew.

The woman's jaw was detached with a loud pop. Rollins screamed and passed out. Sol Herskowitz chased after him with the tape recorder, still trying for a decent sound bite.

The Channel 3 camera panned to the mayor.

"What are you doing here, Mayor?" a reporter called.

"I came to shake the hand of the man who solved the case of the Business Club," the mayor said without missing a beat, "and to thank our fine police officers for their swift response. So, where is this Michael Carolina, the newest reporter in our fair city?"

"How you doing, Mayor?" Carolina said.

Joey Giovannetti turned.

"You?"

"Yup. Been sailing lately?"

Somehow Giovannetti managed a smile. He grabbed the reporter's hand and pumped it furiously for the camera.

"This is pretty weird," Carolina said under his breath.

"This is Providence, kid. You roll with it," the mayor replied. "I'm just glad you didn't go after me."

"Well," the reporter answered, finally smiling for the camera, "there's always next time."

23

The next day, the Reverend Rasmus made radio history. He recounted his brush with death in excruciating detail, including the struggle with Rollins and the agonies suffered by poor Ms. Thompson. Rasmus even tried to call her in her private room at Rhode Island Hospital, where she was being treated for shock and a severely bruised jaw. Rita told him he had a lot of nerve and hung up.

"It took the paramedics half an hour to unhinge her, praise God," Rasmus said, "The woman was a veritable Doberman, I tell you, and I mean that in the most complimentary way."

Then Rasmus played the tape of Rollins as he lay on the apartment floor.

"So tell the God-fearing people of Rhode Island, Mr. Rollins, where *is* all that money?"

Rollins moaned.

"Are you prepared to accept responsibility, sir, before God and His flock, that you and the evil Falcone, you and the evil Flannery, you are all the bastard sons of the Devil?"

"I think she bit clean through," he sobbed.

"No, sir, she's still holding on, I see. Now, are you prepared to repent?"

"Aaaaagh."

When Rasmus's show was over, the GM hugged him as he walked out the studio door. Tears were streaming down his face.

"Sol. Baby. We logged almost a thousand calls. The numbers are gonna be right through the roof. Let me buy you lunch."

"Why the fuck not?" Sol said, grinning ear to ear. "But it's gonna be real expensive. I already got a call from a station in New York. I need six figures and a station car before I even start to think about staying here."

That afternoon, a cowed and limping Jack Rollins was brought before a district court judge on charges of assault and battery, kidnapping, and attempted murder. He pleaded not guilty to all counts. Then came the matter of bail.

Rollins's lawyer was brief.

"Your Honor, I would point out to the court that my client has substantial ties to the community, and, in fact, he has never been in trouble before."

"He's been too busy making it for other people," the judge said.

"Judge, I think this defendant is a very good candidate for personal recognizance."

"I'd object—" the assistant attorney general said. The judge raised her hand.

"Don't bother. Held without bail. And believe me, Mr. Rollins, I'm giving you a break," she said as Rollins was led away. "There's a mob outside the courthouse. And a little old lady carrying a rope."

An hour later, Governor Dunleavy's office issued a press release announcing that Jack Rollins had tendered his resignation. The press release included a statement from the governor that he had no knowledge of Rollins's "alleged misdeeds," adding that his office would cooperate fully with any state or federal investigations.

Later the same afternoon, a reporter from the *Providence Herald* spied Dunleavy's personal limousine pulling up to a side entrance of the State House. He later swore that he observed a state trooper unloading a case of extralarge-sized disposable diapers, the kind generally used to combat adult incontinence. *Herald* editors refused to run the piece with only one eyewitness and killed the story.

Bert and Ernie returned from Montserrat within hours of Rollins's arraignment. They quickly obtained a warrant to search Rollins's brick Colonial on Bristol Harbor. In a safe hidden behind the basement water heater, they recovered just under $500,000 in cash. In a second-floor office, they found a ledger with a series of account numbers, numbers similar to those found in Frankie Falcone's luggage.

As the two agents were stacking the evidence, a U.S. government van pulled up with a team of FBI agents.

"We're here to help," the lead agent said, pushing Ernie aside.

"But this is our case," Ernie whined.

"Forget it." Bert sighed, gazing sadly at his crestfallen partner. "Haven't you heard of the three great lies?"*

Two days after saving Sol Herskowitz's life, Rita Thompson filed a lawsuit against the manufacturers of her denture adhesive and asked for $3 million in compensation for physical pain and suffering, medical costs, and emotional distress. The case settled out of court for an undisclosed amount rumored to be in six figures. Rita moved to Newport and used the proceeds to open a frozen lemonade business.

Sergeant Corvese returned from Montserrat with a tan and a set of fingerprints lifted from Liam O'Shea. The prints matched several taken from the hotel room where Emily Lane Carter had last been seen alive. Using that and an affidavit from Michael Carolina that documented O'Shea's statements in the San Juan airport, the murder cases of Frederick

---

*The three great lies are (a) "The check is in the mail"; (b) "I promise not to come in your mouth"; and (c) "I'm from the FBI and I'm here to help."

Simmons and Emily Carter were closed. The case of Tisha Billings remained open, pending further investigation.

Liam O'Shea was buried outside the town of Plymouth in Montserrat, in a pauper's grave. Per his wishes, Francis Xavier Falcone's remains were cremated. The ashes were scattered in the Caribbean Sea. Falcone's computer equipment was eventually auctioned along with his villa. A rap star from Watts bought the villa. Fergus O'Neill bought the computer gear for a fraction of its original cost. He used it to set up the island's first and only virtual-reality video arcade.

"What are you going to do now?" Shirley asked as she wolfed down prime rib. It was early evening, and Michael Carolina had joined his boss for another dinner at the Capital Grille. This time, dozens of people stopped by their table to congratulate the reporter who had tracked down Frankie Falcone. The maître d' offered a Caesar salad, on the house.

"I don't know what you mean," Carolina said.

"Oh come on, don't play coy," Shirley said. "I know you've had calls from CNN and CBS. They'd kill to get someone with instincts like yours."

"I was lucky."

"You were smart. That's why they want you."

"Next week, there'll be another story, and I'll be old news."

"I don't think so." Shirley munched thoughtfully on a crouton. "I get the sense you really aren't that interested anymore."

Carolina chuckled quietly. "You have good instincts, too. When I was younger, all I dreamed about was getting the big break, getting to the nets, traveling the world. But I'm just no good at following other people's orders. I wouldn't even listen to you."

"That's true. Fortunately, you have a boss who is both benevolent and wise enough to overlook that minor flaw."

"Indeed. I am blessed."

They ate their prime rib. A waiter brought a bottle of Napa Valley Cabernet. It made Shirley giggle as she used it to wash down a vitamin.

"I heard Billy Guano called," she said.

"Yep." He grinned.

"What did he want?"

"Plans to do an interview that sets the record straight. How I broke the story, found the truth, all that crap. 'I really had you figured wrong.' That's what he said."

"So did you agree?"

"Oh sure."

"Really?" Shirley looked genuinely surprised.

"Yes, I did. Told him I was very busy but that I'd meet him in Newport at La Petite Auberge. Said he should go ahead and order chateaubriand, well done, plus a kir and a soufflé for dessert. Told him he could have one hour, starting precisely at eight o'clock, and that the food had better be on the table when I arrived."

"He didn't say yes."

"Sure he did."

"When is this going to happen?"

"Well, it's nine o'clock now," he said, looking at his watch.

Shirley dropped her fork. "Tonight?" She doubled up with laughter.

"He thinks he's getting an exclusive," Carolina said. "Told me he might even freelance an article to one of the journalism magazines. Think he's figured out I'm not coming?"

When Shirley stopped laughing, she had another drink. Then somehow the mood at the table turned a bit more solemn.

"You could stay here," she said. "You're a household name now. People will be leaking stories to you for the next fifteen years."

"I've thought about that," Carolina said. "You know, I think that would be lots of fun. And Shirley, I really owe you a lot. You gave me a chance when no one else would."

"You're turning me down, aren't you?" She slugged down more wine. He nodded sadly.

"I want to go sailing," he said, trying to sound upbeat, hoping it would lift her mood. "There's a boat in Jamestown. Forty-foot cold-molded, gaff-rigged sloop."

"I have no idea what you're talking about."

"It doesn't matter. She's gorgeous. I want to take her to Bermuda, then down to the Grenadines. Maybe do a transatlantic, or through the canal to the Galápagos."

"Are you taking Lilly with you?"

The question didn't surprise him.

"No. I'm going alone."

She nodded glumly. "Well," she said, "at least I'm not losing you to a younger woman."

"I'm sorry, Shirley," he said, and he meant it.

"S'okay," she replied.

They walked out together. Shirley was a little unsteady on her feet. "Will you stay through the month?"

"Sure."

"T'anks," she said sleepily.

"I think I ought to drive you home," he said, taking the keys from her hand.

"Why do I miss all the good ones?" she said to no one in particular as he started the car.

Two weeks after his office was searched, Tommy Flannery was indicted on thirty counts of fraud, aiding and abetting embezzlement, conspiracy to commit embezzlement, and obtaining money under false pretenses. One week later, he resigned as speaker of the Rhode Island House of Representatives, then walked into superior court and pleaded guilty to five counts in exchange for the state's agreement to drop all other charges. An assistant attorney general announced that

Flannery was entering the state's protected witness program and asked that Flannery's record and plea agreement be sealed. A judge granted the motion and continued indefinitely the date on which Flannery would be sentenced.

Sources familiar with the case later told reporters that Flannery was cooperating in the investigation to locate assets from Amerigo Vespucci Loan and Investment and in a companion investigation into the activities of James Flannery. Tommy demanded and received protection after reports surfaced that Jimmy had authorized a contract on the former speaker's life.

Michael Carolina was cleaning out his desk when she appeared before him dressed all in black and using a cane.

"I heard you was leaving," she said.

He stopped what he was doing. "I'm sorry . . . have we met?"

"Name's Anna," she said. "Don't get up."

He did anyway and got her a chair.

"What can I do for you?" he asked, unsure of why she was there.

"You already done it. I had all my money in Amerigo Vespucci. Now that that mick is cooperating, them regulators are saying I'll get it back. It's all because of you. I wanna say thanks."

"A lot of it was just dumb luck," Carolina said.

"Bull," the little woman said, her hands resting on her cane. "You make your own breaks in this world. That's what my husband did. That's how he left me some money. And I almost lost it all."

"Well, I'm glad you're getting it back."

"Maybe if I hadn't been so greedy, hadn't tried to get the better interest rate, I never woulda had this problem to begin with."

"Maybe."

"Live and learn," she said. "So, you full-blooded Italian?"

He shook his head. "Half Irish. My mother."

"No kiddin'?"

"Erin go bragh," he said.

"Just like Frankie," she said. "Don't that beat all."

Carolina just smiled.

"Well," she said, "that's all I wanted to say." She rose to leave. "Oh yeah," she said, digging in an ancient black cloth purse. "I want you to have this. A souvenir."

She left him sitting there, looking at her old Vespucci passbook.

He was down on a wharf in Jamestown, making ready to sail, when the slender woman in jeans came walking up.

"You didn't say good-bye."

"I was going to call," Carolina said. He tried to concentrate on the checklist of stores he'd taken aboard. But he couldn't escape the feel of her stare.

"It's a nice boat," she said.

"Thanks." It was. Forty feet of wood and epoxy, with a carbon fiber mast. The jib was roller-furled, and the halyards were rigged back to the cockpit. A fine offshore boat, paid for with the insurance money from the blast that took *Maeve*. He'd named her *Maeve II*.

"Where are you headed?"

"Bermuda."

"Sounds nice."

"Yeah," he said. She made no signs of leaving.

"I'm sorry," he said after a minute.

"I heard you apologized to Shirley, too."

"You compared notes?"

"Why not? Neither one of us can understand how someone who isn't afraid of anyone when he's working is so afraid when he's not."

"I'm not afraid of you," he said. "I just can't deal with the pain."

"But without that risk, there's no joy."

They didn't talk anymore, but they both knew she was right. He kept checking the list, and she kept watching him. After nearly half an hour, he put the list down.

"I've checked everything three times."

"That's good."

"Usually twice is enough."

"So now you're being careful."

"I'll miss you," he said. "Remember that day on Thayer Street? When I told you that I was beyond redemption?"

"I remember."

"I was wrong. I have you to thank. You put me back on track."

She touched his hand. "Then why leave?"

"I'm still not healed."

She looked away, and he knew she was fighting off a tear.

"Someday it'll be different," he said.

"I hope so."

The breeze was picking up. It blew strands of brown hair across her face. She brushed them away.

"It feels good," he said. "The wind, I mean. High tide breaks in half an hour."

"And that means . . . ," she said.

"I have to go." He nodded.

They were looking at each other, wondering what to do and how to do it. It was an awkward moment, and yet, somehow, comforting to both of them.

Slowly, tentatively, they embraced.

Then Lilly dug her hands in her jeans as he started the boat's engine. The sun broke through a cloud and turned the water to bronze and silver. He slipped the lines and eased the yacht out of the berth.

He motored slowly, steering toward open water, where he could point the bow south toward Block Island. She followed, walking slowly along the pier until she reached its end, and the boat slipped past. She saw him turn and flash one last smile.

"Come back again," she called, and gave a little wave.

"Bank on it," he called.